I0829565

Resubmerged

Reality Has More Than Just Wings

Abby Snow

Snow Publishing

www.abbysnow.org

Dedication:

Being that this is my first book, it has required a lot of help, support, and love from many different people.

For starters, thank you Mom and Dad. You have been angels in this entire process. Thank you for supporting and pushing me to keep writing. Because of you, this book was able to slowly come together and be the piece it is today.

I also want to give a *huge* thanks to my cousin, Christine Hainly. You did an amazing job designing and constructing the cover of the first edition of this book.

Also, to Rose Gordy, thank you for your tips on self-publishing. Your wisdom, encouragement and stories have touched my life in so many ways.

Thank you to Sarah, who edited a very early draft of my story and provided me with honest feedback. You did a great job of bringing attention to imperfections in the story line.

Thank you Aunt Cheri. You were extremely instrumental when it came to editing and further enhancing the story line.

And, I cannot give enough thanks to Connor Skarda, Andrew Kim, and Kelly Schluederberg. Connor, thank you so much for being the face of the first edition of this novel. You did me an incredible favor and I don't know how I could ever repay you. Andrew, you are an extremely talented cinematographer. You did an amazing job designing and producing the video trailer for this book. I cannot wait to see what exceptional things you do in the future. And Kelly, you agreed on a whim to be the model for the book trailer video. You fit the part perfectly and did a fantastic job. I could not be any happier with the final product. Thank you both for taking the time to make such a wonderful visual representation of this novel. The book trailer is so much more than I had ever expected!

And last, but *definitely* not least, a big shout out to all of my friends. You have stood by me during the six years it took me to complete this book. You listened to me rambling through story lines and character edits, and did not take it personal when I disappeared to write at the local coffee shop. Thank you for always being there for me and giving me something to write about. I appreciate all of you more than you realize.

Chapter 1

I PRESS MY BACK UP AGAINST THE COLD STONE *wall. A deep, familiar rumble echoes from down the hall, sending a shiver up my spine. I can't place my finger on exactly what made the sound, but I know that I have to get out of here.*

Another rumble shakes the ground beneath me, obviously closer. I begin running, not sure which way will lead me outside and which will lead me to the creature I'm so afraid of encountering. My nerves tingle and, in spite of everything, I can't seem to collect myself. My mind won't focus, not enough to decide what to do next.

I come to a stop, leaning over to grasp my knees. My breathing slows slightly as I straighten, flattening my back against the wall again. Little, uneven rocks poke my skin through the fabric of my shirt. I can hear my heart drumming inside my head.

A different sound erupts from further down the hallway to my right. Its pitch is slightly deeper and smoother than the one I'd heard before.

The pace of my breathing automatically increases and I try to slow it down. I know they can hear it. They can sense it. If I can't get it under control, they'll find me, and after they do—I don't let myself consider that alternative.

I break into a sprint, darting down the hall as it curves to the left. Shooting a glance over my shoulder, I search for the creature that made the noise, not sure what I'm looking for, but knowing I'll recognize it the moment I see it.

I run into something solid. My body topples back helplessly. I manage to catch myself just before my head hits the floor, elbows slamming into the ground. It hardly hurts like I expect it to. Tracing the object in front of me, I'm finally faced with what I've been running from. The animal is tall; it would probably be my height if I were to stand up next to it. Its fur ruffles as it repositions its body. I grow numb, utterly terrified.

I suck in a mouthful of air, waking to the reality around me. Moisture has gathered on my palms, warm and clammy. My body shudders uncontrollably as I lay under the cover.

My room is still dark. I look over at the digital clock on my nightstand. It reads 5:00, which is just a half hour before I usually wake up for school. I consider going back to sleep, but figure I won't be able to get much sleep, not after that.

I slip out of bed, doing my best to balance on shaking legs. I begin getting ready for school, like I would any other day, except this isn't a normal day. I've made up my mind and my plans are not going to change. They can't.

Pulling on an outfit, I take a quick glance at myself in the mirror. My dirty blonde hair lies in knots on my head. Blue-green eyes, surrounded in dark eyelashes, stare back at me, wide and alert. Meanwhile, my lips are swollen and overly pink. I ignore them and quickly brush through my hair until it's lying flat on my back. I take a last glance around the room, inhale a deep breath, and walk downstairs.

As I'm eating breakfast, I hear heavy footsteps coming down the hallway. My body tenses. Elton, my uncle, appears from around the corner. His head hangs low as he looks at his feet. My spoon clatters against the side of the bowl as I scoop another bite of the cereal. Elton's head lifts, his forty-year-old features shifting emotions as he stares at me, first startled, then worried, then curious.

He glances at the clock on the microwave. "It's five twenty. You're not usually up this early."

"I know. I just—" I shove the cereal-filled spoon into my mouth, giving myself a little more time to come up with an answer that won't worry him. When I'm finished chewing I say, "I woke up early and decided to start getting ready for school."

He looks at me cautiously, examining me. His eyebrow rises.

"What?" I can feel my face growing warm and quickly drop my head. "Seriously," I say, glancing up at him. His suspicion seems to be fading.

Aunt Tamlin tramps into the kitchen. She pushes her brown hair away from her tired face. "What are you doing up?" she asks, spotting me at the table.

"She said she woke up early and just decided to stay up," Elton explains. Tamlin shifts her hazel eyes to him. There's something in the way they look at each other, as if they're silently communicating with each other. I can't read it—their expressions are alien to me—so I just sit, eating, and watch them.

Tamlin's eyes stare into mine. "What time did you wake up?"

"Five."

"And you just stayed up?"

"Yeah. It would have been useless to go back to sleep for a half hour," I try to explain.

She laughs a little. "Maybe, but what teenager doesn't enjoy sleeping?"

Me, I think. Sleep makes me feel unprotected, powerless. Last night wasn't the first time I've had that dream. Nightmare would probably be the better word for it. It scares me; they scare me. And to make it worse, every time I have the nightmare it gets more vivid and lasts longer.

The first time, it was just me standing against the wall, hearing a growl. It had been muffled and unclear, but as the months progressed, the dream repeated, getting longer and more menacing each time. And the worst part is, I know exactly what's going to happen, but I can never change the outcome; never make myself run in a different direction or stop running before I slam into the creature. I always do the same thing and every time I wake up shaking and sweaty.

Tamlin grabs a cup of coffee. "Okay. Well I'm going to go wake up Nora and Lilly," she says before heading back upstairs.

Elton puts together his breakfast and sits down in the chair diagonal from me. It's silent, like it usually is before the girls wake up. A couple minutes later, though, Nora and Lilly hop down the stairs and plop into the chairs at the table. They're always full of energy in the morning. They talk and jump around as they get ready for school and eat their breakfast.

"Girls!" Elton exclaims over the noise and clatter as everyone finishes. "Ready to go?"

Nora and Lilly nod in unison. "Alright let's go then." He opens the front door and I watch as the girls skip out the door, ready for another day of elementary school. Elton shuts the door and follows the girls out to his car. My eyes begin to water. I blink back the tears, knowing that if Tamlin catches me she'll know that something's wrong. And that's the last thing I need.

"Well, I'm headed out too," she says, picking up her computer bag from beside the end table in the living room. She walks to the front door. "Don't miss your bus, okay?" She throws me a pointed look, then laughs. "See you tonight," she adds, giving me a little wave before she closes the door.

No you won't.

Tears well up in my eyes and as hard as I try, I can't blink them back. I can't will them to disappear. I let out a quiet sob before collecting myself.

I run upstairs and grab the little duffel bag that I had packed yesterday, in preparation of today's plans. I hear brakes squeal as my school bus comes to a stop at the end of the block, but I don't bother to sprint out the front door and get on. Not today.

I jog down the stairs and into the kitchen, shuffling through a stack of papers on the counter until I come to a small, crumbled sheet. There's a name printed at the top in red and black ink: Barrier Reef. Below that, in smaller font is written, 'Life is Better with Help.' Beneath that is a paragraph of strange cryptic writing. I shove the paper into my pocket and rummage through the kitchen cabinets until I find a huge stack of money in the corner of one of the overhead cabinets. I grab the bills, close the cabinet door, and shove the money into my bag.

My aunt and uncle will eventually figure out that I took it, but not before I'm on a bus headed somewhere far away from here, the outskirts of New York City.

People hustle all around me. I'm in the heart of New York City, camouflaged by the bodies surrounding me.

The sun begins dipping beneath the buildings, casting darkness over the streets. I push through the crowd until I can wedge myself into the entrance of a store.

A boy in a grey hoodie stands, peering into the store's window. His head raises, his gaze fixating on me. His eyes bore into me intensely, then slowly narrow.

While he doesn't say anything, his lingering stare sends a chill down my spine. I quickly turn and begin walking, eager to leave and once again disappear in the crowd. At the end of the block, I peek over my shoulder. Despite the crowded walkways, I swear I see the boy from the shop following behind me. Looking forward, I try to calm myself with deep breaths, but it doesn't do much. I can feel a prick on the back of my neck as my heart speeds in my chest.

Instantly, I'm running, dodging in and out of bodies, clutching the duffel bag in my hand as my arms swing. My knuckles grow white as I grasp the bag's handle. I need to get away. I need to lose him. I don't know who he is, or if he's even relevant, but I need to get away.

A couple blocks later, I glance back. I don't see anyone, but I don't dare to stop.

A firm object collides with my body just as I reach the corner. My eyes snap upwards, spotting a person stumble backwards and quickly regain their balance as I plunge to the ground, a nearly inaudible thump sounding against the city as I make contact with the concreate.

"Are you okay?" a deep, masculine voice asks, but I can barely hear it over the pounding in my ears and the stinging in my lower back.

I jump to my feet, frantic to continue moving, worried that if I stay in one place for too long something bad will happen. I nod. "Sorry," I mutter, probably too softly for him to hear.

The man's strong hand clamps around my wrist. He stares at me through dark, profound eyes. His features are hard, but soften as he looks at me. His grip intensifies as he pushes me into the alley. I stumble backward, bumping my into the brick wall. My eyes close as tears surface. I let out a cry of pain.

My heart sprints in my chest, suddenly concerned that I might be in more danger than before. Something presses against my lips. At first, I think it's his hand, attempting to silence me, but the odd motion tells me it's not a hand—it's lips.

Chapter 2

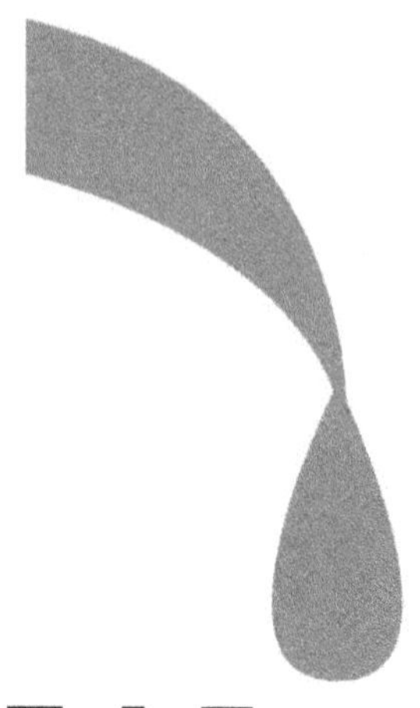

WARM AIR PASSES OVER MY LIPS AS HE breathes only inches from my face. I freeze. As he closes the space between us once again, his lips part and fall closed against mine. I can feel his hands at my hairline. My palms find his chest and push, but he doesn't budge.

His thumb strokes my jaw. Gentle fingers glide through my hair. His bottom lip grazes over mine and falls into my mouth. I clamp my teeth down, blood instantly filling my mouth and coating my tongue as my hand flies up to slap him.

He pulls away from me. In the shadow, I watch as his face contorts. "Ow!"

I peer up at him. He's taller than me by more than half a foot. He lifts his hand to his cheek, which is slowly growing bright red in the outline of my handprint. He glides his fingers across his bottom lip. Pulling back his hand, he examines the shimmering red liquid on his fingertips.

"Well that kinda hurt," he says. There's something familiar about his voice that I hadn't noticed before.

I peek around the man's broad, muscular arms at the sidewalk behind him. I don't see the boy, or anyone familiar, but I can't be sure they're actually gone. My senses are on full blast. My focus returns to the guy who kissed me.

The dim light from the store window illuminates his face just enough to see the edge of his jawline, the pull of his cheekbones, the dip of his eye sockets beneath his eyebrows. Light reflects off of his tousled black hair. His dark eyes stare down at me. I expect him to be angry, but instead, he lets out a laugh.

"Damn Callerie! Was that really necessary?" His eyebrows lift onto his forehead.

I gasp. "Keson?" A smile forms on my lips and I don't bother trying to suppress it.

Since we were little, he's the only one who has ever called me by my last name.

"What are you doing here?" I ask. "What was that for?" I blurt out, throwing my fist into his chest.

Keson hesitates. "What was what for?"

"That kiss."

His lips press together and his shoulders broaden even further. He lifts them in a shrug. "You looked scared. I needed to grab your attention. I couldn't just let you take off and keep running for no reason." He laughs.

"There was a boy following me, did you not see him?"

He shakes his head from side to side. "No. I didn't see anyone."

"Really?" I ask, looking around him at the sidewalks that blend into the busy streets. No one is there, no one is following me. And, although I know that I'm not crazy, the look Keson is giving me expresses that he may be questioning my sanity. I let out a small laugh. "Yeah, of course not. Sorry."

A smirk wiggles its way onto his face. "I always knew you were a little crazy, but Callerie, this is a new level."

I punch his arm, releasing a broken giggle.

"Hey hey hey! That one didn't earn me a slap... the kiss, maybe, but this, no."

I drop my eyes, embarrassed as I think back to that moment. "Yeah... sorry about hitting you, and biting you, and running into you," I ramble off the list of events.

His laughter stops me. When I look up, I catch his dark eyes peering at me. They're the same eyes I remember seeing as a kid. It reminds me of being back in Cylilia when we were younger. He's the same Keson. He's trustworthy and caring and practically my brother, only—seeing him now with his strong arms and handsome features and after that kiss, I'm really glad he's not.

"I… can you talk for a minute?"

"Sure," he replies, nodding.

Still holding his arm, I guide him to the entrance of the doorway he came out of when we collided.

Once we're inside, I drop my bag and pull the crumbled piece of paper out of my jeans pocket. Flattening it in my palm, I examine the cryptic writing at the bottom and remember when I first found out about the pamphlet, only days ago.

It's late; the clock strikes midnight as I sneak down the stairs for a glass of water. The lights in the kitchen are still on, out of place for this time of night. As I grow closer, I hear Tamlin and Elton's hushed voices. I hide in the shadows of the hallway, straining to hear what they're saying.

Elton's voice carries to my ears. "And, you just got this randomly?"

"Yes," Tamlin replies.

Elton hesitates. "But... why? Why would they send it to you?"

"I don't know." She sighs. "I've heard rumors about these safe houses, but I didn't think they were real. They use the old code to tell people where they are."

"But they are real. Aren't they? And, if you got a coded message from them, what does that mean?"

Tamlin speaks after a moment of silence, "I haven't seen this type of writing in years. I don't even know if I can read it anymore." After a moment she says, "I think it's in North Carolina somewhere, but I'm not sure."

"Barrier Reef? What's that?"

"Their name. Casual, but meaningful," she responds simply.

I stare up at Keson with the paper in my hand. "Do you know how to decipher this?" I ask, nearly pleading with him. I know this safe house is in North Carolina—according to Tamlin, anyway—but besides that, I have no idea where I'm headed.

Keson takes the piece of paper from my hands and, after looking at it, turns his attention back to me, gawking. "Where'd you get this?"

I shrug. "Tamlin and Elton got it."

"Do you know what this is?" His eyes are wide with shock.

I shake my head. "Not exactly, but I have an idea."

"This is a coded letter from a secret organization that helps hide Cylilians who are in trouble."

I'm not sure why it's such a big deal or why he is looking at me the way he is. "Well? What does it say?"

"Not quite sure, give me a second." He doesn't say anything for a long time. Finally, he speaks. "There's this safe house. Barrier Reef—which might be code for something, I'm not sure. It's in Raleigh, North Carolina right now, in a warehouse. But it looks like they'll be moving in a few weeks." He stops and goes silent.

"Is that it?" The paragraph seemed longer than that.

"There's more about how they function and move around, but not a lot."

"Thanks," I acknowledge, holding out my hand, palm up. He places the paper in it. "How were you able to read this?" I ask, examining the cryptic writing.

"We used to take it as a class at school in Cylilia. It used to be the main language there, but it kind of faded away over time."

"Why didn't I learn it?"

"It was sort of like a language history class you took after you turned twelve."

"And, I was ten when Cylilia was overtaken, became Dunchoria, and I left. I never took that class." I look at the ground.

"Hey," Keson says, trying to get my attention. "It's fine. It's just a dumb language thing."

But what he doesn't realize is that—even though it would have been nice to learn the language in school—that's not the reason I'm upset. I was ten when my entire life changed.

"Can you teach me how to read it?" I ask, peering up at him through my eyelashes.

He nods. "Sure." A smile plays on his lips.

He reaches down and grasps my bag with a big, strong hand. Then his other hand closes around mine. It feels warm and comforting and good. My heart jumps a little in my chest as butterflies begin gently fluttering in my stomach, as if they'd just been awakened from a long, peaceful sleep. We leave the store and walk the brightly lit street.

My thoughts slip into a memory.

I'm young, or younger at least. Eleven-year-old Keson walks beside me.

"My dad told me I wasn't supposed to see you anymore. He said it'd be bad for us to hang out," he says.

"Bad?" my high pitched eight-year-old voice asks. "How would it be bad?"

"I don't know. He wouldn't tell me. All he said was that we shouldn't."

"But I want to hang out with you. I like playing with you," I whine.

"Me too." He pauses for a moment of thought. He comes to an abrupt stop. I look back at him curiously. "Okay. I have a plan," he says.

"What?" I ask excitedly.

"You have to promise not to tell anyone."

"I won't," I agree.

The memory fizzes out almost instantly. I'm back to reality, greeted by the store-lit street.

Keson releases my hand. We walk side by side for a block in silence. I glance at him every now and again, trying to memorize his features. He's grown up a lot since the last time I saw him.

We reach a little coffee house. Keson comes to a stop at the door, forcing the people behind us to swerve around him, some cussing under their breaths, but he ignores them. He yanks open the door and gestures into the shop. "Ladies first." A small smirk curves the corners of his lips upward. The corners of his eyes wrinkle.

I laugh and walk through the door. Sitting down at an empty table, I place the paper in the center of the circular, polished wood. Keson slides into the chair across from me, dropping my bag at my feet.

"So?" I say, prompting the lesson. "Teach me."

He laughs. "Okay, first thing you need to know, each symbol stands for a letter. So, if you can learn the letters-"

"I can read the words," I finish.

Keson teaches me the alphabet and numbers up to ten, which lasts through two cups of coffee and the sandwich we share, all of which I pay for using the stack of money from the kitchen cabinet. When we're done, Keson attempts to convince me not to leave, with little success. Finally, he succumbs and leads me to a nearby bus stop. After studying the map, I see that this bus line goes all the way up and down the east coast, meaning it'll take me straight to North Carolina, right where I need to go.

We sit on the bench, waiting. Conversation drifts from family to school to gossip about old friends and foes, until the bus comes around the corner, slowing at our stop. I stand, bouncing on my tiptoes, eager—and at the same time scared—to get on. The moment I step foot on the bus I know I can't turn back. But as much I want to turn around and go home to Tamlin and Elton, I know I can't. Getting the letter for the safe house couldn't have been a mistake. In order to keep my family safe, I can't turn back.

The bus doors open and people pour off. I'm about to step onto the bus when a hand clasps onto my arm. I turn to face Keson. He pulls me in for a hug. My skin tingles at the affectionate gesture. Warmth engulfs me from the inside out. The feelings of security and protection fill me. I breathe in the scent of him and promise to remember it. After all this time, I still feel safe around Keson, as if nothing in the world could ever hurt me.

His strong arms release me, reminding me that I'm not invincible; there are things that I have no control over, things that can hurt me. I want to pull him back in, make him wrap his arms around me and allow his safety net to fall back over me. But I don't.

I stare up into his eyes. "Thanks," I mouth almost silently.

He somehow manages to hear it. "You're welcome. Hopefully I'll see you again soon," he states calmly.

Something in the way he watches me makes me think there's something more to that statement; something he wants to say, but instead he just offers a smile. "There's always a reason to keep going," he says. "Just remember that."

I press my lips together in a straight, tight line. "I will," I acknowledge in a soft tone. Tears begin to well up in my eyes. I turn and walk on the bus before he can see them. Taking a seat by the window, I glance down at him standing on the sidewalk. The bus pulls away from the curb. I lift my hand, waving goodbye and offer a small smile. He does the same.

Then he's gone, torn from my sight.

North Carolina greets me—damp and cool—as I step off the bus. I'd practiced reading the letter for the majority of the ride. Even though Keson had given me a lesson on how to decipher the symbols, I wasn't sure I'd be able to remember them. I look down at the letter in my palm, attempting to read the warehouse address.

"Excuse me ma'am," a male voice says from behind me. "You forgot your bag."

I gasp and take it from him. "Oh my gosh! Thank you. I didn't even realize."

The man nods and passes me as he strides down the sidewalk. My focus returns to the symbols. I find the place where the address is written, directly beneath the line 'Life is Better with Help.'

I ask a lady standing nearby if she knows where it is. She tells me it's on the edge of the city and points in the direction I should head. I walk for close to an hour. Just as I'm about to give up, the building appears, right where the lady said it would be.

Nearing the entrance, I hesitate, feeling both ambitious and afraid of what will be waiting inside. A squeal echoes through the building as I push open the large, metal door. The concrete walls are covered in multicolored graffiti. A couple of wooden crates are scattered about the room.

I walk to the middle of the warehouse. There's not a person in sight. Is this the right place? I study the paper. It has to be. But if it is, then why isn't anyone else here? Isn't it supposed to be a safe house? I pause. What if the safe house is *only* a house, a place to stay that's safe? It's possible.

This is not going to help me! An abandoned building? Seriously? I can feel the hope that I didn't even realize I had, now deflating. This was my last option. I was so sure that all my questions would be answered; I didn't even have a backup plan.

I don't know what else to do, or where to go. Maybe I should just go home. Tamlin and Elton are probably wondering where I am. I contemplate for a moment.

I can't go home. The reason I left was to keep them safe.

If I go back, the danger follows me. I don't know why, but they want me. King Chastrin is the reason I lost my mom, my dad, and my sister. He took away everything that mattered to me, and I'm not going to let him do it again.

I take another look around the warehouse. There's something on top of one of the crates on the opposite side. It's a piece of paper. I can vaguely see the red and black words on it.

A squeal echoes in the silence. I jump, startled. Looking toward the door, I watch as it swings open. My heart leaps in anticipation, thinking that whoever's entering is a member of Barrier Reef. Light reflects off something, casting a gold shimmer on the floor in front of me. My eyes narrow as I survey the object. It's a badge. The person wears a gray uniform. A gun dangles from the holster around his waist. It's a police officer.

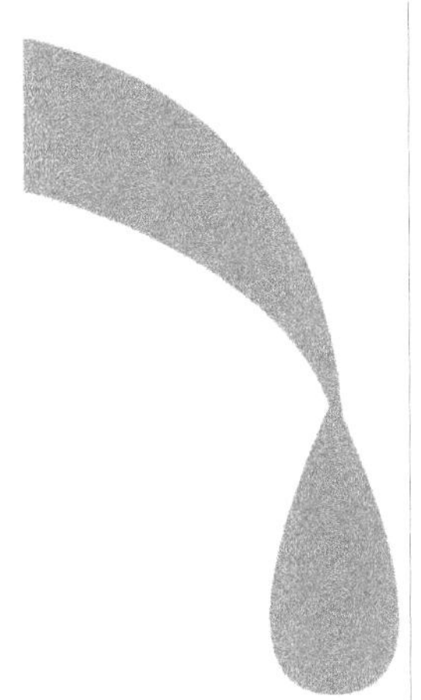

Chapter 3

"**S**HIT!" I SAY UNDER MY BREATH, DIVING around the closest corner. Pressing against the wall, I sink into a crouch, looking at the crate a couple yards away from me. I want to run to it and grab the paper off the top, but I also know that I can't have the officer see me. He'll wonder why I'm here and I can't tell him. I don't even know why I'm here at this point.

He'll think I'm a runaway, which, in a sense, I guess I am. He'll send me back home.

"And you're sure you saw her come in here?" a male voice asks.

"I'm sure," a high pitch woman's voice replies. "Just a few minutes ago."

"Hello," the officer says, raising his voice. "Sweetie? We know you're in here. Just come out." He pauses. "We'd like to talk to you." He waits.

Then, footsteps echo throughout the empty warehouse. I peer around the corner. The cop is walking around cautiously. He tramps over to the crates only yards away from me. I can feel my heart beat increasing with every passing moment. I hold my breath, wishing I could disappear.

He spots the paper, the one I so desperately wish to reach. Picking it up, he examines it, turning it between his fingers. I catch a glimpse of the red and black lettering at the top of the page. My heart skips and stalls in my chest. It looks just like the one I have. Maybe the paper buried in my pocket wasn't lying and this place really is a safe house.

The officer's eyebrows furrow. His hand crumbles the paper and tosses it to the ground. He moves to the next set of crates, searching behind them. I stare at the crumbled piece of paper on the ground. I need to get to it. My balance shifts and I topple over. A thud echoes through the warehouse as my hands hit the cement floor.

The cop spins on his heels, his eyes immediately settling on me. I don't have time to think. Pushing myself up off the ground, I dart toward the ball of paper on the floor. My hand swipes down, fingers skimming the cement floor to pick up the paper. As I run through the opening of the warehouse's metal door, I catch a glimpse of the woman the cop had been talking to earlier. She jumps back, startled.

My bag swings back and forth in my hand as I sprint down the sidewalk.

"Stop!" I hear the officer call over the sound of my thudding heart and pounding feet. "Wait!"

I ignore him and continue running. His footsteps grow closer. I glance behind me, seeing that he's right on my tail. *Shoot!* I pump my fists faster, determined to increase the distance between us.

"I'm trying to help!" He sounds breathless. "Just hold on, one minute."

My footsteps falter, but only momentarily. I bolt, not knowing where I'm running to, just knowing who I'm running from. Finally, I slow my pace and then stop, exhausted, letting my body collapse against the wall of a building. Loosening my grip on the bag, it drops to the ground.

I hold the balled-up piece of paper in my palm, gently unfolding it. My fingers fumble with the creased edges, until the entire paper lays flat in my hand. It looks almost the same as the one I got off the counter at home. Red and black letters line the top, followed by the slogan, and then a paragraph in Cylilian. I stare at it, my chest still heaving.

My heart leaps as I decipher the symbols. Coos Bay, Oregon. That's where the new safe house is! That's where I need to go!

There are people walking, but not many. A woman passes me with a stroller. I jog up next to her.

"Excuse me," I say.

She jumps back, startled. "Oh!" Her hand reaches up and touches her heart. "You scared me."

"I'm really sorry. Do you know if there's a train station anywhere around here?"

She hesitates, thinking. "There's one on that side of town," she says, pointing a finger.

"Okay, thank you!"

I sit, waiting for the train to arrive. A mom and her daughter are at the other end of my bench, a stroller with a baby is parked in front of them. The woman is gently crooning to the baby as the older daughter doodles in a notebook.

Tears spew out of the newborn's eyes. The sound of wailing fills the waiting area. I look over at the lady as she leans forward and picks up the baby. She places her in the crease of her arms and slowly sways from side to side.

Thoughts begin to invade my mind. My vision starts to blur and the noises around me fade until they are replaced by another image; a memory.

My mother sits tensely at the kitchen table holding Evlynell. A younger version of me is perched in a chair next to them. King Henliv's army had lost a battle yesterday and in the midst of it, my father had died fighting.

The front door slams against the wall. My mother jumps up, propping Evlyn on her hip in a swift movement, and quickly reaches down to grab my hand. Members of Chastrin's army—Uniforms—storm into the house.

"Callerie. This is it," I hear one say, malice in his tone, as they enter the kitchen. "Kalene Callerie, you are under arrest for conspiracy plots against Chastrin, the new King of Dunchoria."

In a single blink, the Uniforms invade the room and rip Evlyn from my mother's arms. Evlyn's loud cry fills the house.

One of them walks toward me aggressively and grips my shoulder. Pain courses through my body where he is squeezing me. As I look up at the Uniform towering above me, panic and fear flood through me. My pulse quickens and adrenaline rushes through my veins. Without realizing what's happening, my power kicks in. The Uniform holding me twists in pain and crumbles to the ground.

The vision ripples and disappears. The piercing noise of the baby crying rushes back into my ears. I glimpse over at the mother; she's still cradling the baby, whose hair is pulled tightly back by a headband, adorned with a purple bow. A frustrated expression plays on the mother's face. A continuous wale drones on from the baby, even as the mother attempts to comfort her. The older daughter reaches over and strokes the baby's arm in an affectionate motion. I slide further down the bench until I'm sitting next to the mother.

"What are their names?" I ask.

The mother glances from her baby to me. She seems startled. "This—" She gestures to the newborn in her arms. "Is Lucy. And this—" She places her hand on her other daughter's head. "Is Ivy."

I look at Ivy, who's probably about four years old. She peeks up at me from under her curled bangs, and quickly averts her gaze back down to Lucy when she realizes I'm watching her. The motion reminds me of Lillian, my youngest cousin. She's so shy and timid. Her head always lowers to dodge the curious gazes of others.

"I'm Jacklyn," the mother adds.

"Hi Jacklyn, I'm—" I hesitate for a split second. "Rose," I finish.

"Nice to meet you, Rose," Jacklyn says. A loud cry erupts from the infant in her arms. Jacklyn shifts her attention back to Lucy.

I watch for a minute, and then ask, "What's wrong?"

"I don't know. She's been crying for a while, but I can't get her to stop."

I remember Evlyn crying in the Uniform's arms that night. It was so long ago, but it's still fresh in my mind. "Can I hold her?"

Jacklyn looks at me questioningly. "Sure," she replies slowly, uncertainly. She lifts Lucy from her lap and hands her to me.

I gently cradle the baby in my arms. The crying continues, just as I had expected it to. Focusing on Lucy, I think of comfort and peace and happiness. Slowly, I transmit the feelings to the baby in my arms. The crying softens, coming to a stop as it dissipates into the waiting room. Lucy stares up at me through glossy blue eyes.

They begin to brighten and a high pitch squeal emits from her tiny mouth. I smile in relief and satisfaction.

I glimpse up at Jacklyn. Raising Lucy, I place her in Jacklyn's arms. Jacklyn looks down at her smiling daughter, then up to me. "How'd you do that?"

"I just put her in my arms and cradled her a little," I lie.

"She must really like you," Jacklyn smiles. She gazes back down at Lucy. After a minute she adds, "Thank you."

I smile back. "You're welcome."

The train tracks rattle. A train whistles in the distance.

Sunlight pours through the windows as the train pulls out from under the covered station. Buildings stand tall all around the tracks, then gradually grow shorter and scarcer, until farm fields replace them.

I gaze out of the window at the fields that spread for acres. I consider my current situation; I'm running from something that's almost inevitable. My thoughts drift to memories again.

The Uniform that had touched me now lays coiled on the ground. Another Uniform standing nearby starts pursuing me barbarically. I can see the wild blaze in his dark, unforgiving eyes. Fear spikes in me again. He reaches out and grabs me harshly. I channel all the pain in my body to him and release it, but he doesn't move. Not even his eyes show any sign of pain. My mom steps between us, breaking the contact.

The Uniform speaks, loud and determined. "She just used aggressive tactics against the King's Uniforms and she will be punished."

Another memory comes in quick succession, forming vividly in my mind. I was ten years old. I had been living with my aunt and uncle for two months, but found myself drawn back to Dunchoria.

I'm scared as I pass through the portal to Cylilia. I don't know what to expect. I can't imagine that it has changed much in the two months I've been gone, but then again, Chastrin's Uniforms had searched every home in town to make sure there were no Cylilians that opposed him. Just like he had with my own house. My heart thumps with hope as I think about it. Maybe I'll be able to find them. My mother and little sister, the two people who were stolen from me. Snatched away by Chastrin and his Uniforms.

Pine needle and soil-covered ground greet me on the other side of the portal. It looks just like I remember. The trees stand tall, protruding into the sky above. I begin walking, until the greenery grows scarce and eventually disappears. The town sprawls out in front of me. The stone castle towers in the sky, visible above everything else.

I continue walking, heading straight toward my house, located only a couple blocks away. When I finally reach it, I notice two pieces of wood are placed across the front door in the shape of an 'X.' I reach between the boards and find the doorknob. Pushing the door open, I wedge my body into the house. Chairs are pushed out from the table; a few flipped over on the floor. Wooden boards cover the windows. The house is silent and dusty. Chastrin's Uniforms did this.

Chapter 4

ESPITE THE RUMBLE OF THE TRACKS AS we pass through the Midwest, I sink off into sleep, clutching the Barrier Reef paper in my hands the whole time. When I wake, most of the other passengers are already awake.

Eventually, the train pulls into a station and comes to a slow-motion stop. Everyone stands up, stretches, and grabs their luggage. I pull my little duffel out from above my seat and exit the train. I follow the rest of the crowd as they head for the front of the station. I spot a bathroom door along the wall and manage to cut through the maze of people and into the room. I look at myself in one of the mirrors. My dirty blonde hair lays against my back, nearly straight. It's frizzed a little, and the strange yellow lights in the bathroom make the stray strands glimmer gold. I pat it down as best I can and switch my attention to the rest of my body. Vaguely noticeable black rings settle like shadows above my cheekbones. After I've fixed myself up as best I can, I leave the bathroom.

The halls are nearly empty now, only a few trailing passengers linger on the platform. An exit hallway becomes visible up ahead. I walk toward it, careful to ignore the half a dozen boys sitting and standing against the wall in a cluster. A couple girls sit with them, giggling and talking quietly. Their bodies move loosely, swaying as if they were blades of grass in the wind. I keep my eyes locked on the path ahead of me.

Someone whistles. The group members look at me. My pace increases instinctively. I pass the little clique and hustle forward, leaving them behind me.

A hard hand clasps onto my wrist and twirls me around. A man in his late teens stares down at me. I meet his eyes; fear quickly invading my body. A trigger inside me begins to pull, tightening, ready to let loose and fire. I force it to stop and focus on remaining calm.

The boy releases my hand but stays close. "Where are you going?" he asks, breathing in my face. His breath smells like a mix of alcohol and marijuana.

I collect myself and try to steady my quivering lips enough to talk as casually as I can. "Just catching a train," I lie. I smile a little, proud of my delivery of the words.

"Which one?" he presses. "Maybe I could escort you." I look over his shoulder. Thank goodness all of his friends stayed where they were. They're still watching us, but they haven't bothered getting up.

"No, that's okay. I'll be alright. I don't need an escort," I insist.

The boy takes a step closer, glaring down at me. His eyes are determined and filled with persistence. I take a step backward, creating distance between us. When I turn to leave, I feel his hand find my wrist again. "Which one?" he repeats, his voice rough and unrelenting.

I look at him, trying my best to absorb his words. Fear, panic, and pure helplessness elevate inside me, starting in my stomach and crawling up through my body. *He's only human,* I remind myself. *At least you're not facing off against Uniforms.* Then again, if he were a Uniform, I'd have no problem releasing what I'm trying my best to keep inside. The guy stares down at me, waiting for me to answer him. His eyes are sharp, bitter, and merciless. I drop my eyes to the ground, but I can still feel his gaze on me. I think about is him, his gaze, and his grip on my wrist.

Then, I let go. The feeling inside me floods from my body. The hand enclosed on my arm releases and his body me falls away. I lift my eyes slightly and watch as the boy drops to the floor. He rolls and clamps his hands on his head.

His group rises from where they're sitting. Some stumble and bump into each other, obviously drunk. They move toward us slowly. I look back down at the man on the ground, his body rigid in pain.

I hesitate. Then, I'm running, fleeing from the mess I just created.

I slow my pace to a quick walk when I feel I'm far enough away and glance behind me. I can no longer see the platform or the people residing at it.

The front doors of the station come into view. Taxis wait outside on the curb, begging for customers. I push through the doors and am greeted by the scent of burning wood and the chill of the frigid wind as it blows across the pavement and rushes against my skin. Outside, on the wall above the doors, a sign hangs. In big, bold letters it reads, 'Oregon Station.'

I come to a halt, watching as people stand, waiting for family members. Trunks slam as people pile into the taxis. After a moment, I jump into the back of the closest empty cab.

I drop the duffel on the seat next to me. The cab driver twists around to look at me. "Where to?" he asks.

"Coos Bay, the downtown area," I reply instantaneously.

He nods, turns to his GPS and types in 'Coos Bay'. The engine hums to life and the cab begins to pull away from the station. I gaze out the window as the station disappears from my sight.

No matter how far I travel from New York, I still feel like I'm too close to keep my family protected. I feel alone in this world, the one that's not mine. I have a world of my own, or at least I did. I'm not so sure about that anymore.

My mind wanders uncontrollably around the question that's been nagging at me for a long time. I've always had a feeling that Chastrin would come looking for me.

The cab comes to a slow stop. My eyes snap to the window and I find myself watching as people leisurely walk past the car and down the sidewalk. Shops line the street. People trot in and out of them, carrying shopping bags.

The driver glances down at the mechanism in the middle of the dashboard. He then looks at me in his rearview mirror.

"Ma'am," he says. I jump at the sound of his voice. Jerking my attention off the flow of pedestrians, I meet his eyes in the mirror. "Is this location okay? It's the center of the Coos Bay shopping area."

"Yes, this is fine," I answer.

I pull my bag onto my lap, find my wallet, and pay him.

I stuff the rest of the cash back into my bag and begin to inch toward the door. I stop myself and pull the coded letter out of my pocket. I ask him if he knows where the address on the paper is.

He gives me directions, then says, "It's a store called 'Tracy's Accessories.' Would you like me to take you there?"

"No that's okay, I can walk."

I slip out of the taxi, grasping my duffel bag. The cab pulls away from the curb, slowly merging with the other cars.

My senses kick in at the realization that I'm alone... again. My family is on the other side of the country. Hopefully they're safe.

A husky woman saunters past me carrying four shopping bags; two on either arm. She gives me a nasty look as she passes. I realize that I'm standing still in the middle of the sidewalk, forcing people to swerve around me. I take a quick glance around, trying to memorize my surroundings before heading in the direction that the taxi driver had mentioned.

My feet begin to move, matching my pace with the other people bustling around me. I fix my gaze on the horizon. My breath comes out in faint puffs of white; the temperature here is colder than it was in North Carolina.

The block ends and I follow as the people in front of me cautiously cross the street. They ignore me as I copy their steps, close on their heels.

A tiny, one-story building rests on the corner. A painted sign hangs above the doorway. The purple and navy-blue letters read 'Tracy's Accessories.'

I enter the store, my attention settling on the lady standing behind a register at the back of the store. Despite the eye-catching, elegant necklaces and purses throughout the room, I walk toward her.

"I, uh—" I stutter, not knowing what to say to her or how to explain the reason I'm here. The name tag pinned to her shirt reads, *Chloe*. "Are you the owner?" I ask.

"No. I'm the manager. What can I help you with?"

"Is the owner here?"

"No, she should be in tomorrow."

"Okay," I say, my hope draining. "Thanks. I'll come back tomorrow." I start to leave but turn back around. "Do you know where I can find a hotel?"

The woman pauses, her eyes watching me curiously. She gives me a strange, uncertain look. "You don't have a place to stay?"

I don't answer.

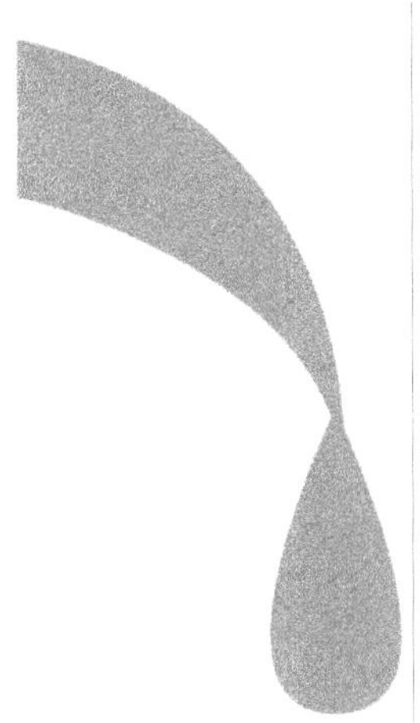

Chapter 5

I PASS THROUGH THE LARGE FRONT DOORS OF the hotel and enter the lobby. A middle-aged man sits in a chair behind the reception desk. As I walk in, he looks up from the computer in front of him.

"Can I help you?" he asks.

"I'd like a room," I answer swiftly.

"Can I see your ID please?"

"Uh, sure." I shuffle through my duffel until I find my New York driver's permit in one of the hidden, inside pockets.

I pass the card to him over the counter. He examines it for a moment. His facial expression contorts into disappointment. I know almost immediately that his expression is meant for me. The man's eyes pull away from the card to peek at me. With an outstretched hand, he returns the ID.

"You have to be eighteen to rent a room here," he says apologetically. "I'm sorry. I don't know what else to tell you."

Dang it! My mind races as I try to figure out what I can do or where I can go. I give a slow, understanding nod, and turn for the exit. As I amble forward, my mind swims with ideas.

The sun has fallen under the horizon, but the faint light of dusk still lingers, casting an orange glow over the street. I walk in the direction of the town's center. As I walk, my stomach grumbles. It's the first time I've heard it today, but it makes me realize that I have barely eaten. Breakfast was some cheap food from the train, and I completely skipped lunch.

I spot a pizza place across the street and head over. Two slices of cheese pizza later, I'm feeling better, ready to face reality again.

The cool night air hits me.

I wander down the empty sidewalk. My footsteps echo in the silence. I walk past store after store. Some have lights blazing in the dark night, others are pitch black, matching the outside world.

My eyes drift to a spot a block ahead of me, where the shops vanish and are replaced by a cluster of trees. There's a short, waist-high fence lining the sidewalk. I trek forward and cross the narrow side street, not too concerned about cars. I'm the only one navigating the sidewalk and I haven't seen a car in almost five minutes.

I place my hands on the fence and stare into the trees. Memories of the park back home, in New York, enter my thoughts. All the pleasant, playful memories, along with the scary, dangerous ones flood back into my head. Stepping beyond the fence I feel a mixture of comfort and panic. My body stalls as my mind tries to come up with a way to calm myself.

Listening to the silence around me helps. It's completely quiet. I know that I'm alone, which isn't necessarily comforting, but it's better than being surrounded by people you can't trust.

A white object catches my eye. I study it for a minute, not understanding what it's doing in the middle of the trees. I approach it slowly, with caution. When I get a few feet away from it, I can make out the silhouette of a bench. My tension fades and I saunter up to it. Some of the paint has peeled off, leaving the wood beneath exposed.

Realizing this is probably my best option, I settle onto the wooden planks. I place my head on one end and extend my legs, my feet dangling off the other side. I arrange my bag on my chest and fold my arms around it. The wooden beams press into my back. My body is stiff and sore from the long day and constant tension. Exhaustion sets in and my muscles fall limp. My eyes slide shut.

My eyelids whip open in a panicked frenzy. Sunlight floods into them and a gasp escapes my lips. My heart pounds in my chest. My eyes blur as I try to focus on my surroundings. I look around with fuzzy vision and attempt to figure out where I am.

Forcing myself to breathe in deep, steady breaths, I begin to calm, relaxing enough to regain my senses. My eyes focus on the bag, still in my hands. My ears concentrate on the environment. A bird chirps in a nearby tree, another answers from deeper in the woods. *The woods…* that's where I am. I slept on a bench last night—which explains my sore, tight back.

I sit up, and my vision goes black momentarily. Light and color slowly begin flooding back in, revealing the dark orange and brown leaves that still cling desperately to the trees, which cast distinct shadows against the dirt covered ground. I walk to the exit of the park.

Cars zoom by on the main street. The sidewalks are as crowded as they were yesterday when I first got here. I move forward, letting the early morning sun hit my back. My feet move as quickly as they can, anxious to get to Tracy's Accessories.

Chloe, the cashier from yesterday, had said that the owner would be in today. And that's exactly who I need to talk to.

When I enter the store, Chloe is standing at the counter in the back. I walk up to her and ask, "is the owner here yet?"

"Yes." She lifts her arm and points a finger toward the door in the back. "She's in the office."

I nod and walk toward the room. A woman in her thirties sits behind the desk, her attention on a sheet of paper in front of her. She bounces a pen in her hand, concentrating.

I knock on the doorframe. Her brown eyes skip to me. "Oh! Hello." She pushes the piece of paper to the corner of her desk. "How can I help you?"

"Are you the owner?" I ask.

"Yes." She stands up, extending her hand. "I'm Tracy."

I reach out and shake her hand. "Hi Tracy. I'm Rose." Reaching my hand into my pocket, I pull the coded paper out in front of me. Her eyes observe the paper in my hand. "I was hoping you'd be able to tell me—"

Her eyes widen. "Close the door!" she whispers harshly.

I do as she says and turn to her. "Sit," she says, gesturing to a chair opposite her. I take a seat and stare at her slim figure perched in the chair on the other side of the desk.

"So? Do you know what it is?"

She watches me momentarily before responding with another question. "What did you say your name was?"

"Rose," I answer hesitantly.

"Is that your full name?"

I shake my head.

"What is it, then?" Her eyes scrutinize me as she waits for the answer.

I pause. "Roslanie Callerie." The words flow from my lips. It's been a while since I've said my full name.

"Roslanie," she says, so low it sounds like a whisper.

I nod.

"You're one of Kalene's girls, aren't you?"

I gawk at her. "Y-You knew my mom?" I stutter.

She nods, a smile slipping across her lips. "We were classmates, back in Cylilia."

"Really?" I ask in disbelief.

"Yeah." She lets out a sigh. "I haven't seen her in forever."

"Neither have I," I respond under my breath. I'd prefer not to have to try to explain what happened.

"So?" Tracy asks. "That paper. May I see it?"

I nod and hand her the coded letter. She skims it for a moment.

"May I ask how you came across this?"

"Well," I start, trying to decide where to begin. "I found it at the safe house in North Carolina."

"Are you from there?" Tracy asks.

"No, I'm from New York."

Her expression shifts to one of curiosity as her eyebrows furrow in thought.

"My Aunt and Uncle were sent a letter about the safe house being in North Carolina. I figured it might be meant for me, so I left home in hope of finding it."

"How old are you?" Tracy asks, raising an eyebrow.

"Fifteen," I answer.

"You were ten when Chastrin took over, right?"

"Yeah."

"And when did you leave Cylilia? Or Dunchoria by then, I guess."

"That same year."

"You never learned how to read Cylilian?"

"No. Not in Cylilia anyways. But Keson helped me learn the letters back in New York."

"Keson?"

"Yeah, he used to live in Cylilia. He's practically my older brother," I explain. The memory of our kiss slips into my head. I begin blushing and push it out of my thoughts.

"Oh. I see."

"What is this whole safe house thing?"

Her eyebrows lift, shocked. "You don't know?"

I shake my head.

"And yet you came here? Looking for it, but you had no idea what it was?"

I nod. "I knew that it was a safe house for Cylilians who were in trouble, but that's about it."

"Well, that's quite courageous of you. But why'd you leave home for something that you may have never found?" Her eyes watch me carefully as I answer.

"I didn't really have another option. Chastrin's Uniforms came looking for me. I wanted to make sure my aunt and uncle and cousins didn't get stuck in the middle of it."

Something in her expression shifts. "He's looking for you? Why?"

"I, uh—" I contemplate whether I should tell her. "I did something when I was ten and he thinks I owe him for it." I decide to clarify, knowing that she's only going to question me more. "He wants me to do something for him I guess." I sigh. "I'm not even sure."

"And you want help from Barrier Reef?"

"I don't know what I want. All I know is that I don't want to help Chastrin." He has done so much to disrupt my life. The last thing I want to do is help him.

"What is your power?" she questions calmly.

"My power?" I hesitate, wondering why it's relevant.

"Yes, we have to know what—or who—we're getting ourselves involved in."

"Oh. I'm a Mind Inflictor," I convey.

She stares at me for what feels like a long time. I'm almost worried she's going to deny helping me, until she finally replies, "Okay, we'll help."

"We?" I ask, trying to gain clarity.

"Yeah. You didn't think this whole organization was run solely by me, did you?"

I shrug. "I guess not."

"There's a procedure we have to follow for these kinds of things."

"What kind of procedure?"

Chapter 6

I LOOK AT MY REFLECTION IN THE MIRROR. Chocolate brown eyes stare back at me. Shoulder length brown hair frames my face. My complexion seems paler against the dark hair and eyes. I don't look like myself anymore. I look like a completely different person.

Tracy had taken me to a private salon to get my hair done. Afterwards, we had gotten contact lenses and she had taken me clothes shopping—my duffel didn't fit more than two outfits—before she brought me back to her house. I've been staring at the mirror for almost an hour now. I keep trying to memorize the face looking back at me—trying to tell myself that this is me now—but I'm finding that extremely hard to do.

I lift my arm and swipe a loose strand of dark hair off my forehead. Tracy had explained to me that when they admit a new person into Barrier Reef they have to change the person's appearance, identity, name, and personal background. It's like creating an entirely new person. It will keep me, and my loved ones, safe.

I am a new person with a clean slate.

The door creaks open. I spin around to face Tracy. "What do you think, Macy?" she asks, using my new name.

"It's… nice. It doesn't even look like me."

She laughs. "Well, that's the whole point." She pauses. "Okay, so what's your story? Do you remember?"

Of course I remember. Tracy had already asked me a hundred times throughout the makeover. I had it practically memorized by now. "My name is Macy Anne Woods. I lived in Michigan with my mom and dad up until a month ago when they died in a car accident. I came here to live with my aunt and uncle. I have no siblings, I attended East Jackson High School with average grades, and I don't play any sports. Am I missing anything?"

"Nope. I think you've covered it all. The family that's going to take care of you will be here soon. They know your real identity, but they know they aren't allowed to share that information with anyone." She pauses. "Oh, and they're human, so be gentle." She lets out a small laugh, but I know it's not a joke. She's just attempting to lighten the mood.

"Humans? Why humans and not Cylilians?"

She leans against the door frame, casually explaining. "They've been friends of mine for a long time. They actually helped me when I had just moved here from Cylilia. They're… Cylilian sympathizers, in a sense." She smiles. "I don't know where I would be without their help, they're very valuable to the organization."

"How long ago did you move here?"

"At the start of the war."

I nod. "What's your power?" I'm curious. I could probably guess. With her compassion and ability to blend so well into society, maybe a Chameleon or a Singer.

Just at that moment, the doorbell rings. Tracy smiles, ignoring the question, and leads me to the front door, opening it.

A man and woman stand in the entrance.

The man looks at me through hazel eyes. His hair is graying, but it may have been blond at one time. His eyes skip to Tracy. "Hey Tracy." He takes a step forward and shakes her hand.

"Hi Peter," Tracy greets.

The woman standing next to Peter watches me with her dark brown eyes, a large, toothy smile forming. "Hello," she says. "You must be R… Macy." She catches herself before she says my real name. "I'm Linda."

"Hi," I reply.

"It's nice to see you again Tracy."

Tracy smiles, matching Linda's. "You too, Linda." She lifts her arm, gesturing for Peter and Linda to come in. We all walk to the living room and sit down. "So, let's get down to business." Tracy lifts a manila folder from the coffee table. "These are Macy's manuscripts from her previous school." She passes them to Linda. "Her grades, records, everything you need to register her for school without suspicion."

"How'd you—" I start.

"It's not that hard to create a fake transcript," Tracy responds, knowing what I'm about to ask. "We do it all the time."

I nod, but it strikes something inside of me. How many other Cylilians crouch under Barrier Reef's protection? How many other children, teenagers, and adults are dependent on this single organization? And, how many of those are sitting idly in Coos Bay?

"You guys are planning to enroll Macy in school, right?" Tracy asks Peter and Linda.

"Of course!" Linda answers. "What else would a fifteen-year-old do?"

"And you do know that you can't breathe a word of Macy's real identity to anyone, right?" Tracy's eyes switch between Peter and Linda as she speaks.

"Yes," Peter replies.

"It's not our first time doing this," Linda says, her voice low. A soft smile plays on her lips. Her eyes are almost doe-like, innocent and gentle.

"I know," Tracy replies, standing from the couch. "I just need to remind you. Safety precautions and all."

"We know." Linda follows Tracy's lead and stands up from the sofa.

We walk to the front door and I pick up my bag, following Linda and Peter out. Just as I'm about to step onto the porch, Tracy grabs my wrist. I turn to face her.

She looks at me for a moment, a smile forming on her lips. "Good luck," she says as she lets go of me.

"Thanks."

"If you ever need something, you know where to find me."

I nod and walk out to the couple's car.

I press my back up against the cold stone wall. A deep, familiar rumble echoes from down the hall, sending a shiver up my spine. I can't place my finger on exactly what made the sound, but I know that I have to get out of here.

Another rumble shakes the ground beneath me, obviously closer. I begin running, not sure which way will lead me outside and which will lead me to the creature I'm so afraid of encountering. My nerves tingle and, in spite of everything, I can't seem to collect myself. My mind won't focus, not enough to decide what to do next.

I come to a stop, leaning over to grasp my knees. My breathing slows slightly as I straighten, flattening my back against the wall again. Little, uneven rocks poke my skin through the fabric of my shirt. I can hear my heart drumming inside my head.

A different sound erupts from further down the hallway to my right. Its pitch is slightly deeper and smoother than the one I'd heard before.

The pace of my breathing automatically increases and I try to slow it down. I know they can hear it. They can sense it. If I can't get it under control, they'll find me, and after they do—I don't let myself consider that alternative.

I break into a sprint, darting down the hall as it curves to the left. Shooting a glance over my shoulder, I search for the creature that made the noise, not sure what I'm looking for, but knowing I'll recognize it the moment I see it.

I run into something solid. My body topples back helplessly. I manage to catch myself just before my head hits the floor, elbows slamming into the ground. It hardly hurts like I expect it to. Tracing the object in front of me, I'm finally faced with what I've been running from. The animal is tall; it would probably be my height if I were to stand up next to it. Its fur ruffles as it repositions its body. I grow numb, utterly terrified.

Blue eyes stare at me. The animal's head and neck look like that of an eagle. Light brown feathers with streaks of gold cover its head, while pointed ears protrude upwards. As my eyes follow its body downward, the feathers dissipate and are replaced by the same golden shade of fur. Its body resembles a lion's, but feathered wings fold alongside either rib cage. Eagle talons poke out of the animal's lion-like paws. Its tail looks like a lion's, the tip a mixture of feathers and fur.

My eyes falter on a white, furless patch on the animal's right shoulder, just as it releases a deep, trembling growl. I look up at it, terrified.

Chapter 7

M Y EYES FLY OPEN. I VIOLENTLY THROW the sheets off my body and swing my legs over the edge of the bed, pushing myself into a sitting position.

The back of my neck is moist and I can feel a bead of sweat roll down my spine and slide beneath my shirt. My legs are numb and my entire body is shaking. I clasp my hands together, feeling the warm, clammy moisture gather in my palms.

Where the hell am I? The walls are plastered in light brown paint. There's a deep, mahogany colored dresser across the room. My bag lies on the ground next to it.

My mind wanders back to last night, to Linda and Peter. I'm in their house. They brought me here last night, after Tracy helped transform me.

I slowly stand up from the bed and take deep breaths, trying to calm my nerves. My mind keeps wandering back to the nightmare and I have to continuously pull it back into focus.

I need to get out.

I quickly get dressed and put in my new colored contacts. As I'm brushing my teeth, I can't help but stare at myself in the mirror. It's strange to look in the mirror and see an unfamiliar face, one that doesn't belong to me, yet is me. *This is me now.*

I grab a granola bar from the cabinet Linda showed me last night on a tour of the house. Then, my hand grasps the knob of the front door, eager to open it and get out of the house.

"Where are you going?" I hear Linda's voice asking behind me.

Peering over my shoulder, I see her standing in the hallway, her arms folded across her chest in a relaxed, nonchalant manner. "Oh, hi. I just need some air. I'll be back soon."

She nods. "It'll be good for you to get familiar with your surroundings here," she comments. With that, I open the door and leave.

The cold, chilled morning air clings to my skin. It's not comfortable, and I forgot to bring my coat, but I kind of like the feeling. It forces me to think about it; focus on it, instead of the nightmare.

I walk the streets, not quite knowing where I'm going, but eventually I find the downtown area. Shops line the sides of the street and the sidewalks grow more crowded as I continue walking. I watch the people around me, thinking about them instead of myself and my fears.

Ahead of me is a woman walking with her two young daughters, who are holding hands. The younger girl looks up at her sister and, with her free hand, reaches up and pulls a couple strands of her sister's hair. It's not hard enough to be mean, just enough to get her attention. The older sister glances down at her, makes a face and sticks out her tongue. The younger copies the expression. They both laugh.

A sad smile forms on my lips. It makes me think of my cousins. The memory of the day before I left New York, now nearly a week ago, fills my thoughts.

Aunt Tamlin and Uncle Elton have tasked me with keeping track of the girls as they shop. The department store smells of fresh leather as we meander about it. I walk at a steady pace, past row after row of sofas and couches. Nora and Lilly run toward me, they each grab one of my arms and hug it for a second before releasing me.

"Rose, can we go look at the toys? Please," Lilly begs in her sweet, innocent six-year-old voice. Her big, pleading brown eyes watch me in anticipation.

I curve my lips into a smile. "Sure."

They both smile back at me. "Thank you," Nora says, grabbing Lilly's hand and running off toward the toy aisle of the department store.

I follow them, glancing around to see if their parents are anywhere in sight. They're probably off window shopping at another store. I don't mind watching the girls; they're so young and adventurous, the way I used to be. Lilly is still oblivious to the real world, and Nora is beginning to see how life really works. Nora's only nine, but she acts older; it probably has something to do with having a younger sister to watch over.

I reach the toy aisle and see the girls gazing from shelf to shelf. Lilly points up at a doll that sits just out of her reach. Nora nods and plucks the doll off the shelf, handing it to Lilly and making the six-year-old grin from ear to ear. Lilly hugs the doll so tight that if it had been alive, she would have strangled the thing to death. Lilly's short legs race toward me, her newfound doll trailing behind her. She holds the toy out to me.

"Can we buy her?" Lilly asks, fluttering her eyelashes as she waits for my answer.

I stand up and slide my hand into the pocket of my jeans, pulling out a ten-dollar bill. I nod. Lilly pulls the doll back in for a hug and strokes its hair. "What's her name going to be, Lilly?" Nora asks.

Lilly freezes, thinking. "Jenny."

"That's a good name," Nora agrees.

"Okay," I say, slipping on a smile. "Let's go to the checkout line and buy Jenny, so she can become an official member of the family."

We make our way to the front of the store, which is emptier than usual.

The winter sun gleams through the double glass doors at the entrance of the store. As we get closer to the cash registers, I squint out the doors and across the street to a quiet little wooded park. Dozens of people dressed in navy blue and white uniforms file out from the park.

They divide, each heading in a different direction, as they emerge into the street. A realization quickly hits me, and I know exactly what's going on under the cover of the trees deeper within that park.

The people appear to be humans, but I know they're not. I know what they really are.

The figures are different heights, and ages. Every person that comes out of that park is a Uniform; the authority figures of Dunchoria.

This is not good!

Three of the Uniforms cross the street and walk to the front of the store. They yank open one of the doors and walk briskly into the building. My heart stumbles and beats faster in my chest.

I grab onto the girls' wrists and pull them into the closest aisle, out of sight. Peering around the corner, I watch as the three men raise their heads; looking around, as if they're searching for something they've lost. And I guess in a way, that's exactly what they're doing.

"What's going on?" Lilly whines.

"Shh!" Nora covers Lilly's mouth.

There's no way Nora knows what's going on, but she knows that now is not the time to ask questions.

I pull my head back into the aisle, staring at the items on the shelf across from me. The Uniforms are looking for me. I can feel it. Something nags at the back of my head. Am I paranoid for thinking this? Maybe, but my gut says otherwise. Lilly grabs my arm, reminding me that I'm not alone. Not only am I in danger, but they are too. My breath comes in quick, rasped bursts. I can feel my blood pulsing in every part of my body.

It's my fault that I had to leave. Only a couple days prior to the Uniforms showing up in the store the other day, I had shown my friend Nick my power. He had approached me, stating that I had been acting strange and he had been noticing odd things. The questions followed, stemming from my childhood to my abnormal abilities and influences on people. I hadn't meant to show him. I hadn't known that anyone had been watching. But apparently Nick had.

He was a good friend, but he was human. And humans aren't supposed to know about us. They aren't supposed to see the things we do. But once they know, they talk. Secrets become gossip, and as the word travels, the danger of discovery elevates. I trusted him, but I didn't trust the Uniforms and the timing was too perfect to ignore. Maybe I had just been paranoid, but I wasn't going to risk it. There was too much at stake.

My feet have grown numb from the cold as I glance into the shops in Coos Bay, attempting to focus on something other than my own thoughts. One window catches my eye and I abruptly stop. Behind the glass, pictures are propped in elegant frames.

As I enter the shop, the bell above the door rings. The woman manning the checkout counter is too busy with a customer to even toss me a glance. I walk over to a picture hanging on the wall, glad to have the moment of solitude. The picture is dangling slightly above eye level. It captivates me, making my body freeze, but my mind buzzes in thoughts and memories.

Half the picture is underwater. Shells lie on the sandy ocean floor while the sun beams through the bright blue water, casting a slight shine on the shells' surfaces. Fish swim between strands of seaweed, chasing each other. Their mouths break the water's surface as they take gulps of air. A fishing pole is propped in the dirt by the water's edge. A man and a young child sit next to the pole, waiting for a fish to bite. The string hanging from their pole sways in the water, creating ripples.

A memory forms in the back of my mind. I pull it forward and watch as it plays out in my head, reminding me of the fishing trips my dad and I used to have.

I'm eight again. My dad and I are sitting on the edge of the pond. I'm holding a fishing pole securely in my hands, careful not to let it go.

"Daddy?" I ask, disappointment coating my voice. "When are the fish going to start biting?"

My dad looks down at me. "In time," he answers simply, offering no further explanation.

I look at him curiously. I don't understand. In time? What is that supposed to mean? An impatient feeling floods my body. I begin to bounce up and down anxiously. My gaze travels down to the water. Fish swim back and forth under the liquid surface beneath me. I frown as I lean back into a sitting position beside my dad.

"Give it time," he adds supportively.

I sit, holding the pole, for another five minutes. A slight tug rips my attention back to the pond. My grip tightens on the pole. Another tug tells me that something is on the other end, yanking at the hook.

I giggle, surprised by the catch. My hands fumble with the thick pole. "Daddy, I got one! I got one!" I holler in excitement. My pitch is high and closer to a squeal than a yell.

He leans over to me, his hands finding the pole. "Okay," he says calmly. "Now pull up the line. Be careful."

I make an attempt to lift the pole out of the water, but the fish has added some weight and I'm struggling. Dad sees that and helps me. The fish emerges from the pond, tossing water into the air as it wildly flips its tail back and forth. Its body is all silver, except for a white strip that runs down the arch of its back. The sun gleams off its shiny, wet scales.

Dad pulls the line closer to us. I drop the pole and reach out for the dangling fish. I extend my index finger and stroke the side of the slimy fish. A giggle bubbles up in my throat and bursts out. I have never touched anything like that before; the slimy feeling is new to me.

Dad places the fish on the ground. It flops up and down on the dirt and gags air in and out of its mouth. I look at it confused. The helpless motion of this beautiful creature suddenly makes my chest tight. "It can't breathe daddy!" I exclaim.

"No, it can't," he confirms.

My eyes grow wide. "Put it back in the water!" I exclaim. "Don't let it die!"

An amused smile crosses Dad's face. He gently lifts the fish back into the air and lays it down in his hand, which folds around the fish. With his other hand, he swiftly wiggles the hook out of the fish's mouth.

"Hold out your hands," he insists.

I make a cup with my hands. A slimy sensation fills my whole body as the fish is placed into my cupped hands. I squirm at the feeling.

"Now, lower your hands to the water. Be gentle and careful; you don't want to hurt it," he instructs.

I do as he tells me. The fish slowly slides off my hands and enters the water. I smile as the fish swishes its tail back and forth, swimming through the water as if nothing had happened. Still grinning, I look up to my father's face next to me.

"Excuse me," a voice says, interrupting the memory and bringing me back to reality. I turn away from the painting to look at the lady behind me. Her eyes examine me, uncertainly. "Do you need help?" she asks exhaustedly.

"Oh! No, but thank you," I reply.

She nods and walks back to the checkout counter, while I head to the door.

My hand rests on the doorknob. As I take a last glimpse of the picture, a smile slips over my lips. As I push the door open, it collides with an object on the other side.

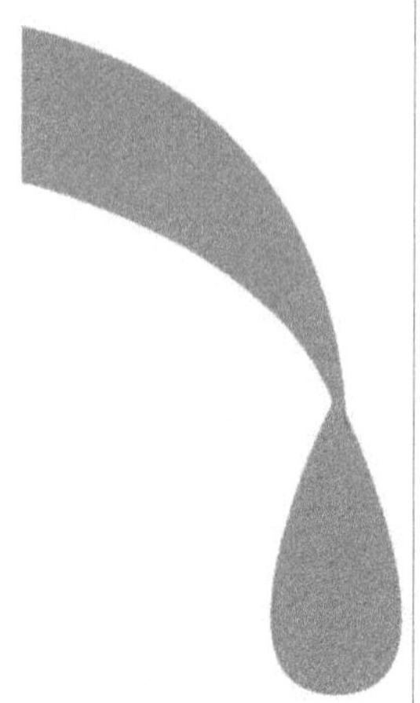

Chapter 8

MY EYES JERK FORWARD JUST IN TIME TO see a figure stumbling backwards.

I slowly push the door open. Warmth fills my cheeks. I try to calm the feeling.

"Are you okay?" I ask, my cheeks growing hotter.

"Yeah, yeah, it's okay," the boy in front of me replies in a voice so beautifully smooth it makes a chill crawl down my spine. He lifts one hand to feel his head. His toned bicep flexes ever so slightly.

"No, seriously, are you okay?" I reach out and rest a hand on his shoulder, trying to get his attention and make him look at me. A moment later, I break the contact, knowing that if I touch him for too long, I might pass my emotions onto him, and that's the last thing I need right now.

He drops his hand from his head, causing his spiked brown hair to ruffle. My heart jumps in my chest. He's about my age, with glistening caramel brown eyes. His pupils stare at me for a moment, the rims around his irises darken slightly.

A slight breeze sweeps my hair off my shoulder. The wind settles, leaving me with the lingering scent of him; just enough Axe cologne mixed faintly with pine wood.

"I'm fine." He runs his hand through his hair, suddenly more relaxed. "Really, I am," he assures me gently. A smile holds on his lips and spreads to the rest of his face. Dimples form at the corners of his mouth. His eyes brighten, grinning in their own silent language.

My heart goes crazy. All I want to do is get closer to him, fill the empty space between us. I try to collect myself.

My words come out shaky. "Are you sure?" I take a deep breath, willing the rest of the sentence to come out steadier. "I hit you pretty hard with that door." I can feel my cheeks growing hot again as he watches me.

"Yeah, I'm sure. It's fine, don't worry about it."

I nod. He walks toward the store's entrance again. Placing his hand on the handle, he pulls the door open.

"I'm sorry," I apologize, just before he passes through the entrance of the picture shop.

He turns back to me and offers a smile, and a single, accepting nod. "See you around," he adds before disappearing into the store.

After the door closes behind him, I turn to face the blinding sun. The image of the boy fills my head. The way the light from the setting sun glistened against his hair. The look in his eyes as he watched me.

My heart leaps and stumbles in acknowledgment.

I'm not sure how long I was in the shop, but the crowd on the sidewalk seems to have died down. I head in the direction of Peter and Linda's house. I've managed to shake the fear from the dream and a new feeling has replaced it.

Butterflies.

Butterflies flapping their gentle wings in the pit of my stomach.

I reach the house and head straight to my room. I dig through my bag, looking for a clean outfit to change into and grab the bleached white towel from the end of the bed. Walking to the bathroom, I shut the door behind myself. I glance at my reflection in the mirror above the counter. How long has it been since I left home? Five days? Has it really been that long since I last saw my aunt and uncle and cousins? I wonder how they're doing, especially the girls. They hadn't understood what was happening. They didn't understand any of this, and I don't expect them to. I hope they're okay and safe.

After I take a shower, I head downstairs to where I can hear Linda and Peter chatting away in the kitchen. They immediately draw me into their conversation, planning what I need before I start school. The rest of the day is a whirlwind of shopping—more clothes, books, notebooks, and pens. Peter and Linda are sweet and extremely generous. They treat me like I imagine they would treat their own child. It's comforting and makes the adjustment slightly easier than expected.

The next morning, the buzzing of the alarm clock frightens me from my sleep. I quickly turn on the little lamp resting on the nightstand and search for the off button. I yawn and look at the time. It's six o'clock. The sun is still asleep behind the hills outside. The horizon is dark.

Peter and Linda had told me that I had a meeting with the guidance counselor at the local school today. It was the first step in getting me registered for classes.

I get dressed and comb through my hair. I head down the stairs in a quick, unbalanced mess. For breakfast, I help myself to eggs in the fridge, trying to tell myself this is my house now—at least for the time being. I mix up an omelet with whatever else I can find. As I'm eating, Linda walks into the kitchen, dressed nicer than I'd seen until now.

"Good morning," she greets.

"Good morning," I reply.

"Are you ready for your first day?"

"Yeah, I think so," I say, willing myself to believe it. I was never much a fan of school, and this new identity is only going to make things harder.

I finish getting ready and wait for Linda by the front door. She comes around the corner, jingling her keys.

"Alright, let's get a move on!" she exclaims, opening the door and stepping outside. I follow, waiting at the car while she locks the front door of the house. Eventually, she turns toward the car and clicks the unlock button on her key set. The headlights blink twice and a cha-ching sound echoes in the quiet air.

Five minutes later, we pull into a school parking lot.

The sun has begun to rise above the trees next to the quaint brick building, casting a light blue haze across the sky. Linda parks the car in a free space and shifts her body to look at me. "Are you okay?"

I nod before I'm able to answer. "Yeah."

"Should I come in with you?" she asks. "I tried to get you here a little bit early so you don't have to hassle with the student traffic. And so you'll have more time to find the guidance office," she explains.

My gaze flickers to the school building. I watch as a group of kids go through the doors. "No, I think I'm okay. I'll figure out where I need to go. But thank you!" I respond.

Linda nods. I step out of the car and close the door behind me.

She rolls down the window. "Either Peter or I will be here in a couple hours to pick you up," she confirms. "Just text us when you're done."

I nod, patting the cell phone in my pocket. "Got it." I head in the direction that I saw the other students entering the school. It's early December; halfway through the school year. I have no idea what to expect.

Almost instinctively, my eyes begin darting around the parking lot and skimming the front wall of the building. My hearing sharpens, listening to every car and every voice. I'm not in a dangerous place, and I try to remind myself of that. It's just a school filled with students. There's nothing to be afraid of, at least not according to my standards. None of them know what I'm going through; they don't even know who I am. I'm a new person, unrecognizable to even those who knew me.

Inside, some students are clustered in groups, while others are roaming the halls. I place my hand on the door handle and take a deep breath. Pulling open the door, I enter the bright, crowded front lobby. Nobody turns to look at me; they simply continue what they are doing.

A group of girls ahead of me on my left break out in laughter. My eyes snap to look at them, my body tensing. One of them, a slim girl with light brown eyes and wavy blonde hair, begins talking. I can't hear what she's saying, but all the other girls laugh at her comment. She casts a glance in my direction and her eyes lock with mine. Her smile disappears and her lips press into a straight line. Her eyebrows pull together and rise. I interpret that as my signal to keep moving.

I walk through the halls, swerving between the groups of kids hanging out along the walls, with no clue where I'm headed. The hallway I am following comes to a dead end. I turn around and head back toward the main entrance. Or what I think is the way back. This building feels like a never-ending maze.

A boy rushes out of the doorway next to me, hitting me broadside. I almost fall, but he manages to catch my arm and keep me from toppling over.

A male's voice comes from the doorway that the boy came out of. "Real smooth, Colton!"

The boy who hit me—Colton, I'm assuming—turns to the door, still holding my arm. "Shut up, Nathan!" He raises his voice, but it doesn't sound threatening.

"Sorry about that," he says in a smooth, familiar voice. "They find that kind of stuff funny. Are you okay?" I don't understand why I recognize the voice, but something about it makes my heart skid.

I gather myself, steading my feet on the ground as I look up at him. "Yeah." My heart comes to a halt. His caramel brown eyes find mine, holding me in a soft, mesmerizing gaze. His brown hair rests on top of his head, just like I remember it from when I saw him downtown a couple days ago. Dimples form at the corners of his mouth.

"Hey," he says playfully. "You were downtown not too long ago. You hit me with that door, right?"

"That's me," I answer, casting a glance down at the floor to keep from getting too embarrassed.

"Well," he continues. "I guess now we're even." I can hear the smirk in his voice. "My name's Colton. My friends call me Colt."

"Macy," I say after a long pause, nearly forgetting my new name.

"Are you new here? I've never seen you around."

"Yeah, today's actually my first day."

"Where are you headed?"

"The guidance office, but I have no idea where that is." I cast a glance into the room Colton came out of. The boy who pushed him must have retreated to his desk because he is no longer standing in the doorway.

I try to focus on what Colton's saying, but it's hard to hear anything against the pounding of my heart in my ears. "Go down this hall, take a right at the end, follow the hall until it splits off and you should find yourself at the main entrance. Then you want to take a left and it'll be right there. You'll see it, there's a sign on the door that says, 'Student Services.' Just tell the lady at the desk that you came to see the guidance counselor. She'll tell you where to go from there. You got that?" he asks, unsure.

I hesitate. "Probably not." I laugh. "But I'll figure it out. Thanks." I spin, about to start walking away.

A hand finds my forearm, sending a spark across my skin. I swing around, my focus settling on Colton's mesmerizing caramel brown eyes. My attention sinks to his fingers wrapped around my arm.

Catching the motion, he quickly removes his hand, clasping his palms together in front of his body. "Sorry," he collects himself. "I can walk you there if you want."

"Don't you have class?" I ask, gesturing to the room.

He shrugs. "I've got time."

I can feel the smile forming on my lips. "Well in that case, I would appreciate it."

His lips pull upwards to reveal a charming smile. "I was hoping you'd accept. This way," he says, jerking his head down the hall. We walk side by side down the hallway, talking about where I came from, why I was downtown, and numerous other topics. We reach Student Services, both of our bodies coming to an automatic halt as we finish our conversation. "This is it," Colton asserts, glancing at the door.

"Okay, thank you," I reply, reaching for the door's handle.

He grins. "Any time." Before spinning to walk back to class, he pauses to look at me. "See you around Macy."

Chapter 9

"**I**'M HERE TO SEE THE GUIDANCE counselor," I say to the woman at the front desk.

She nods. "Just give me a minute." She stands up from the chair at her desk and shuffles down a little, narrow hallway. I can hear the sound of hushed voices, and a moment later, the receptionist waves me down the hallway. Inside, the guidance counselor tells me to take a seat.

"Good morning, Miss...?"

"Macy," I say. "Macy Woods," I add quickly.

"My name is Mrs. Smith," she says. "We were expecting you. Do you have a manuscript from your previous school with you?"

"Yes." I hand her the manila folder that Tracy had given Linda.

Mrs. Smith opens the folder and scans the papers for a moment.

Her focus switches back to me. "Alright, so we've created a schedule for you—"

She runs through my schedule and recites rules on the dress code and academic policies. There's paperwork I have to fill out and some forms for Peter and Linda. Mrs. Smith hands me my schedule and tells me that I might want to get here early tomorrow so that I can figure out where some of my classes are. I take my schedule from her and leave the office when instructed, glad this is all I have to deal with today. Sending a quick text, I meander toward the exit of the building.

I get outside just as a silver car pulls up in the car loop. Linda's sitting in the driver's seat. I open the door and sit down on the seat. I get buckled and we drive off. "How was it?" Linda asks glancing at me with eager eyes. Her lips split, revealing her signature toothy smile.

"Nothing much happened. I had a tough time finding the guidance office, but eventually figured it out." I leave Colton out of the conversation, there's no need to get into that. "There's some paperwork that you guys have to fill out and I got my schedule," I say looking through the list of classes and numbers associated with them.

Back at the house, I hand the paperwork to Linda, who fills it out and gives it back to me. The remainder of the day flies by as I divide the time between watching TV and helping Linda cook and set the table for dinner.

The next morning, Peter drives me to school and I feel slightly more confident. Once I'm inside, though, I'm quickly overwhelmed again. I shuffle through my backpack until I find my schedule. Looking at the first item on the schedule I do my best to memorize it. *Social Studies, Mrs. Lane, A23*. Now all I have to do is figure out where that is.

The bell rings. Teenagers begin dispersing into their classes, eventually leaving the halls completely empty. The late bell rings three minutes later. Finally, I stumble upon the room and walk in. The teacher's standing at the front of the classroom talking. The sound of the door clicking shut behind me causes her and a couple of the students to stare at me.

"Sorry," I say when the teacher gives me a questioning look. "I didn't know where the classroom was," I explain.

"What's your name?" Mrs. Lane asks me.

"Macy Woods."

"Well Ms. Woods. First day at school and you're already late." She shakes her head. "Not a good way to start off your year here."

I nod. She continues talking. "You can have a seat in any empty chair." I do as she says and take a seat in an empty chair in the second to last row.

I pay close attention to her lesson, most of the stuff she's saying I've learned about vaguely in my classes in New York. It's strange, the types of events that have occurred in this world. All the wars, it's crazy! In Cylilia there had been battles, but they had never been huge, more like little skirmishes between villages. They rarely ever involved the king. But here, it seemed like leaders pitted against each other in every decade of history. Between revolutions and World Wars, I wonder how this world isn't in ruins.

The bell rings. Everyone in the class stands up and quickly leaves the room. I take a quick glance at my next class's room number, B15. I try to keep up with the rest of the students as they funnel out of the class and into the hallway. Once in the hall I head for the back of the school.

This time, I find the classroom faster. The bell sounds and the teacher, Ms. Phillip, closes the door.

She begins to talk about cells. "What's a bacteria cell called?" she asks.

"A germ," one of the boys in the back of the class says with a chuckle.

Ms. Phillip ignores him and looks around for someone to answer. Her eyes skim over me and come back. "Oh!" she exclaims. "The new student, right?"

"Yes," I reply.

"What's your name?"

"Macy Woods," I say.

"Okay, well Macy do you know the answer?"

I think for a minute. "Is it a prokaryote?"

"Yes," she replies with a smile. "It is. A prokaryotic cell," she says, "is a cell that has no membrane-bound nucleus. This causes the DNA to—" she continues, explaining the structure and function of prokaryotic cells. The class passes quickly and the bell rings.

As I'm packing up, a girl appears in front of my desk. "Hey," she says with a wide smile. Her brown hair pours over her shoulder. She observes me with jade green eyes.

"Hey," I reply, slinging my backpack over my shoulder.

"You're Macy, right?"

"Yeah."

"I'm Bree," she says. "You were in my Social Studies class last period."

"Really?" I ask.

"Yeah! With Mrs. Lane."

"Oh! Yeah, I'm the tardy girl from last period."

She laughs. "What do you have next period?"

"Um—" I say, glimpsing the schedule in my hands. "English with Mrs. Taylor in room B02."

"Okay. I'm walking right past there to get to my next class. We can walk together," she offers.

I nod and we begin walking. In the short distance from my second period class to my third, Bree catches me up on things they've learned so far in both Social Studies and Science. A lot of the lessons I am already familiar with from school in New York.

We reach B02. Bree and I stop at the doorway of the classroom. "Alright," she says. "This is it. Hopefully I'll see you in another one of my classes. If not, see you tomorrow," she adds before walking away.

I enter the classroom and take a seat. Shuffling through my bag I pull out my notebook and a pencil. Out of the corner of my eye I see someone come to a stop next to me. "You're in my seat," he says.

"Oh my gosh, I'm sorry!" My cheeks grow warm as I stand. A hand rests on my shoulder and I can feel the warmth where his skin touches mine.

Laughter comes from the boy behind me. "No, no, don't stand up. It's fine. We don't have assigned seats. I'm just messing with you," his smooth voice explains.

Colton! I don't know what to say. "You're in this class?" I finally ask, surprised.

He lets out a short laugh and glances around the classroom. "Sure looks that way."

Colt takes the empty seat next to me. And even though he's sitting right next to me, I still feel the urge to get closer to him; to move just an inch toward him. He reaches into his backpack and pulls out a binder and a pencil. Placing them on the desk, he drops his backpack to the floor under his desk.

"What classes do you have the rest of the day?" he asks after a minute of silence.

I pull out my schedule, unfold it, and place it on my desk. Colton leans closer and reads it over my shoulder.

"We're in the same math class," Colt says, pointing to my schedule. "Fifth period."

My chest tightens excitedly. "Seriously?"

He nods.

The late bell rings. The English teacher—Mrs. Taylor—saunters over to the door and closes it. My eyes follow her as she walks up to the front of the room. On her desk, there's an attendance sheet. She lifts it up and observes the class. She scans for missing students and marks a few spots on the paper.

Still holding the sheet in her hand, she begins to speak, "Today class, we have a new student joining us." Her hand gestures to me. The entire class shifts in their seats to look at me. "What's your name?" she asks.

"Macy Woods," I answer for the third time today.

"Well, Macy, welcome to tenth grade English." After a moment of silence, she continues, "Would you mind coming up to the front of the classroom?"

"Sure." I nod and stand from my seat. I walk hesitantly to the front of the class, wondering why she wants me to come up.

Once I am in the front, she begins questioning me. "Tell us about yourself. Where did you go to school before this?"

"East Jackson High School," I reply, finding it hard to ignore all of the sets of eyes staring at me.

"Oh! And where's that?"

"It's in Michigan." I recite from the backstory Tracy had given me.

"Fun," she says, but I'm pretty sure she doesn't really care. She asks me a couple more general questions, making me grow nervous. Finally, she finishes. "Alright, well, I hope you have a successful year here at Oak Landing High School. You can go back to your seat now."

I nod and quickly walk back to my seat. I find Colt smiling at me. When I reach my seat, I plop down and shrink away from the class's watchful eyes.

"Don't let that make you feel singled out," Colt says under his breath. "She does it to every new kid. She made all of us do that at the beginning of the year."

I smile. "Thanks."

I focus my attention on Mrs. Taylor for the remainder of the class and try my best to keep up with everything she's saying, even though I've never read Fahrenheit 451, the book they're discussing.

The bell rings, finally releasing me from this boredom. "See you in fifth period," Colt says before standing and leaving the classroom.

I find my next class fairly easily and endure the usual pattern of the new kid at school.

At lunch time I find Bree and sit down next to her.

"Oh! Macy this is Claire and Hannah," Bree introduces, gesturing to two girls as they take a seat across the table from us. I grin back. I'm making friends. I slip easily into their conversations as we eat, laughing along with their jokes and chatting about everything from parents to where I'm supposedly from in Michigan—that one takes some creativity on my part.

As we're exiting the cafeteria Bree asks me what my next class is. It turns out we both have math together, so we walk through the halls side by side. I'm glad to have the help navigating, even though I'm starting to get my bearings here.

In the classroom, Bree and I sit down together in an empty row toward the back. After we've gotten settled into our seats Bree starts calling over people. Apparently, I've befriended quite the social butterfly.

"Hey, Katie, come here," she hollers to a slim blonde girl across the room. The girl approaches us promptly.

"Yeah Bree?"

"I just wanted to introduce you to Macy. It's her first day here."

"Oh." Katie looks at me with deep blue eyes. "Hey," she says.

They start gossiping about a girl who supposedly had a party that got busted the past weekend. Bree seems to know everything that happens in this school. I'm not sure if that'll be good or bad.

As Katie's walking away, Bree focuses her attention on the door. I follow her stare and find myself gazing at a familiar face.

"And coming in now is—"

"Colton," I finish.

"Hey Macy," he says as he walks toward us.

"Obviously you've already met each other," Bree says from my other side.

"Yeah," Colt confirms, shoving one of his hands into his jeans pocket. "We have English together."

"Oh," Bree says, raising her eyebrows at me.

He drops into the chair and slings his arm over the back. "She doesn't like being excluded from things," he whispers in my ear. The sensation causes me to shiver, but I do my best to suppress it.

"What are you whispering about?" Bree questions, scooting closer to try to hear.

"See? I told you."

I laugh. Colt's good at making light of things. And, considering the incident when we first ran into each other in town—actually I ran into him—he's been nicer to me than I expected he would.

The students stop filing into the room and the bell rings. Class starts. Math isn't my strongest subject, but this has to be my favorite class so far. Bree and Colt are both in the class with me. The hour seems to fly by and I'm off to sixth period in what feels like a matter of minutes.

The rest of the day goes by slowly though, and I'm relieved when the final bell rings. Linda's waiting outside for me.

"How was your first *real* day?" she asks as she pulls out of the school's parking lot and onto the main road.

"Good."

"Anything eventful?"

"Um... I made a couple friends." I say.

"Oh! That's good!" she responds. Her voice sounds happy and excited.

"Yeah." I nod.

Chapter 10

ON WEDNESDAY, I ENTER THE SCHOOL building more excited than the previous days. My heart speeds as I walk to first period, eager to see Colt, even though I know I won't see him for another two periods. Bree and I chatter during Social Studies and Science, but I can't seem to take my thoughts off of English; off of seeing Colt.

The feeling's strange, waiting to see someone, wanting to see them so much that my heart beats fast because of it.

When third period finally comes, I race to my seat. But the bell rings and Colt never shows up. The same thing happens in fifth period. The feeling of my heart pounding slows and I'm left exhausted by the effort.

On Thursday, my anticipation to see Colt has dwindled. I'm expecting him to be out again today, but when I walk into English, I'm happily surprised to see him already sitting in his seat.

"Hey, where were you yesterday?" I ask, taking a seat in the chair next to him.

It takes him a minute to respond. "Family issues," he finally says, his expression serious.

"Oh. Is everything okay?"

"Yeah, it's fine. I just needed some time to… figure things out." There's silence. "But glad to see you noticed my absence." He turns to face me. His expression lightens and a smile forms on his lips.

"Well, I doubt I was the only one," I reply. At the front of the room, a girl stands, staring in our direction. Her amber eyes sail past me and straight to Colt. The minute his eyes find hers, a grin plays out across her lips. My heart drops and a weird feeling flairs inside of me, making my stomach flip and my chest squeeze… jealousy? "Looks like you have an admirer," I convey, willing my voice to remain steady as to not reveal my inner emotions.

His gaze turns to me. "Yeah, I know. A not-so-secret admirer." His eyes roll and then brighten in humor. My heart lifts and I laugh before I'm able to stop myself.

The bell rings and class begins as Mrs. Lane walks into the classroom. I catch the amber-eyed girl staring at us. She sends me the evil eye before she swings her body around to face forward.

Friday, I hurry to third period English, and from the hallway outside the classroom, I can see Colt already seated at a desk. I wiggle through the crowd and into the room. I sit down next to him.

"Hey," I greet with a smile. My heart drums against my chest.

"Hey," he replies, looking up from a book in his lap.

"What're you doing?" I sneak a glance over his shoulder at the book he's holding.

"Trying to catch up."

"Procrastinating?"

"Yeah," he admits with a smile and a short laugh. "I don't really have time to do it when I get home."

"Why not?"

He takes a deep breath and glances up at me with his soft caramel brown eyes. His lips press in a straight line before he speaks. "My family life isn't all that great."

"Oh." I'm quiet for a moment. "I know what that's like," I convey without thinking. Surprised by how easily that came out and scared that I shouldn't have said it, I glance up at him to see his expression.

His eyes are locked on me. They hold a hint of wonder and curiosity. "You do?"

I nod, suddenly feeling uncomfortable.

Colt's eyebrows pull together slightly. He bites the inside of his lip, thinking. It's obvious that I don't want to talk about it, so he doesn't ask any further questions. The bell rings and English starts. There's barely any conversation between us for the rest of class.

At lunch I sit next to Bree.

"Are you excited for the weekend?" she asks in a friendly tone after we finish eating.

"Yeah, I guess so."

"Yeah, I guess so," she mimics playfully. "It's the weekend! You have to be more excited than that."

"Yeah," I say, and realize that it still sounds dull. "I am," I correct, trying to sound happier.

"Do you have any plans?" Bree asks.

"Not that I know of." There's a short silence. "What about you?"

"I think I'm going shopping tomorrow and then I have a family dinner Sunday night."

"That sounds fun," I respond.

Bree nods. "You can come shopping with me if you want," she offers.

I shake my head. "No, that's okay, but thanks."

"Sure," she says. "Anyways, you seemed a little confused in science today."

"Yeah. I just didn't understand the whole cell cycle thing."

"I can explain it if you want me to. I think I get it."

"Could you?" I ask.

Bree nods and starts explaining the intricacies of mitosis to me.

After she finishes, I look at her. "You've been so helpful. And I can't tell you how nice it is to have met someone like you."

She smiles. "Same here, I've never known anyone like you, you're different somehow."

I smile, holding back a laugh. Of course I am. "How?"

"I don't know. You just are."

The bell rings. Bree and I grab our bags and head to class.

In the math room, we sit down in the same seats we sat in yesterday. Colt walks in moments after us and takes his seat next to me.

"Hey Macy," he says as he sits down. Bree raises her eyebrows at him expectantly. "Hey Bree," Colt adds when he sees her.

"Is there something going on between you two?" Bree asks slowly.

I swing my head to Colton. Is there? Do I want there to be?

He just makes an indecisive expression. I guess he doesn't know either. It's only been a few days; it's hard for anything to happen in that amount of time.

A dirty blond-haired boy yells from across the room. "Colt's got himself a chick!" A couple of the girls around him snicker, but I think it's because of the way he said it, not the fact that he said it. I stare at the girls. It takes me a minute to realize where I've seen them before. They're the girls who stand in a cluster at the front of the school every morning. One of the girls is Colt's "not-so-secret admirer" from English.

Colt glares at the guy who said it. "Mind your own business, Nathan!"

A dark brown-haired boy standing next to him talks next. "Come on Colt. It's pretty obvious!"

"No one asked for your opinion Drake," Colt shouts harshly.

The dark-haired boy—Drake—saunters up to Colt's desk. He sends a nasty stare at Colt just before his chestnut eyes switch to me. They hold the same intense expression while they examine me, almost as if he's trying to memorize what I look like. The lights in the classroom flicker, as if the electricity is being drained from them. A tingle runs through my body. The feeling is unfamiliar; making me a bit uncomfortable. I sink down in my chair.

His eyes skip back to Colt. "You don't want to get on my bad side, Colt," Drake nearly hisses.

"But you obviously want to get on mine," Colt responds. His eyes glance at me then back up to Drake. Something in the way Colt looks at me makes me reach for his hand under the desk. I place my hand on his and give it a gentle squeeze. I can feel butterflies in my stomach and my face beginning to flush. I focus on keeping my emotions to myself. Colt's gaze automatically returns to me, his eyes flashing in thought. I discretely shake my head from side to side, trying to let him know not to go any further.

Colt's glare settles back on Drake just as the late bell rings, but he doesn't say anything.

Chapter 11

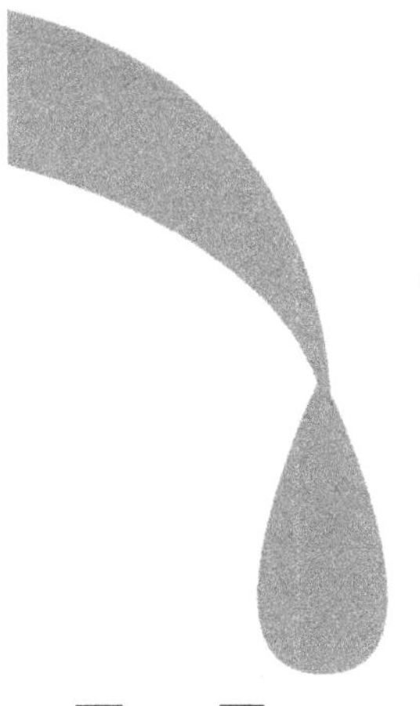

MR. WILLIAMS—OUR MATH TEACHER—walks into the classroom just as the bell stops. He looks at Drake hovering over Colt's desk. "Mr. Maddox, would you please take a seat?"

Drake's eyes narrow. He then walks back to his seat across the room.

"What was that about?" Bree asks. "I've never seen him like that."

Colt shakes his head. "I don't know."

"So that's not normal?" I ask.

"No," Colt answers, his eyes watching Drake across the room. "He's never been that riled up before."

Mr. Williams speaks, "Okay class, lunch is over. Quiet down."

I don't get a chance to ask Colt what he means. Mr. Williams begins droning on about triangles and I sit quietly for the rest of the period, thinking over what had happened.

The bell signals our release from math a little less than an hour later. Bree says goodbye and rushes out of the classroom.

I'm packing up my books when Colton speaks. "Hey. There's a party tonight at Nathan's, if you want to come."

I've been here a week and he just asked if I wanted to go to a party. "Um." I hesitate. "Yeah, sure. That'd be fun."

"Okay, cool." He pulls out his phone and starts scribbling something on a sheet of paper and then hands it to me. "This is his address and my number, in case you have any questions." He starts walking toward the door. "Party starts at eight."

I nod and shove the paper into my backpack.

I step out of the car and am immediately greeted by the thumping of music.

"Just please be careful, okay?" Linda asks from the rolled down window of the car.

"I will be."

"Oh, and if there are any problems or you want us to come pick you up, just call us."

"Okay, thank you," I reply, turning to face the house. Linda drives off, leaving me standing alone on the sidewalk in front of the house.

I begin walking up the driveway. I'm about to knock on the door, when someone comes stumbling out. They look kind of drunk, but I move past them and slip into the house.

Inside, the music is even louder. People clutter the house. I observe the living room and see people dancing everywhere. Along the walls, couples are making out. I quickly turn on my heels and continue down the hallway.

A group of five teenagers—three boys and two girls—huddle around the peninsula in the kitchen. In their hands are the typical red, plastic solo cups.

One of the boys jabs two of his fingers into another girl's side. Her golden hair bounces as she jumps up, surprised.

She giggles. "Jason stop!" she whines, in a flirty, playful tone. She sounds tipsy. Her curled eyelashes flutter as she looks up at him

It dawns on me that she's the same girl in my math and English class, the same one that was looking at Colt.

"Come on Mackenzie," the boy says.

Mackenzie casts him her signature glare.

"Fine," Jason replies. "You can poke me. Go ahead." He holds his arms up, away from his sides.

Mackenzie folds her arms across her chest. "What if I don't want to anymore?" She lifts her eyebrows.

A smile slips across his face. "You know you want to."

Some of their friends start laughing. The other girl grabs Mackenzie's arm and wiggles her eyebrows at her.

"Do it!" one of the other boys exclaims.

Mackenzie smiles at Jason. She extends her arms, ready to poke his sides. He brings down his arms, trapping her wrists between his waist and his forearm. She giggles a little and tries to pull her arms back, with little success.

Jason laughs and quickly lifts his arms, grabbing hold of Mackenzie's wrists. They stand there for a minute, staring at each other. Then, Jason pulls Mackenzie into him. His lips find hers and hoots and hollers explode from their friends.

A hand touches my shoulder. I jump and spin around. Colt stands there smiling at me.

I release a breath. "Oh my gosh! You scared me!"

He laughs. "Sorry." There's a moment of silence. "I'm glad you came."

I smile, looking away from him to observe everyone around us.

"How long have you been here?" he asks.

My eyes skip back to him. "Only a couple minutes."

"Oh. In that case, you haven't danced, yet."

I shake my head.

"Well," he urges. Jerking his head toward the living room, he begins walking. I follow him, smiling a little.

The beat grows stronger as we enter the living room. The other people all seem too occupied to pay attention to anyone other than themselves and their dance partner. As I'm watching them, I notice that I have no idea how to do the moves they're doing. The style of dance is different than anything I've ever done.

Anxiety grows inside of me as I realize that I am about to make a fool of myself.

Colt looks over at me. I stare at him. *What am I supposed to do?* He leans over and grabs my hand. He gently pulls me into him and offers a reassuring smile. "Just move with the music," he says into my ear, sending shivers down my spine.

I nod and turn my back to him. I follow the other girls' motions, watching the way they move their bodies. I do my best to mimic them. The beat drops and I watch as they all drop to the floor and come back up. By the second song my body automatically falls into rhythm with the beat of the song and I find that the dancing begins to come naturally.

At some point, I have to stop myself. I turn to face Colt, who peers down at me. "What is it?" he asks.

"Nothing. I just... need a break."

He nods and leads me over to one of the couches positioned along the wall. Another boy and girl sit, cuddled into one another on the opposite side of the couch.

The boy looks over as we sit down. "Hey!" he says, a bit too happy. "Colt, my boy! How's it goin'?" He sounds wasted.

"It's going good Nathan," Colt responds. I can hear the smile in his voice. "Are you drunk?"

"Nah man!" Nathan laughs drunkenly. "Okay, maybe a little. But I only had two—wait maybe it was four—Who cares? It's all good!"

I can feel Colt shake beside me as he laughs. "Okay man, whatever you say." His attention turns to me. "How do you like it?"

"The party?"

"Yeah."

"It's good. I like it." I peer over at Nathan on the other end of the couch, who's gone back to talking to the girl next to him. "This is his party?" I ask glancing back at Colt.

He laughs. "Yep."

"Well, I think he's enjoying himself."

"Sure looks that way," Colt replies.

I laugh. Across the room, Mackenzie and Jason are dancing. He spins her around as they sway and move on the dance floor. She seems to be enjoying the attention.

I guess she's over Colton.

"Does Mackenzie still like you?" I ask. My eyes flit over to where Mackenzie and Jason are.

Colt doesn't even bother looking. "I don't know. And, honestly, I don't care. I'm interested in someone else."

My heart sinks and I avert my eyes to a random spot in the room. What was I expecting him to say? That he was interested in me? Am I really that naïve? My face grows hot as the embarrassment sets in.

I feel his hand on my cheek as he pulls my face back toward him, forcing me to look at him.

"I was talking about you," he says smoothly. I blink, letting his words settle in. Something in the way he looks at me—his eyes observing every inch of my face— makes everything around us stop. The music becomes a faint buzz, the sounds blending together until they are nearly undetectable.

He leans closer to me. My heart goes crazy in my chest as he guides me closer. His brown eyes peer down at me intently. I stare at him, frozen. All I can hear is the pounding in my eardrums. I know what comes next. His fingers graze the skin under my chin. He looks into my eyes as his fingers run through my hair.

He bends his neck, getting even closer to me. So close I can feel his breath caressing the skin on my cheeks and the tip of my nose. His lips find mine, brushing them gently, as if testing the waters. He backs up, just enough to be able to look into my eyes. His eyes scan my face as he searches my expression for any sign of rejection or refusal. Finding none, he leans in again. His hands cup my face. His lips locate mine. They move, slowly at first, then grow more intense and hungry.

My eyes shut. My arms wrap around his neck as we kiss.

He pulls back. And, even though I don't want him to, I let him, allowing us both to catch our breaths. I stay close to him, not wanting to venture too far. The caramel in his eyes is barely noticeable in the dim light, but I don't need the light to know how they look. A smile pulls at the corners of my lips. He kisses me again, just a peck, but it still makes my heart go crazy in my chest.

His eyes flash to the spot behind me. "Oh no," he mutters. I follow his eyes and find the other end of the couch empty. "Where'd Nathan go?" he asks.

I shrug.

"I better go find him, before he gets himself into trouble." He stands up, looking around the room. He turns back to me. "I'll be back in a second."

I nod.

He walks out of the room. I sit by myself, watching the bodies sway in a beautiful mass of movements.

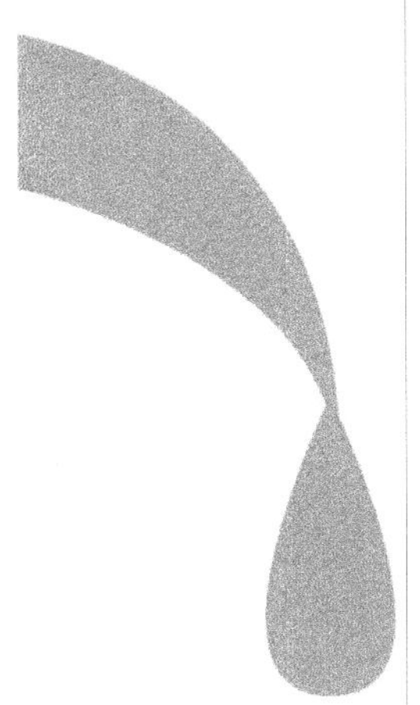

Chapter 12

I STAND FROM THE COUCH AND MAKE MY WAY to the upstairs bathroom. After splashing water on my face and checking myself in the mirror, I leave and descend back down the stairs, shuffling through the bodies, eyes searching for Colt. I make my way to the kitchen. The same group of teenagers who were standing around the peninsula when I first got here are standing around it again. Jason's arm is slung over a different girl's shoulder. Mackenzie stands on the other side of the girl, talking and giggling, obviously not fazed by the fact that Jason has replaced her so quickly.

"Kristen," Mackenzie says through giggles.

The girl who's under Jason's arm looks over at Mackenzie. "I'm not kidding! Colt can tell you," Kristen says, her voice thick. Her eyes skip over to someone across the peninsula from her.

My eyes follow hers and find Colt standing there, his brown hair ruffled and a small smile on his lips. "It's true."

Laughter explodes from the group. I walk over to Colt and place my hand on his shoulder. He turns to face me, a plastic, red cup in his hand. Behind him I can see three more cups on the counter.

"Hey!" he exclaims, throwing his free arm over my shoulder. He smells sweet, like honey and Axe. "What've you been up to?" His words are slurred, as though he had chugged a few drinks while I was upstairs.

"I should be asking you the same thing." I gesture to the cup in his hand and the ones on the counter.

"I'm just havin' some fun," he replies.

"Colt—" I begin.

"Is it hot in here? Is anyone else getting hot?" he asks louder.

He begins tugging at the bottom of his shirt. His arms lift above his head, taking his shirt with them. My eyes slip down to his bare, muscular stomach. His six-pack is faint in the dim lighting. A drop of sweat slides down his abdomen, following the outline of his abs. He slaps his shirt down on the counter and gulps down the remaining alcohol in his cup. Whoops and hollers erupt from the people around us.

Colton's arm wraps around my waist and he pulls me toward his bare torso. The palm of my hand collides with his chest. His skin is smooth and soft underneath my hand. The crevices of his muscles shift. He places his hand over top of mine and moves it to his pecs. He looks at me, his pupils overly dilated. A smile slips onto his lips. The muscles in his pecs flex underneath my hand. I smile and pull my hand away.

"You like that?" he asks, taking a step toward me.

I laugh. "You obviously do."

He smiles, grabbing my arm. He pulls me toward him slowly, his eyes locked with mine.

"What are you—" His lips press into mine, bringing my question to a halt. His lips move on mine sloppily. I can taste the alcohol, heavy on his breath.

I push away from him. "You're so drunk," I comment.

He smiles. "Maybe, but you're still the prettiest girl at this party." He turns his back to me as someone shouts his name from the other side of the room. I stare at his toned, bare back. An area of darkened skin on his shoulder captures my attention. It's not a tattoo, but almost like a brand or birthmark. As I get a closer look, I notice that it has a distinct shape: it's a single claw with a drop of liquid seeping from the sharp tip.

Colt turns back to me and we kiss again, the image of the mark on his back only a fuzzy memory.

I spend the weekend further exploring the town, making sure to visit Tracy's store when I'm downtown to give her an update on how everything is going. Monday morning greets me with the buzzing of my alarm clock and the sound of rain hitting the roof. I get to school a little earlier than usual. First period doesn't start for another fifteen minutes, so I meander the hallways while I wait for the bell to ring. As I'm rounding the corner of one hall I see a group of kids on the opposite end. Their voices carry to me and I recognize Colt among them.

"Dude Friday was crazy!" one of the boys says. The rest of the group laughs, and start eagerly exchanging stories from the party.

I walk up to Colt. He notices me right away. "Oh! Hey," he says to me, before turning to the rest of the group. "I'm going to go guys. See ya later." I catch Mackenzie giving me an evil eye right before Colt grabs my wrist and tugs me down the hallway behind him.

I speed up so that I'm walking next to him. He drops my wrist, his pace slowing. "Look…" He hesitates. "Friday… I got wasted. Did I do anything that I shouldn't have?"

I shake my head and let out a little laugh. "How much do you remember?"

"The first hour or so, I remember going to look for Nathan and then I came back to get you and you weren't there. I went to the kitchen and everyone was there, I started drinking…. And, past that…"

"Well, past that, I found you. You were drunk, so you took off your shirt." The image of the mark on his shoulder flashes into my mind.

His expression grows worried. "I took off my shirt?"

"Yeah, you were hot." A smile slips across my face. That has double meaning, but I'll let him decide which I meant.

"Did you take off your shirt?" he says with a smirk.

I laugh. "No! I didn't." He smiles at me. "Actually," I continue. "We went outside and I convinced you to put yours back on."

"Mhmm." He pauses, thinking. "Too bad," he mutters.

I look at him, eyes wide.

His smile grows, his lips thinning. "I'm joking," he says, his tone light. His hand reaches for mine. His thumb rubs across the back of my knuckles.

"Mhmm," I acknowledge, copying the noise he made. I shake my head and let out a short laugh.

The bell rings, signaling the start of the day.

He laughs. "Okay, well I'm off to class, I'll see you later."

Bree's already sitting in her seat when I get to class. She taps the desk next to her when she sees me walk in.

"What's the deal with you and Colton?" she asks the minute I drop into the chair.

"What do you mean?"

She rolls her eyes. "It's pretty obvious that something's going on. Do you like him?"

I shrug my shoulders.

She rolls her eyes again. "Come on Macy. I saw you guys holding hands under the desk on Friday."

I laugh. There's so much more that she doesn't know. "You saw that?"

"Yeah I saw it! So what's going on?"

"I, um..." I stutter. "I don't know."

"Well you better figure it out," she urges. "And, in my opinion you like him and he likes you. I've known him for a while now and he's never acted the way he acts around you."

"What do you mean?"

A little smile forms on her lips. "Um hello?!" she exclaims. "Did you miss everything I just said? He rarely pays attention to girls the way he does with you."

My cheeks warm. I can feel my heart begin to drum in my chest.

"So?" Bree continues. "Do you like him?"

I think about it. "Maybe… I'm not sure. It's a little too soon." I pause.

I'm not sure if I should, a voice in my head corrects. I get this strange feeling when I'm around him.

"What do you mean you're not sure?" she asks playfully.

"I need some time to figure everything out, including how I feel about Colt."

"That's fair," she says, nodding.

The late bell rings. Mrs. Lane stands up from behind her desk and grabs a piece of chalk from the tray below the chalkboard. She begins scribbling words on the board and we spend the next 40 minutes wrapped up in discussions on the Civil War.

"Have fun," Bree tells me when we part ways before third period. I know exactly what she means by those words.

Colt's not here yet. I sit in my regular seat and pull out my notebook and pen.

"Hey," Colt says, sitting down next to me.

My head's down, looking through my bag, but my heart skips when I hear his voice. His eyes are bright and happy when I look up at him. Dimples quickly form at the corners of his mouth and his lips hold a smile. I can't help but smile back at him.

Was Bree right? Do I like him? Do I like him like *that*?

Of course I do. And if Friday wasn't enough proof, isn't this? My heart beats fast every time I see him. That has to mean something. When he smiles I can't help but smile back.

"Hey," I greet.

We don't talk much during class, possibly because memories of Friday night keep popping into both of our heads. Reminding us what had happened.

Third period ends and I float through the hallways to fourth period and lunch. When it comes time for math I walk to class with Bree, as usual. I notice that Drake is leaning up against his desk staring at me. My heart thumps in my chest and I can feel my cheeks warming.

A tingle runs down my spine. I quickly drop my eyes down to my hands and take a seat at my desk.

Bree takes advantage of the silence. "So? Have you figured things out yet?"

"Yeah." I hesitate, contemplating what I should tell her. A smile plays on my lips. "Yeah, I've figured it out."

She lets out a little squeal. "You like him!" She quickly refocuses. "See? Now how hard was that?"

"Not very," I reply. *Malina*, the name floats into my thought. She would have loved this type of thing. Oh man! How would she have reacted if she learned that I liked a guy? I wish I could tell her. I wish I could talk to her about everything.

The conversation comes to an abrupt end as Colt strides into the room and drops his bag on the ground as he sits in the chair next to me. "Hey," I say with a smile.

"Hey," he replies, grinning. "How's your day been?"

"Interesting," I offer, glancing at Bree to let her know she's the reason why. She holds her hands up in surrender.

"What about you?"

"It's been alright. Nothing special."

"We are in school," Bree chuckles. "Not much is supposed to happen."

"True," Colt says.

Tuesday sneaks up on me and instead of there being rain when I wake up, there's snow floating gently down to earth. But inside school, the snow doesn't change anything. During math, Colt and Bree sit next to me, like they have the past three days.

After class, I'm about to step out into the crowded hallway when Colt says my name. "Macy." I turn around to look at him. "Come here."

I slide out of the line of students trying to leave the class and walk over to him. "Yeah?" I ask.

"I was wondering… do you wanna go on a date with me?"

I look at him for a minute, making sure he means it before I answer. The hesitation must be making him nervous. His eyes begin to search my face, trying to read my thoughts. My eyes lock with his. I can see the questioning, nervousness, and doubt in his expression.

"Of course I do." I give him a reassuring smile.

His lips automatically lift into a smile. A sigh of relief escapes before he can catch it.

"But I have one question for you," I interrupt before he can start talking again.

"What?" he asks, a little surprised.

"Did Bree talk to you? Did she tell you?"

His expression becomes confused. "Tell me what?"

"Never mind." I pause, shaking my head to regain my thoughts. "When would this date be?"

"Friday? Five o'clock?"

"Okay! What are we going to do?"

"It's a surprise," he answers with a sly smile. "I'll come pick you up though. What's your address?"

"I'll text it to you," I reply.

The day finishes, butterflies fluttering in my stomach.

On Wednesday, I can't wait for fifth period. Finally, it's lunchtime and I hustle toward the table where Bree and I always sit.

"So? Have you gone on a date?" she asks once we're both eating.

"What?"

"You and Colt."

I hesitate. "Not officially."

"What?" she questions, surprised. "What does that mean?"

"He kinda just asked me on one yesterday," I reply.

"When is it?" she asks, nearly jumping out of her chair.

"Friday night."

"I told you that he likes you!" she exclaims with a grin. "He doesn't just ask out girls. Not to be his plus one at parties, and especially not to take out on actual dates."

I laugh.

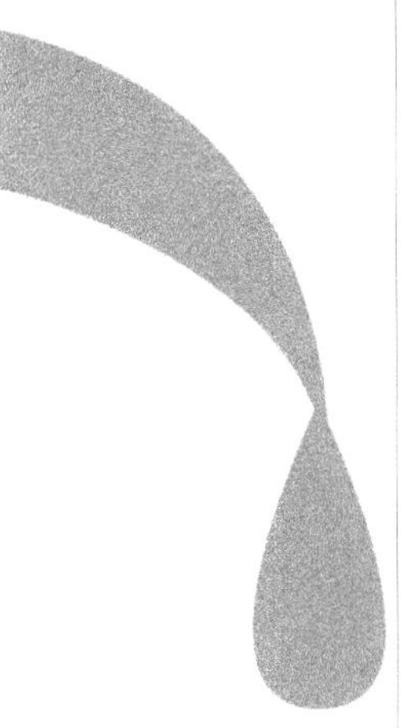

Chapter 13

THE REST OF THE DAY—AND THE REST OF the week—feel like it's just building up to my Friday night date with Colt. And things keep going great with him; in classes, we talk more than ever. It's different talking to him now that I know he likes me. I somehow find the pounding in my chest and the butterflies in my stomach comforting. I like the feeling I get when he's around.

At the end of English on Thursday, he reaches for my hand as we walk the hallway. His fingers intertwine with mine. My heart flutters. I can feel my legs go numb as his hand folds into mine.

"I'm walking you to class," he says with a gentle smile. My heart squeezes in my chest.

The rest of the day slips away and Friday replaces it. Lectures on the Civil War in History, and viruses in Science, buzz by, with—of course— snippets of conversation with Bree. She seems to be really interested in the date tonight. I can't offer her very much information; Colt told me next to nothing about it.

Before I enter one of my last classes of the day, a flash of orange hair catches my attention. I search for the person it belongs to. My eyes widen and I suck in a breath. Could it be? The girl's grey eyes observe me, but constantly break contact to flicker to the people passing her. A young boy on his phone brushes against her shoulder. Instinctively, she flinches and takes a step away, her back pressing into the lockers behind her.

It is her!

Malina.

The first memory I have of her slips into my mind.

My tenth birthday had just passed. Ever since I was little I'd looked forward to that day. In Cylilia, ten was one of the most important years—it was when your powers developed. My excitement was at a peak for weeks after my birthday. But, as the days passed, and I still had no power, that excitement began to dwindle. I was one of the youngest of my friends, so they all had their powers before my birthday even came. They would mess around and brag with each other about their abilities—some became Passives and could glide through walls; others found out they were Shadows and could make themselves disappear; and a select few were Visionaries, and could pass images onto others. A few weeks after I turned ten, my friends began to abandon me one by one; I was left alone. I couldn't relate to them anymore, not with all the new changes. I was alone for the next week; I had no friends, no one to talk to, and no one to relate to. One day I was sitting against a wall outside of the school and a red-haired girl, around my age, came and sat down next to me.

"I know how you feel," she told me as her gaze landed on a group of ten-year-old children playing a couple yards in front of her. They were laughing and bumping into each other.

I had followed her watchful grey eyes. "Are they your friends?" I observed.

"They used to be," she answered.

I nodded, understanding the situation. After all, that was where I was too.

After a quiet minute the girl turned to look at me. "My name's Malina Onsho."

For the next four months, we were best friends. We would have sleepovers on the weekends. We would sit on each other's beds talking, gossiping, revealing who we had crushes on, and sharing our deepest, darkest secrets. We had been inseparable. But that had changed when I left for New York. The friendship was short-lived, but strong.

In one swift, smooth movement, Malina whips around in the hallway and starts speeding toward the main entrance of the school. I follow her as she pushes through the main doors.

The sun's reflection is nearly blinding against the crunchy, stale layer of snow that rests on the ground. After a minute, my eyes adjust to the change in lighting. I can see my breath in big white puffs as I exhale into the fresh, cool afternoon air.

I increase my pace, trying to catch up with the orange-haired figure in front of me. She has to know I'm following her, but she doesn't stop or look back to check. Her movements seem quick and hurried. Maybe she wants to lose me. Suddenly, she's running, sprinting across the sidewalk.

My legs sail through the air as I attempt to match her pace. A small dirt path forms at the tree line behind the school. Rather than slowing her speed, like I would expect, Malina continues sprinting through the woods. A hemlock tree with a wide, exposed trunk sits a couple yards in front of us. Malina rushes towards it, her body lifts as it hits the trunk of the tree. Instead of the loud crack of her body slamming into the tree's bark, there is only silence and Malina vanishes.

It's a portal.

My feet slow in surprise, but only for a moment before I run full force toward the tree. My body mimics the motions of Malina's just before the scenery changes.

The snow-covered ground of Oregon is quickly replaced by dry dirt. My balance fails and my body falls, colliding with the soil. Standing up, I wipe the dirt from my clothes and look around. I'm not in the woods on the outskirts of the city, like I had expected. Instead, small, simple houses surround me. I imagine that no one lives here; the houses look tattered and unkempt. Except... someone would have lived here at some point. Where are they now? What happened to them?

I don't have time to consider the answers for my questions. A faint scream echoes from the woods to my right. I stand silently, listening for something, anything. At the sound of a second scream, I'm sprinting across the cracked road, the trees quickly growing closer before I'm completely immersed in them.

I force myself to stop, turning in place to look at my surroundings. I need a hint. A sign. Something.

My eyes settle on a large object lying on the ground. I walk toward it, careful to remain quiet. When I'm a few feet away, I realize it's a body. I rush toward it, dropping to kneel on the ground. The man lays on his back, his face turned upwards toward the blue sky that hides behind the thick canopy of leaves and limbs. His short, black hair frames a calm, peaceful face. Pale skin pulls over defined cheekbones. The face is familiar. Too familiar.

My stomach churns. A sick feeling washes over me.

Keson.

Chapter 14

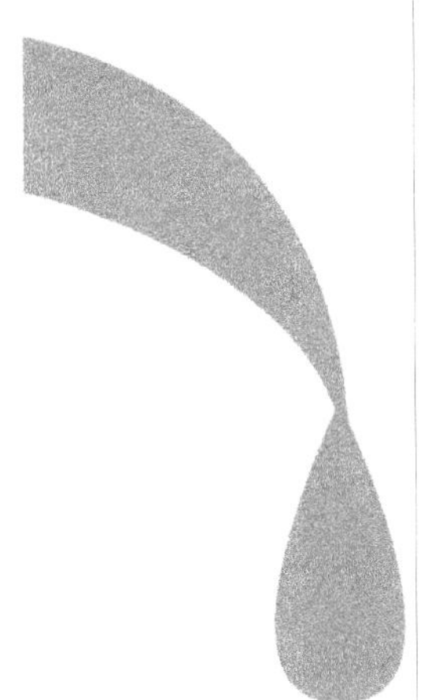

I GO INTO OVERDRIVE.

"Keson?" I say softly. "Keson?!" I grip his shoulders and shake him gently. Nothing happens. He doesn't open his eyes, doesn't move. "Keson!" I shake him harder. "Keson!"

I don't know why he's lying here. Or how he got here in the first place, but I do know that I can't leave him here.

After a moment, his eyes begin fluttering. They open, dazed. Looking around, they settle on me after a couple long seconds.

"Callerie?" he asks, his voice strained.

I nod.

"What are you doing here?"

"What are *you* doing here?" I throw back at him.

"Honestly—" He pauses. "I have no idea."

I can feel my eyebrows pull together as I look at him. "What do you mean?"

He shakes his head, beginning to push himself off the ground. "I don—" He drops back to the ground, his hand flying to his abdomen. He lets out a pained groan.

"What? What is it? What's wrong?" I ask him worriedly.

"My stomach."

I trace his arm down to where his hand is clutching at his stomach. I can just vaguely see the glimmer of dark liquid underneath his hand. "What's wrong with it?" I place my hand on his. "Can I see?"

He nods, but doesn't move his hand.

"Keson. Let me see it," I plead softly.

He moves his hand away from his abdomen, revealing what looks like a dark, stained patch on his shirt. I grab the bottom of his shirt and lift it, exposing his skin. I pause. The faint light shimmers against the pale skin, reflecting off the liquid gathering in a puddle on his abdomen.

I can feel my body start to go numb as I stare at his stomach. "Oh my god," I breathe, my voice quivering. "You're bleeding."

He stares at me, his pupils so big they nearly take up his entire iris. He lifts his head and looks toward the area my eyes are fixated, at the expanding mass on his abdomen. I watch as a drop of blood runs down his side and drips onto the ground.

He lets out a deep breath and allows his head to drop back to the ground. "I remember."

"Remember?" I stare at him with wild eyes. "Remember what?"

"How I got it."

"Wha-how?"

"There was a man. He had a knife. He stabbed me with it."

"Stabbed you?" I begin to panic.

My breathing quickens. "What should we do? Should I go get help? What if I can't get back before—" I trail off.

"Rose, calm down. That's the first thing you need to do." I take deep breaths, trying to calm myself, but I don't know how much it helps. "It's not that bad," he says.

"*Not that bad*?! Keson! Did you look at it?"

He lets out a laugh, but stops abruptly, his face contorting uncomfortably. He places his hand on his stomach, trying to dull the pain. "Yes. I looked at it, Callerie."

"Can you walk?" I ask.

"I'm not sure."

I get into a crouching position and place my hand on his neck. "Ready?"

He nods slightly and begins pushing off the ground. I support his head and back. When he's in a sitting position, I wrap my arm around his waist and help him stand. He sways a bit, but manages to get himself upright.

"Okay," I say slowly. "Now try to walk."

He does as I say. We walk through the woods, slowly growing closer to the town. He comes to a sudden halt, causing me to stumble. His body goes tense.

"What? What's wrong? Does it hurt more? Should I put you back down?"

Keson doesn't reply, his eyes remain forward, wide with shock—or is it fear? I can't tell.

I follow his gaze, but don't see anything yet. "Keson?" I ask, beginning to worry.

He remains tense, not acknowledging me. *He can hear something*. He's a Soundwave; able to hear things far before they can be seen. And right now is a perfect example of his ability. Something—or someone—is coming. "We've got to go," his voice comes out in a whisper.

My eyes strain to see beyond the grand tree trunks and quickly darkening surroundings. I need to see what he hears. I need to know what it is that is scaring him so badly, making him freeze.

A figure appears at the edge of the tree line. The silhouette grows bigger as the person walks toward us. Keson's body goes rigid, his feet stumbling as he attempts to back up. A chill runs down my spine and I know this is wrong. Keson is nervous, and that worries me. He doesn't scare easily. This is the person who stabbed him.

I turn as quickly as I can, considering that Keson's entire body weight is on me. We try to run, but Keson's hiss tells me that the fast pace is hurting him. His body goes limp, causing me to lose my grip on him, and both of us to fall to the ground.

"Keson! Get up, come on. Get up!" I look over my shoulder to the man who continues to pursue us. "We need to go." I yank at his arm, wrapping it over my shoulder before standing, doing my best to pull Keson up after me. I'm cut off by the sound of a scream ripping through my throat as a sharp pain erupts in my side.

I drop downward, losing my hold on Keson. My vision blurs as my head slams against the pine-covered floor. After a moment, I manage to turn around and push myself up from the ground. I grit my teeth, doing my best to hold in another scream. My side is burning.

Looking down, I find a slash splitting the fabric of my shirt, where the pain is coming from. Deep red liquid soaks the material.

My breath quickens. I can feel myself growing lightheaded. With shaking hands, I grab the bottom of my shirt and pull it up. Trails of blood trace down my skin. It's hard to see the actual cut through the pooling blood, but from what I can guess, it's deep.

A twig cracks, causing my attention to snap into focus. My gaze halts on the man standing in front of me. His expression is determined and stern. I can see the slight hint of pleasure in his eyes.

His hand twitches. My eyes fall to the blood-covered knife in his hand. My breathing quickens, frightened.

He is the one who stabbed Keson.

"W-what do you want?" My voice sounds weak.

He smiles at me, but doesn't say anything.

"You're the one w-who stabbed Keson," I stutter, barely able to get out the entire sentence. I can feel my eyelids growing heavy; slowly beginning to droop.

The man nods.

"Why?"

The man hesitates, but it looks like he's willing to answer. "You don't know anything," he finally replies.

"Anything. Wha-what's that supposed to mean?"

"It's funny, you know," he says. "How someone can be so integral, so critical to everything, yet they don't have a clue."

"W-what? M-me?" My eyes close slowly, my body starts falling back toward the ground.

A hand finds its way to the middle of my back, catching me before my body can lie completely flat on the ground.

I conjure up enough energy to open my eyes one more time. The man peers down at me, satisfied. I want to get up and run from him, but I can't focus on anything for more than a few seconds and my body refuses to do what I tell it to. "Now, now," he says, so softly that it's almost comforting. "It's not time for that, yet. You can't give up quite that easily. They have to see this first," he adds quietly.

As I look up at him, tiredly, his pupils seem to grow even larger, blackness claiming his entire iris. "It's done," he whispers, more to himself than to me.

Something jabs my leg, creating a sharp, painful sensation. Another scream erupts from my mouth. I don't try to suppress it, knowing that even if I tried, I wouldn't be able to.

"*Oh no!*" the man hisses, his attention shifting to my legs. He grabs onto something and yanks his arm upward. The pain in my leg intensifies, and then dulls. The knife is back in his hand, fresh blood dripping off the tip.

He jumps to his feet and runs. I force my eyes to focus on the tree canopy above me. I listen to my breath, my eyelids slowly shutting, making the world go black.

Chapter 15

THE WORLD IS DARK WHEN MY EYES OPEN again. Slowly, I lift my hand to my side and feel the place I was stabbed. I suck in a breath as I press down on tender skin. I can feel the dampness on my shirt. My fingers trace the slash mark in the fabric of my shirt.

Did that man mean to kill me? And if so, why am I still alive?

I push myself off the pine-covered ground. My eyes scan the area around me, stopping on a bump a couple feet away. I squint, trying to get a better look at it.

"Keson." His name spills out of my mouth. I scramble toward him on my hands and knees. He's laying on his back, his head turned to the side, facing me. His eyes are closed. When I finally reach him, I examine his body. I watch as his chest lifts and drops. *Good, he's alive.* My eyes travel down to his stomach. The blood stain on his shirt looks like it has expanded. I lift his shirt. Rivers of red trail down his side. A small puddle has gathered on the dirt beneath him. With every dip of his chest, blood gathers in the wound and spills out as he inhales.

I take a deep breath, trying to calm my tense nerves. "Keson?" I whisper.

Nothing happens. Despite his Soundwave abilities, he doesn't acknowledge that he's able to hear me.

"Keson?" I say louder, giving him a little shake.

Nothing.

"Keson?!" I shake him again.

I don't know how much time has passed, but judging by the amount of blood on his shirt and the ground, I'm guessing he's not in a good condition. I feel tears starting to fill my eyes. I had just seen him less than three weeks ago. He was fine. He was happy. He helped me. He's the reason why I was able to find safety.

I've known him for almost my entire life. He's always been there for me. He's never left my side. In times of need, he was there.

My vision blurs with tears as another memory fills my mind.

Keson—eleven years old at the time—walks next to me after school. He has just finished telling me that his dad doesn't want him hanging out with me anymore.

That the age difference is too dangerous. "Okay. I have a plan," he says.

"What?" I ask excitedly.

"You have to promise not to tell anyone."

"I won't," I agree.

His eyes light up. He leans over, crouching to my level. "Here's what we're going to do," he says with a smile. "We have to have a secret spot." He pauses. "That way when we hang out we won't get in trouble because no one else will know."

"Where?" I question, my eyes wide at the thought.

He shrugs, looking around for ideas. "You know that park way down there?" he asks, pointing down one of the streets that leads to the far end of town.

I smirk. "Of course."

"There. That will be the spot."

Now, I stare at Keson's motionless body lying on the ground in front of me. He's still breathing, but his chest is moving slower than before.

"Keson?" I probe again, placing my hand on his shoulder. "Keson?" My voice raises. I drop my forehead to his chest. "Please," I whisper.

I hear his breathing pick up. His chest vibrates as he coughs. I lift my head and look into his dark, tired eyes.

"Keson!" I exclaim. My arms fly around his body.

He hisses against my ear. "The cut."

I pull back instinctively. "Oh! I'm so sorry. How is it?"

"You tell me."

I observe the wound on his abdomen. It's hard to see anything. "I'm not sure. How does it feel?"

"Numb," he moans.

"Numb," I repeat. What does that mean? I let out a frustrated groan. "I'm sorry. I don't know what to do. Whether I should go get help or stay—"

"What's that?" Keson interrupts. I trace his gaze to the slash mark on my shirt.

My fingers fumble with the frayed fabric. "Oh. I got cut too. I think it was the same guy that stabbed you."

"What?" The exhaustion from Keson's voice fades and is replaced with anger. He begins pushing himself off the ground, but I force him back down, keeping my hand resting on his shoulder.

"Shh, calm down," I shush him.

He says breathlessly, "He *cut* you."

"Yeah, but it's not too bad."

Keson coughs violently, sucking in short breaths in between each. His eyes begin to drift shut again.

"Keson!" I cup his face, willing him to stay awake.

"Go," he whispers. I can barely hear him. "Get out of here." His head slumps to the side, his breath catching as the side of his face falls to the ground.

"No, no, no! Keson! Don't! Keson!" I grip his shoulders. I feel tears forming in my eyes as I stare at his completely still body lying in front of me. I don't want to stand up. I don't want to leave him here, but I know that if I don't leave now I won't be able to. The man could still be nearby.

My hands fiddle with Keson's shirt and come to rest on his chest, attempting to see if he's still breathing. His lungs are flat, frozen in place. His face is pale.

I don't want to leave. But I don't want to stay. My heart sinks further, dropping to my feet. Keson's body remains motionless, signaling no sign of life.

He's dead. He's gone.

I rise, barely able to feel my legs beneath me. Without another glance toward Keson's body, I sling my backpack over my shoulder and force my legs into a sprint.

I burst out of the woods, ignoring the fiery pain that erupts in my leg with every step. I swerve through the streets. The portal is straight ahead. I dart toward it, eager to get away from all of this, to make it a distant memory. I don't want to live in this realm a moment longer. I leap at the trunk of the portal.

My feet land on snow covered terrain. I stumble, tripping over myself and hitting the ground. I remain on my hands and knees, finally feeling the heaviness in my chest. My breathing comes in labored, forced bursts. Tears stream from my eyes before I can stop them. The chilly night air feels like needles against my lungs as I gulp it in. After a long couple of minutes, my limbs relax, relieving the tension as the tears slow and my breathing returns to normal. I push myself back into a standing position, walking back to the house with a slight limp.

My pace slows as I near Peter and Linda's house. I come to a stop at the door. Scanning the surroundings, I try to catch my breath. Nothing seems out of place; everything is normal, just as it had been yesterday. My phone buzzes from inside one of the pockets of my backpack. I reach in and retrieve it, looking at the message.

Colton: Just stopped by your house, but you weren't there. Where are you?

My stomach turns as I start to feel sick. I missed the date. On top of everything else, now I have this to deal with too. I shove the phone back into my bag and push the thought out of my head.

I turn to the door and ring the doorbell. Waiting for someone to answer, I think about what I'm supposed to say about where I was and what happened.

What happened?

Malina was here, in the human world. I followed her to Dunchoria.

Keson got stabbed and died before my eyes. I couldn't help him.

I got stabbed too… but I'm still alive. I couldn't save him.

I can feel tears rushing to my eyes, moistening them and threatening to spill over my cheeks.

A shadow fills the glass next to the door. The door opens, and Peter stands with his hand braced on the door handle. He casts me an inspecting gaze, showing concern. His body relaxes, his arm loosening on the door as his guard drops. "Oh my," he whispers as his eyes linger on my blood-soaked clothes.

"Who is it?" Linda asks from a little further in the house. I hear footsteps as she walks up behind him. Her face lights up when she sees me. Pushing Peter to the side, she wraps her arms around me. "Are you okay?" she inquires, unfolding her arms and examining me.

I nod. "Yeah." I can feel the tears gathering in my eyes and I'm pretty sure they can see them too, but they don't say anything.

Her eyes look me over, hovering on my shirt, and then growing wide. "What happened?!" she asks, horrified.

I drop my gaze, seeing the red stains on my shirt.

"You're bleeding!" she exclaims, one hand flying up to her mouth and the other grabbing my hand, pulling me into the house. "And your leg!" she adds, her voice high. "Let's get you cleaned up and taken care of."

She rushes me to the kitchen and has me sit on one of the dining room table chairs while she wets a cloth and Peter goes to get the first aid kit. She dabs the blood, which is almost dry, from the skin surrounding the gashes. She then places bandages and healing ointments on the cuts.

"How did you get these?" she asks when she's done.

I pause, not wanting to answer her. Knowing that if do, more questions will follow.

"I don't want to talk about it right now," I reply. "Can I just go to bed? I'm exhausted."

She hesitates, her eyes sinking in defeat. She nods. "Sure. We can talk about it later," Linda says, leading me to the stairs.

Crawling into bed, all my feelings and thoughts seep into my consciousness. Malina is my best friend. But, why did she come to my school in Oregon? Why did she run from me? She's a Tracker and, being my best friend, she can sense where I am. Maybe she was just curious where I was. She isn't a threat. She can't be. I am still safe here. I have to be. The tears that I had been trying so hard to hide from Linda and Peter begin spilling out once again and this time I can't stop them.

Turning my head to look at the clock on the nightstand, I focus until I see the digits. It's nearly noon. I take a deep breath and push myself out of bed.

My hands fumble as I dress myself in a new, clean pair of clothes. Footsteps echo down the hall as I brush my teeth in the bathroom sink. I listen as the footsteps stop and the sound of rummaging through the cabinets replace them. When I walk into the kitchen a few minutes later, I nearly bump into Peter.

He takes a step backwards and laughs.

"Oh, sorry," I say.

"It's okay. Are you feeling better?" I watch as the specks of worry in his eyes are quickly overshadowed by hope.

I nod, unable to say the words. I don't feel any better. My head aches from last night's tears and my heart throbs for Keson. "Where's Linda?"

Just then, the front door opens and a set of footsteps becomes audible down the hall.

Linda walks into the room. "How are your cuts?"

"They don't hurt," I answer.

"That's good." She pauses. "Can we talk?"

I nod in approval. She sits down in one of the other chairs at the kitchen table, and Peter sits down on the other side of me.

A minute of quiet passes before Peter says, "What happened while you were away?"

I hesitate, willing myself not to get emotional over the answer. I take a deep breath. "My friend from back home... I saw her at school and followed her into Dunchoria," I finally reply.

"Did you hurt yourself?" Linda asks, gesturing to the cuts.

I shake my head, feeling my eyes grow wet. "No." My voice cracks at the word. "There was a man."

"A man?" Linda asks, looking anxious. "Who?"

I shake my head, unwilling to answer. There's no way I'd be able to talk about it. Not now. I'd never be able to hold back the tears, and I really don't feel like crying again.

"I don't know," I say, shaking my head violently, as if to push back the memories. "I just need some time alone," I announce, my voice cracking as I stand from the table.

"You're going to have to talk to us about it eventually," Linda says. "But for now, just breathe. I'm sure Tracy can help you if you need it."

I nod, rushing up to my bedroom and shutting the door behind myself. It's Saturday, so I don't have anywhere to be. I curl up on the bed and stay there for the remainder of the weekend, only dragging myself to the kitchen to eat, which isn't often. I'm not hungry. It's hard doing anything besides laying in my bed. My head feels empty and foggy.

Chapter 16

T HE SKY IS DARK AND GLOOMY, JUST LIKE MY mood, when the alarm clock wakes me up Monday morning. Swinging my legs over the edge of the bed, my feet touch the carpeted ground. I let out a sigh, walking to the mirror and lifting my shirt to expose the bandage that covers my wound. When I lift the gauze, I'm surprised to see that the once bloody, severed skin is now nearly sealed shut. I replace the dressing and make my way out of the room and down the stairs.

"Are you ready?" Linda asks as we eat breakfast.

"Yeah. I can do this," I reply, knowing that her question has multiple meanings behind it.

"You know that you don't have—" she starts.

"No. I want to. I'm fine." It comes out forced, but I know that I have to do this eventually and as of right now, I'm ready.

Linda nods. "Just call us if you need anything."

She drives me to school. Just as I'm about to get out of the car, I turn to her. "I'd like to walk home today."

"Okay," she says with a nod. Not asking any further questions.

I jump out of the car and walk to the entrance of the school. Then a thought hits me, causing me to stop.

Colt! My stomach flips. I missed our date! Everything happened so quickly and I was so drained after I got home that I never texted him back or gave it a second thought. What am I going to do? What am I going to tell him? How am I going to explain?

I sigh and start walking again. Entering the school, I head straight for my first class. I'm later than I've been in the past; most of the students are already in their classrooms. Bree's already sitting in her usual seat when I enter the classroom. I pull out the chair next to her and take a seat.

The minute I drop my backpack on the ground she swivels her body to face me.

"How was the date?" she asks, her face lighting up with excitement. I jump at the sound of her voice.

I collect myself. "I don't know," I reply.

Her expression quickly becomes confused. "What do you mean?"

I think of a response that won't require me to think too much about the actual reason I didn't go on the date. "I left town. I missed it."

"Oh," she says. "That's right. You weren't in fifth period." She pauses. "I was wondering what happened to you."

I nod, not knowing how else to respond.

"So, what now?" she asks, as if this is her problem.

I sigh. "I don't know."

The closer it gets to third period, when I know I'll have to talk to Colt, the more anxious I get. I still have no idea what I'm going to say to him. He'll want an explanation and I can't tell him the truth. He'd never understand, let alone look at me the same again if he knew who I really was.

When Bree and I part ways, she looks me in the eye. "Good luck," she says.

I nod and walk into the classroom. Colt isn't here yet. Minutes pass.

"Where were you on Friday?" a voice next to me asks. I jump slightly at the nearness of the sound.

My eyes flash up to Colt hovering above me. "Did I scare you?" he asks, taking his seat next to me.

"A little."

"Sorry about that," he apologizes. His expression hardens. "So where were you?"

My heart pounds harder than it ever has. The way he stares at me makes my cheeks flush. I gulp and take a deep breath. "I left town." I use the same excuse I had with Bree.

He raises his eyebrows. "Where'd you go?"

I hesitate. It's not like I can tell him. And, honestly, I don't think I'm ready to tell anyone about what really happened. I can't even think about it without getting worked up. I just shake my head, unwilling to put words to the thoughts running through my head.

He doesn't respond. He doesn't understand. How could I expect him to? He didn't witness everything like I did. He doesn't know who I really am, or what I'm going through. He's oblivious to my secret life; my internal battle and the friend I lost.

Keson's dead. I lost him.

The bell rings and class begins. We don't talk for the rest of class and, in a way, I'm thankful for that. I'm pretty sure that if I had to speak, I'd break down in tears.

Toward the end of lunch, after I've finished eating, Bree turns to me, trying to break the silence I've brought to the table. Her emerald eyes observe me carefully.

"What?"

"How'd it go?" she asks. By the expression of her face, it's obvious that she already knows exactly how my conversation with Colt went.

"Not good."

"What happened?"

I explain our conversation to her. "It's like I'm losing everyone I care about," I add.

"Everyone?" Bree questions curiously.

"I lost an… old friend this weekend too." I pause as tears make their way to the surface. I hadn't wanted to say it, but I felt like I could tell her without being pushed to talk about it.

Bree leans toward me and wraps her arms around me. After a minute she unwraps her arms and places her hands on my shoulders. "I'm here for you."

"I just—I can't do this right now."

"Do what?" Bree asks, lowering her arms to her sides.

"This!" I exclaim waving my hands in the air. "All this with Colt," I sigh. "I just can't deal with it right now. Not with all the other stuff going on."

The bell rings. Bree and I walk to fifth period together. Another class with Colt. I roll my eyes at the thought. At least this time I have Bree to help ease the tension, if there is any. We arrive at math and take our usual seats. My pulse beats a little faster with every minute that passes.   Finally, Colt waltzes into the classroom. He glances at me and quickly looks away.

I watch as he strides to a desk at the front of the room and takes a seat. My heart sinks. He can't even sit next to me anymore. Did missing the date really hurt him that badly?

Just then, his 'not-so-secret' admirer saunters over to him, places her hand on his shoulder and slides it down his arm. I watch as her glossed lips move. Colt gives a single nod and she sits down next to him.

Apparently he's already over me.

I tear my gaze away from them and try to distract myself.

Bree eyes me. "I guess that answers the question you had earlier," I say gesturing to Colt.

I watch as Bree's gaze follows to where I'd gestured. Her eyes narrow. "Mackenzie," she replies shaking her head. "I thought they were over."

"Over?" I ask, confused.

"Yeah. They used to date," she says, a hint of bitterness in her voice.

"They did?"

She nods. "About two months ago, but they didn't last very long."

"Oh."

Class starts and I do my best to focus on the angles and equations Mr. Williams is scrawling on the board. Halfway through class, though, I find my focus drifting back to Colt and Mackenzie. I don't even try to break my stare; I watch them.

Mackenzie leans over and whispers something in Colt's ear. He turns to her and gives an uneasy smile. A couple minutes pass. Mackenzie leans back into Colt and whispers in his ear again. Before she retracts, our eyes lock. A sly smile slips across her face. We hold each other's stares for a moment.

Then, she swings her head forward and straightens. Knowing that I'm still watching, she turns to Colt, whose attention is focused on the blackboard, and grazes her hand along his thigh. His attention snaps to her. He pushes her hand off of his leg and shakes his head. She waits a second before cuddling close to him. She wraps her arms around his bicep. I watch as her lips form the words 'I'm sorry.'

Mackenzie swivels her neck to look at me again. A smug smile plays on her face. I rip my gaze off of her and Colt.

Finally, the day comes to an end and I walk home in the freezing cold, shivering most of the way, but glad to feel something other than the pain inside. When I finally get to the house, Peter's there to let me in but I go straight to my bedroom, exchanging as few words with him as possible. But, after laying on my bed for close to an hour, I decide I need to get out of the house. I pull off the bandages on my injury, but freeze when I see what appears to be a big paper cut as the only evidence of the incident from a couple nights ago. I don't bother rewrapping it.

I grab my jacket, jog down the stairs, and yell into the house, "I'm going out!"

I walk, not knowing where I'm going or where I want to go. But, somehow, I find myself downtown. The streets are bustling with traffic. There are fewer people on the sidewalk than there are cars on the road.

After a couple minutes, I notice the store on my right. I sigh, coming to a stop. It's the picture store, the one where I first met—or ran into—Colton. *Colt. What went wrong?* I ponder the question.

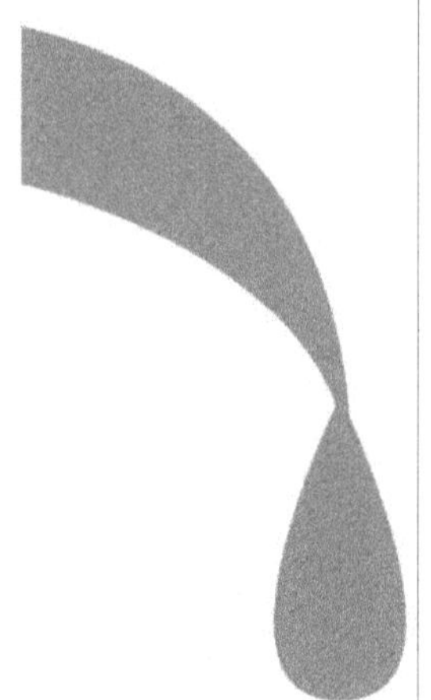

Chapter 17

M Y THOUGHTS RUN CRAZY, BUT eventually they settle on one overpowering concept.

For the first time since my trip to Dunchoria, I accept the fact that Keson is dead. It hits me like a huge brick colliding with my head and I can't stop the tears from flowing. They roll down my cheeks as I rush to get home and have privacy. He's dead. Keson's dead. He'll no longer be there for me, with his witty jokes and sarcastic comments. I'll never see him again, his vibrant, enthusiastic brown eyes or the way his lips curve upwards, exposing his dimples just before he smiles. I have a flashback of his kiss in New York City and a sob escapes my lips. He's gone.

Tuesday morning, it's warmer out and there's a slight breeze. I walk to school, enjoying the change in weather.

When the third period bell rings, I numbly walk to class and take my seat. My heart pounds as I wait for Colt. Just like yesterday afternoon, he enters the classroom, glances at me, and picks a seat on the opposite side of the room. I let out an involuntary sigh and sink in my chair. I sit by myself, wondering how I can fix this. The class begins, but I find myself having a hard time focusing.

In fifth period, Colt chooses the same spot he sat in yesterday, at the front of the room instead of our usual back row.

Bree, seeing my longing eyes trace him, asks, "No luck with Colt, huh?"

I shake my head. No luck getting Colt back, but I still can't seem to get him out of my head.

Mackenzie struts to the classroom door with a couple of her friends. She looks at Colt, smiles, and turns to her friends. Pointing a finger at him, her and her friends exchange a couple words and they all giggle. She waves goodbye to them and enters the room, heading straight for Colt and sits down at the desk next to him. She strokes her hand along his arm. His toned bicep presses against the fabric, displaying every crevice in his muscle.

My stomach turns, making me feel sick at the interaction.

I can't take it! I'm not going to sit here all class and watch this!

I stand and walk to Colt and Mackenzie. I grip Mackenzie's arm in my hand and move it off of Colt. Before I'm able to stop it, the emotions begin seeping out of me. My anger transfers into a burning sensation as it passes from my hand to Mackenzie.

I quickly release her arm, cutting off the transfer. She grabs the spot I had touched. "Ow!" she screams. "What the heck, Macy!" Her eyes are wild.

My eyes grow wide as I realize what I just did. "Sorry," I apologize, but it's not nearly as sincere as it would have been had I actually been sorry. Mackenzie's eyes narrow.

Not wanting to stand here any longer, I turn to Colt, who has been watching me the whole time. "We have to talk."

His brown eyes study me. "Sure," he agrees, standing up.

"Colt!" Mackenzie yells as we walk away.

He sends her a look and she sinks back into her chair.

I walk into the hallway, knowing there are a couple minutes left before class. Colt follows me. The hallways aren't too crowded and no one seems to pay any attention to us. Mr. Williams is down the hall talking to another teacher.

"Look," I say, turning around to face him. "I'm sorry for missing the date. I really wanted to go, I just—I left town and I couldn't get back in time. Something happened."

"You didn't answer my text."

"I didn't have service." It's not a lie. Human cellphones don't work in Dunchoria.

"So what happened exactly?" he prompts.

I hesitate. I can feel the tears welling up in my eyes. I want to tell him, but I can't bring myself to say the words. "I-I can't. But please believe that there was a good reason for it."

He observes me for a minute, not saying anything.

"Please," I plead. "Forgive me."

He's silent, but his eyes watch me intently. We stand in the nearly empty hallway looking at each other. My heart thumps in my chest. "It doesn't work that way," he finally says.

"Then how does it work?" I ask, peering up at him. "I told you that I can't tell you. I can't give you any other information."

"You know what? I don't play games. If you want to lie... or hide the truth, fine. But I'm done putting up with all the secrets."

I hesitate, unable to respond.

The bell rings. Without a word he takes a step away from me and strides through the classroom door, leaving me alone in the hall thinking about what he had said.

"Can we talk?" My voice quivers a little as I stare at Colt's back as he rummages through his locker at the end of the day.

"Do we have to?" he retorts, turning to face me.

"Yes." My eyes search his face for anything that shouldn't be there. His eyes look into mine, waiting for me to say something. "What do I have to do to prove to you that I'm sorry and I deserve your forgiveness?"

He stares at me, thinking. "Be honest." His body twirls around and he starts down the hall.

"Wait," I say, racing after him. "What do you want me to be honest about?"

He whips around to face me. "Everything, but for starters, what happened to Mackenzie today in math?"

I hesitate. I can't just tell him. "I don't know," I finally reply.

"Exactly," he scoffs. "That's what I thought." He stalks off, blending with the other students headed out of the school. I'm about to run after him, but stop myself, realizing that distancing myself from him is probably the best thing right now. The last thing I want to do is have him find out what I'm able to do. What would he think after he found out?

Chapter 18

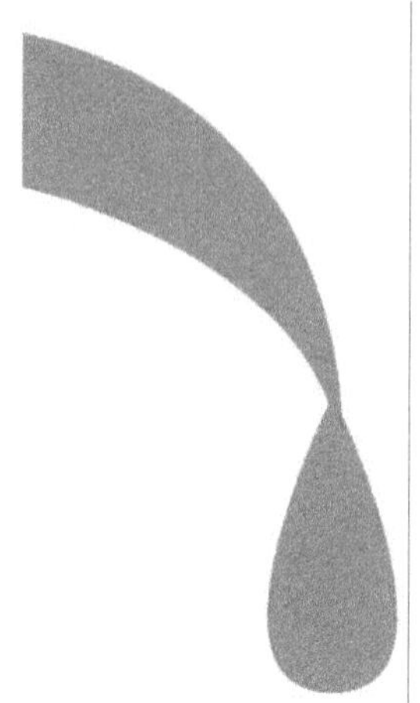

I DO A PRETTY GOOD JOB OF DISTANCING myself from Colt the next couple of days. When math class comes, my eyes don't even drift in his direction, but no matter how much I try to push him out of my head, he keeps creeping back in.

I leave school twenty minutes later than usual, after staying to get some extra help from my Spanish teacher. The parking lot is nearly empty except for a few lone cars. I drop the skateboard from under my arm, hoping onto it. I've been attempting to learn how to maneuver it for the past few days. I needed a new hobby, something to distract me from Colt's absence. There's not a person in sight as I wheel my way across the blacktop and onto the sidewalk. The wind is stronger than usual today. I dip my head as an aggressive burst of air rushes over the pavement. My balance shifts, causing my body to lean backwards and the board to curve to the side.

All I can feel is myself falling as the wheels sink into the crack on the curb, sending my body flying across the asphalt. Every one of my nerves buzz to life, ready to jump to action and brace myself for the landing, but they're cut short when my head bashes against the cement and my vision disappears.

Everything goes black.

Bright, white light floods into my eyes as I open them. I blink in surprise. My surroundings are unfamiliar, white brick walls, long bright ceiling lights, and thin white bed sheets.

A woman walks up next to me, holding a clip board. She's wearing a blue outfit. She examines me with cautious eyes. She turns to the board in her hand and begins scribbling.

"Where am I?" I ask, unsure.

"The hospital," she replies, still looking down at the board.

"How'd I get here?"

"Your friend brought you here," she says in a hushed voice, nodding her head in the direction of a brown-haired boy sprawled across the couch a couple feet away. *Colton.* Seeing him here makes my heart stop. I'm not sure if it's because I'm excited or nervous. Probably both.

"What happened?" I whisper.

"You've been unconscious for a few hours," she tells me, not fully answering my question.

"When am I going to be let out?"

"Tomorrow? Your friend over there—" the nurse explains, gesturing to Colt. "Had your guardians' numbers. He gave them to us and we called them to let them know where you were. They are on their way and can sign you out when we clear you."

I nod. The nurse continues scribbling on the paper clipped to her board. After a couple more minutes, she drops her clipboard to her side and looks at me. "Get some sleep." She pauses. "It's not much fun around here at night anyways." A smile slips onto her face. She turns for the door and leaves the room, closing the door behind her.

I sit in the brightly lit room. The memory of what happened comes back to me. I remember the curb and the skateboard. I remember the feeling of falling to the ground.

The sound of mumbling pulls me back to reality. I turn my gaze to Colt, who is still sleeping on the couch.

His position has changed since I last looked at him. He tosses from side to side.

His mouth opens and odd sounds escape. He mumbles in what almost sounds like a foreign language.

A couple minutes later, the mumbling fades. Colt's eyes flash open and I catch his gaze.

"Hey," I say.

"Hey." He sits up. "How are you?"

"Good," I answer. "How are *you*?" I ask him.

"Fine," he replies, but I know he's bluffing.

"Thanks for helping me. How'd you find me? Back at the school?"

He hesitates. "I was walking out to my truck at the end of the day and I saw you laying in the street by the school. I assumed you fell or something, which would explain all of your scratches and bruises. You wouldn't wake up or respond, so I put you in my truck and drove straight to the hospital."

I watch his reaction. It seems worried, and… upset? "Why'd you help me? I thought you didn't want anything to do with me."

"Even *if* that were true, I still wouldn't have left you lying unconscious in the street in the middle of winter."

"Alright, fair enough. But why are you still here? Why didn't you leave yet?"

He stands up from the couch and walks over to my bed. His hand reaches for mine. Our palms touch and our finger intertwine. I look down at our hands, so warm and secure, and then up into Colt's eyes.

"I would never leave you alone." He freezes, then clears his throat. "Sorry, that sounded… clingy. I just meant—"

"I understand," I assure with a smile. "So, what does this mean? Am I forgiven?" I lift my eyebrows playfully. His words imply that I am, but I need to hear him say it.

He smiles and his head drops. When he looks back up, the smile is still present. "Yes. You're forgiven." The elated tone of his voice makes me smile in delight.

"Good. So… what I'm hearing is that the next time I need you to forgive me for something, all I have to do is get a couple scratches. Simple enough." I shrug.

"Please don't," he begs. But the spark in his eyes hold humor. "Let's try using another strategy first, okay?"

I laugh. "Got it. So, how bad do I look?"

"You look beautiful."

"Don't lie," I reply. But I can't help laughing a bit.

He shakes his head. "I'm not lying. I mean you're a bit scratched up, but it'll heal."

His free hand touches my forehead. His eyes follow his fingers as they swish gently across my skin. They hover in the upper corner of my forehead.

"What?" I ask.

His eyes are still focused on my forehead. "This scratch," he replies.

"What about it?"

"When I found you in the road earlier today it was a huge gash. It was bleeding a lot, but now it just looks like a little scrape."

"Maybe the blood made it look worse than it was?"

"Yeah, maybe," he replies.

A cell phone rings. Colt reaches into his pocket with his free hand and pulls it out. He glances at the screen. "It's my dad," he says. "Hold on. I should get this." He lets go of my hand and walks out into the hallway, closing the door behind him. Holding the phone up to his ear, he begins to talk.

I watch Colt through the glass window. His lips move as he talks. He pauses to let his dad speak. He hangs up and stuffs the phone back into his pocket. His shoulders rise as he takes a deep breath before walking back into the room. He returns to my bedside, placing my hand in his once more.

There's silence.

"You look exhausted," I finally say. "You should get some sleep. You can go home if you want."

His eyes hold something I can't read. "Yeah, I guess so," he answers. "But I'll be back in the morning." I look at him confused. "You're going to need an escort to school tomorrow," he explains.

I smile at him. Then another voice joins us.

"That's okay. I'll take her."

I whip my head around. Standing in the doorway is Linda. "Hey," I greet.

"The hospital called me. Are you okay?" She turns to Colt, who is standing at the side of my bed. "Hi," she says.

"Hi," he replies.

"Thanks for getting Macy here and getting in touch with us. I'll take it from here," Linda says sweetly.

Colt's eyes shift to me for confirmation. "Thank you," I whisper. "I'll see you at school tomorrow."

He nods and releases my hand. As he exits, he gives Linda a slight bob of the head and smiles.

Chapter 19

ORNING COMES SOON ENOUGH. WHEN I wake up, I find Linda—who spent the night here—already awake.

"Good morning," she greets.

"Good morning," I reply. "How long have you been awake?"

"About an hour," she answers.

The nurse from yesterday walks in. Seeing that I'm awake, she flips on the light. I squint under them.

"Sorry," she apologizes, glancing down at her clipboard. "Your lab work looks fine. You have a very minor concussion. But not nearly what would have been expected based on your symptoms when you came in. You're a lucky girl. You're good to go."

"Thank you," I reply. She leaves the room.

Linda checks me out of the hospital and grabs a note for the school explaining why I'm late. When I arrive at the school, I give the note to the front desk secretary and head to English. Mrs. Taylor gives me a suspicious look as I enter the classroom, but doesn't say anything.

Fifth period—math—finally comes. Bree and I get to class before most of our other classmates. The minutes tick by. Just before the final bell, Colt slips through the door. He heads straight toward us and sits down in the chair next to me. As he tosses his backpack on the floor, I look up and find Mackenzie staring at me. Her amber eyes narrow when they meet mine. Her shiny, glossed lips press into a tight, straight line.

Colt's hand finds mine and gives it a reassuring squeeze. My eyes flit to him. His eyes tell me that he knows exactly what's going on. He smiles encouragingly.

Monday, I wake up with the alarm clock. The room is dark. Not one ray of sunshine comes in from the window. I get dressed and head downstairs, but while I'm pouring myself a bowl of cereal, Linda comes into the kitchen and tells me that school's been cancelled for the day.

With nothing to do, the day goes by at a snail's pace. Colt and I exchange a couple text messages back and forth throughout the day, but it's not nearly as nice as actually being able to talk to him in person.

My head is constantly roaming and thinking and remembering. I try to pass the time with catching up on schoolwork, but end up watching television and helping Linda cook. All the sitting around at home almost drives me crazy. So when Tuesday morning comes, I eagerly hop out of bed and get dressed, hoping that we actually have school.

Linda comes downstairs. "You have school today," she says with sleepy eyes.

"Good!"

"There's snow still all over the ground, though, and it's pretty cold. I can drive you to school if you'd like."

"Yeah," I say. "That'd be nice."

"Okay, just let me know when you're ready."

"Alright."

Before I get out of the car at school, Linda tells me she can pick me up too, but I swiftly decline the offer.

The day is a welcome relief from yesterday's boredom, full of chatter and lectures and lunch with Bree. At the end of the day, I'm late leaving my seventh period art class after offering to stay a few extra minutes to wash the paintbrushes. So when I leave, the hallways are nearly deserted. I'm hurrying down a staircase to meet with Colt when a figure emerges.

"Hey Macy," he says as he gets closer. His voice is familiar.

I roll my eyes when I realize it belongs to Drake. "What do you want?"

"Want? Is that the only reason you think I talk to you?"

I stare at him for a moment. "You always want something."

"Okay, okay," he says, holding his hands in the air in surrender. "You're right, I do want something."

I stop short and raise my eyebrows. "Oh? And what would that be?"

His eyes drop to the ground, slowly lifting to watch me from beneath his dark lashes. "I want to kiss you right now." He stares at my lips for longer than I'm comfortable with. "Really badly actually... but I know I shouldn't." He cocks his head to the side, waiting for my reply.

I remain silent, unsure of how to respond. His tall, muscular figure lingers in the frame of the stairwell.

He runs a hand through his dark hair, turning it into a messy, almost alluring, array on the top of his head. Propping his elbow on the wall, his biceps flex, and a small smile crosses his lips. "Or should I?" He pauses. "You want to kiss me too, don't you Princess?" He takes a step toward me, slow and cautious. All the while, his dark eyes stay fixated on me, examining my reaction. My heart skips, not because I'm threatened by the interaction, but because I'm confused and... intrigued? "You really are beautiful." He shakes his head. "No wonder Colton is interested in you." *Colton.* He's waiting for me.

The lights above our heads flicker in response to his words. My attention jumps to the ceiling, observing the lights, perplexed.

"Sorry," he whispers, causing my attention to return to him. There's something in the way he looks at me that makes my cheeks grow warm. It's almost like he's looking inside of me. "I just don't see why you would want to settle just yet. Before you actually know everyone. I want to get to know you, maybe we can even be more than friends someday." His words are gentle and comforting. His expression is genuine, but his demeanor shows charm and etiquette, almost as if he knows what he's doing. He knows the effect his proposition will have on me.

His words catch me off guard. *Settle?* Is that what I'm doing right now? With Colton?

Drake takes another step toward me, but I don't move. My thoughts slam into one another as I contemplate what to do. Run? Or stay?

He closes the distance between us. Do I let him touch me? Or, do I shy away?

I can't decide. I can't move. His words have me craving his presence—his touch—but my gut tells me to not trust him.

His hand reaches for me and I still don't know what to do. I remain still, unmoving. My thoughts go blank as his fingers touch my skin. I can feel a spark at the contact.

I'm stuck. Drake gazes down at me, his focus flashing from my eyes to the place his hand rests on my arm. His thumb strokes tiny circles against my skin. "Then again, there's nothing wrong with a little competition," he whispers in his raspy voice.

A force hits Drake, throwing him across the stairwell. I gasp in surprise. A hand closes around my wrist and pulls me. Arms wrap around me protectively. A familiar scent fills my nose. *Colton.* I look up into a pair of comforting caramel eyes. They stare at me for a moment, then switch focus. My eyes follow Colt's until I'm staring at Drake, who's holding his hand to his jaw, wincing.

There's silence for a couple long moments as the two stare at each other.

"What the heck man?!" Colt finally says.

"Dude—" Drake begins.

"What were you thinking?"

Drake hesitates, his eyes switching between us. "I wasn't," he replies, but something in the way his gaze lingers on me tells me he was fully aware of his actions. His expression contorts, his lips pressing into a tight, straight line as he glares at Colt's arms wrapped around me.

"Clearly you weren't. Talk to her like that again and you're dead."

Drake's eyes narrow, as if the threat is a reason to not give in. But he doesn't advance toward us. His fingers press the skin on his jaw, feeling for tender spots.

Colt's hand finds mine and his fingers lock with mine. I trail after him as we walk through the hallway and out of the building.

Colt is silent for a good portion of the drive home. "Drake," Colt finally snarls. There's a long pause, as if he's trying to decide whether he wants to say something. "He always wants what he can't have. We're 'friends' and all, but he's always trying to find ways to get on my last nerve. I guess he found a way."

I don't say anything.

"His cousins are the same way," Colt adds.

"He has cousins?" I ask, surprised.

"Yeah, he has four cousins that go to school here too. They're always together."

"Always?" I hadn't ever noticed anyone else with him.

"Yeah."

Moments later, we arrive in my driveway. I reach for Colt's hand and grasp it. Leaning toward him, I give him a short kiss. "Thank you," I say, jumping out of the car.

"Hey," Colt says, reaching for my arm. "What are you doing tonight?"

"Nothing… why?"

"Well, we never had a first date, did we?"

"No…" I reply, not quite sure where this is going.

"I was thinking we could do that."

"Okay. What were you thinking?"

"It's a surprise, and this time don't ditch me."

My cheeks grow warm. My gaze drops to the ground. He cups my chin in his hand and lifts it so that I'm looking up into his eyes. "It's a joke," he says with a smile.

I nod.

"Seven o'clock tonight?" he asks.

"Last minute, huh? Shouldn't you be planning dates a little further ahead?" I joke. "What if whoever you asked wasn't available?"

"Then I'd ask someone else." I stare at him. A smile forms on his lips. "I'm just kidding, lighten up." He pauses, gazing into my eyes, a small smile forming. "I'd wait for her."

I smile. "Good answer, see you at seven."

The minutes don't tick by fast enough. I watch the clock, waiting for it to turn seven. Finding nothing else to do, I busy myself with homework and shuffling through my duffel bag.

Finally, seven o'clock comes. I reach into my duffel and find the stack of money I took from the cabinet back home in New York.

The feeling of the stack brings back another memory and I'm transported back to when I was eleven, shortly after I got to New York.

I'm sitting on the sofa in the living room. The TV's on, the volume turned down low. It's late; Tamlin and Elton are putting the girls to bed upstairs.

Footsteps thump down the stairs, another set follows. Tamlin and Elton come into the room.

"Can we talk?" Tamlin asks. Her eyes hold something I haven't seen in them before.

"Yeah," I reply, reaching for the remote and turning off the TV.

"You're old enough now to understand how this kind of thing works," Elton says.

"Your mom and I used to be very close when we were younger. Before I left Cylilia to come here, she told me that your father, Ryker, was still fighting in the war. She knew that Chastrin's army was advancing and gaining strength. Tension was rising. She told me that if something were to go wrong she'd tell you how to find me. She wanted to make sure that no matter what, you were safe." She pauses. "And, now I'm telling you the same thing." Taking a deep breath, she continues, "We've stashed money in the bottom right hand corner of the kitchen cabinet that is on the left side of the refrigerator. If anything ever goes wrong and you need to leave right away, just take the money and we'll know what happened." Her eyes look at me; observing me for some sign of clarification, of recognition that I know what she's saying.

I nod. An unsettling feeling starts in my stomach. A feeling that hopes it'll never come down to that, that I'll never have to leave my family again.

The memory fizzles out, but that feeling stays with me. I hold the stack of money I've taken from the duffel, pulling out a twenty-dollar bill. Stuffing it into my pocket, I wedge the rest deep into my bag.

The thrum of an engine catches my attention. I look out the window and watch as a blue truck pulls into the driveway. I quickly check myself in the mirror and rush downstairs.

There's a knock at the door. I place my hand on the doorknob and open it. "Hi Colt," I say, looking at him standing in the door frame.

"Hey," he replies, smiling at me. His eyes look past me and at Linda, who is walking toward us. "Hello Mrs. Woods," he acknowledges politely.

"Actually, it's Mrs. Miller," I correct.

He appears a little confused, but then collects himself and says, "Okay, hello Mrs. Miller."

"Hello," Linda greets when she reaches the doorway, dipping her head in acknowledgement.

I pause. "So Colt and I are going to go hang out, I'll be back around—" I turn to Colt for help.

"Nine," he offers.

"Is that okay?" I ask her.

"Sure. Have fun," she says as I step out of the house.

As she closes the door, I turn to face the driveway. Colton slips his hand into mine and we walk out to the driveway together. Unexpectedly, he escorts me to the passenger's side, opening the door. He then rounds the vehicle and jumps into the driver's seat, starting the engine and merging onto the road.

"So back there in the house," he begins. "What was that about?"

"What do you mean?"

"With the last names. I know your last name is Woods, but your mom's is Miller?"

I flinch at the word. "She's my aunt actually," I reply.

His eyes shift to me, an expression I can't read is present on his face, but he doesn't ask any further questions. Then, his attention returns to the road.

A couple minutes pass. "You want to tell me where we're going?" I ask, attempting to change the subject.

He shakes his head. "Nope, it's still a surprise."

"What's up with you and surprises?"

"Things are more interesting when you don't know what you're in for," he explains with a smirk.

After a couple more minutes he pulls into a crowded parking lot. The building is lit up with florescent lights that form the words, 'Al's Alleys.' There's a bowling ball next to the words.

"Bowling?" I ask Colt as we get out of the car.

"Yeah, good or bad?"

"Good," I answer. I've never been bowling before. We'd never had enough time to go bowling back in New York.

"Good, because it's half off tonight." He smiles, wrapping his fingers around mine.

"Wow! What a cheap date," I chuckle.

"Nah, just a frugal one." He winks at me as we walk into the loud, crowded bowling alley.

There are barely any open lanes, but eventually we find one and set up a new game.

"So, I have to warn you," I mention after we're ready to start. "I've never done this before."

"You've never bowled?" Colt looks at me surprised.

I shake my head.

"You'll do fine," he says, giving me a reassuring smile.

We begin playing. At first, I hit the gutter every roll, but eventually—with Colt's help—I'm able to knock down some pins.

Then, the competition begins. It's my turn. I grab a ball and go to the lane. Releasing the ball from my hand, it glides along the slippery hardwood floor and strikes the pins, all except two clatter to the ground. I grab another ball and survey the remaining pins. Swinging my arm forward, I release the ball. It rolls, knocking down the last two pins.

I turn to Colt. "Not bad," he says.

"You think you can do better?" I challenge him.

"I don't know, let's see," he says, his velvet voice low, and a smirk slipping onto his lips.

A feeling starts in my stomach and sends jitters all through my body. Just the way he said the sentence makes my heart speed in my chest. My fingers twitch, itching to touch him. As my eyes travel to his lips, I remember the first time we kissed at the party, the way his lips felt on mine. The way my stomach flipped.

I want to feel that way again. I want to touch him, but instead, I walk past him and sit down on the bench.

Grabbing a ball from off the rack, he walks to the thick line at the start of the bowling lane. He scrutinizes the pins for a moment. As he lifts the ball behind him, the muscles in his arm become prominent. I watch as his arm drops forward and the ball goes flying down the alley. It strikes the pins, knocking all ten of them to the ground. The machine begins to clean up the fallen pins. He turns around and walks back.

"How's that?" he asks jokingly.

"Not bad," I laugh, standing up and walking to the ball rack. I pick out one and go to the start of the lane.

I repeat my earlier motions, but instead of the ball heading for the pins it heads straight into the gutter.

"Now that was a better throw than mine," he jokes from behind me.

I smile at him over my shoulder and try again. My hands are shaking, but I manage to get them under control and release the ball. It skims the gutter, but rolls and hits a pin, which wobbles and topples over.

"Wow! That sucked," I say, turning around to face him.

He grins in amusement, his attention centered on me. My heart spikes in my chest. I can't seem to slow it, not when he's watching me like this. My cheeks grow warm, but I'm not sure if it's because I'm embarrassed or flattered. "You're not doing all that bad for someone who's never bowled before," he acknowledges.

"I guess that's a compliment."

"It is," he says, grabbing my hand and giving me a peck on the lips before he continues toward our lane to take his turn.

Walking to my chair, I glance up into the mass of people standing along the balcony at the front of the building, watching us. One face in particular catches my eye.

Drake.

Chapter 20

DRAKE WATCHES ME CLOSELY, CLEARLY unconcerned whether I catch him looking. As I stare back at him, his eyes stay locked on mine. His expression is intense and observant. Almost menacing, but I'm not sure the look is meant for me.

A weird feeling tingles in my stomach. The way he's watching me, it feels... strange.

I quickly sit down in my chair and wait for Colt to finish his turn. All the while I can feel Drake's eyes on me.

I decide not to tell Colt about Drake. I'd rather not cause a scene tonight.

When our game is over, Colt goes to buy us some pizza. I take a seat at an empty table and wait. A figure sits down across from me. At first, I think it's Colt, but when I look up, I find Drake staring back at me.

"Hey Macy," he says, placing his hands on the table.

"What are you doing here?" I ask, suddenly worried. My eyes dart around the room, trying to find Colt and make sure he isn't watching.

"How's the date going?" Drake asks, a smirk sliding across his otherwise displeased face.

I frown at him. "What are you doing here?" I repeat.

"Just keeping an eye on you."

"Why?"

He shrugs. "You never know what could happen."

"Are you trying to upset Colt?" I reply, slightly annoyed that he didn't learn his lesson earlier.

"I mean, that would be okay with me."

I shake my head. "Drake, please don't. He told you to not talk to me again."

Something in Drake's expression switches. His eyes flash in excitement. "I know he did. But would you really be okay with that? If I never spoke to you again?"

I go silent, my thoughts bouncing against my skull as I try to come up with an answer. I want to say yes, that he should leave me alone. But I can't bring myself to do it. Something inside of me doesn't want to let him leave.

He smirks. "That's what I thought." He pauses. "I'm just trying to look out for you Princess," he finally adds. There's something to the words, some hidden meaning, but I can't place it.

"I don't even know you," is all I can say.

"That doesn't mean I don't know you."

I shake my head, confused. "Do you remember my second day at school?"

His eyebrows lift, pushing me to clarify.

"You had that fight with Colt," I say.

He nods. "Yeah, what about it?"

"First impressions go a long way. And yours isn't doing you any favors."

"But what does the scene from earlier today tell you?"

I stare at him. "Honestly Drake, I don't know what that was. You're so bipolar. Part of me wants to believe your words, but the other part wants to build a wall so thick that you would never be able to break through it. Never be able to get to me."

His cocky façade cracks ever so slightly. "Please don't." He eyes me. "Don't block me out. Not yet."

I shake my head, unsure. "For right now, you need to leave. Get out of here before Colt comes back and sees you, okay?"

"Let him see me," Drake says, draping his arm over the back of the chair, his posture relaxing.

I stare at him, straight-faced. "Drake, you're building that wall yourself."

He freezes, as if his movement is going to add a row of bricks to my metaphoric wall. "Okay, okay. I'm leaving," Drake replies, standing from the chair. He sends me a small, almost indiscrete nod. "Until next time," he says right before walking away.

Colton comes back with the pizza a couple minutes later.

"Do you remember the first time we met in town?" Colt asks while we're eating.

"Yeah and I ran into you with the door," I say after a bite of pizza.

He nods, laughing and lifts his hand to his head, as if he can still feel where the door hit him.

"You ready to go?" he asks as I finish chewing the last bite of my slice.

"Sure," I reply, standing up.

The sun is long gone by now, leaving the world dark. Street lamps illuminate the road as Colt drives me home. He doesn't need any directions this time; he seems to know exactly where he's going.

We pull into my driveway just as the digital clock in Colt's truck changes to nine o'clock.

"I had fun," I say shyly.

"Me too."

I lean over the center console and kiss him softly. My heart leaps in my chest as our lips make contact. As I jump out of the truck, he rolls down the window on the passenger's side.

"See you at school."

I nod and walk to the front door. It's yanked open before I even knock.

"Just on time," Peter says. "Linda told me what time you'd be home."

I laugh. Walking up the stairs I can't ignore the sensation of Colt's lips on mine; the taste of his breath and the feel of his lips. I can't seem to shake it, and I don't want to.

I take a quick shower, brush my teeth, and slip into my pajamas. I can't help but think about some of the things Drake said.

One of the lines runs back through my head, "Just keeping an eye on you."

Why would he need to keep an eye on me? Why does he care?

The other thing he said pops into my mind, "That doesn't mean I don't know you."

Was that supposed to have some meaning behind it?

Is he just trying to get in my business, or maybe even my head? I push him out of my thoughts, not willing to let him get his way.

Sliding under the bed covers, I turn off the light on the night stand. But I can't quite fall asleep. An image from my past fills my thoughts.

I'm walking through one of the parks in Cylilia. My father is holding my hand, swinging it back and forth. I'm eight years old. In front of us, Evlyn, who is two, is in a stroller that is being pushed by my mom.

My dad's goofing around and telling jokes. Everyone, including me, erupts in laughter. Even Evlyn, seeing that everyone else is laughing, begins to giggle. My dad looks down at me and tussles my hair.

"Daddy!" I exclaim in mock protest, fixing the hair he has disheveled.

But that family has been torn apart. Other memories cascade into my head, replacing the happy family that no longer exists.

I'm ten. The Uniforms have just broken through the front door of our house. Evlynell is crying in the arms of the Uniform who ripped her away from our mother. I've just inflicted pain onto one of the Uniforms. My mom is positioned between the Force Field and me.

"She's only a child; she just turned ten a few months ago," my mother pleads. "She doesn't understand the rules and consequences."

The Force Field grabs ahold of my mother and says, "It doesn't matter what age she is, it's still a crime." He pushes her aside and heads toward me. I back away. My mother reaches for him and yanks him back, preventing him from getting to me. He swings around and grips her arm, making her yelp in pain and shock.

"Run! You know where to go," she hollers to me over the Uniform's shoulder.

Instantly, I run for the back door and burst out of the house. A few steps away, I look back, taking a final glance at the life I'm about to leave behind. I watch as three Uniforms file out of my house. One is holding Evlyn, who is still crying, and two other Uniforms are holding my mother. None of them are chasing after me. They probably figure that I won't get far.

My mom stares at me and suddenly her voice is in my head, accessing her Singer abilities. Singers are similar to Visionaries or Mind Inflictors (like myself), only they can "sing" to you; get inside your head and have a conversation. It's similar to what humans call 'telepathy.'

"Go find a portal, the ones that your father and I showed you. After you pass through the portal ask for directions to 39258 Maple Lane, Nyack, New York. Aunt Tamlin, my sister, lives there with her human husband, Elton. They'll offer you shelter. Explain everything to them. Just remember, no matter what, your father and I love both you and your sister. I don't know what will happen to Evlyn, but they won't kill her. She'll be waiting for you to find her."

The vision blurs, but the line remains in my head, "I don't know what will happen to Evlyn, but they won't kill her, she'll be waiting for you to find her."

Finally, I drift off to sleep. But the next morning, the line is still repeating and I can't stop mulling it over.

It reminds me of one thing. Evlyn's still alive and she's out there somewhere, presumably in Dunchoria, just waiting to be found. She'd be ten now, which means she'd probably have her power.

Tuesday and Wednesday there's no sign of Drake at school, which makes me both relieved and suspicious.

On Thursday, I spot Drake while walking to lunch. He's with three other boys. Immediately, I see the family resemblance; it's three of his cousins, leaving the remaining cousin nowhere to be found. Drake spots me too. He turns around to look at me, revealing a black and blue bruise on his jaw from where Colt punched him. Drake slips on a sly, knowing smile. I give him a puzzled expression. One of the boys standing next to Drake looks over, giving me a half smile. I break eye contact with Drake and walk to lunch.

The rest of the day goes by uneventfully. As I'm leaving the building at the end of the day, though, I see Drake and his cousins walking along the sidewalk. I take a deep breath and speed walk to catch up with them. My curiosity makes me brave for a moment.

"Drake," I say when I'm directly behind him. He turns around, a little surprised. "Why do you think I need you looking out for me?"

He slows down a little so that he's walking next to me. His cousins are a couple steps ahead, but their attention is completely focused on us, their necks craning around to watch.

Drake examines me for a moment before answering. "I have a sixth sense," he whispers with a smile. His cousins snicker.

I stare at him. "Can you be serious for one minute, please?"

He smiles again, then lets his lips fall into straight line. "Completely serious," he says.

"So answer the question."

"What question?" One of his eyebrows lifts to his forehead.

I roll my eyes and let out a sigh. "Seriously?" I ask, annoyed.

"In all seriousness," he replies.

I punch him in the arm.

"That was very painful, Little Miss," he says. Drake's cousins laugh in front of us. I shoot them a look and turn back at Drake, whose lips are pulling up into a smile that he's trying his best to smother.

"You know, that bruise—" I gesture to the one on his jaw. "It suits you very well. Now people will be able to tell you're a jerk just by looking at you."

I turn in the opposite direction and walk away from them. I can't believe I just wasted my time trying to get the answer out of him. He probably has no idea what my secret is, and he never will.

"Rose?" I'm sitting in art class the next day, but the voice I hear calling me isn't from the classroom. It's a young, high-pitched female voice that has snuck into my head. It sounds familiar, but I'm not sure why. "Rose, if you can hear me, come to Dunchoria." There's a pause. "This is Evlynell. I'm in the castle."

Then the voice stops, replaced once again by the teacher's droning lecture. My heart pounds in my chest. Evlynell. My sister? She just... she was in my head, talking to me. The final bell rings, bringing an end to the day. I meet up with Colt and walk out of the school with him. I keep thinking about what Evlynell said. I need to go to Dunchoria. I need to find her.

Colt stops and turns to me. "Is everything alright?" he asks, concerned.

I hesitate. "I, um, I don't need a ride home today."

"Why? Is something wrong?" Colt tries, taking a step toward me and grabbing my hand supportively. "If it's Drake—"

"It's not," I cut him off, shaking his hand off of mine. "I need you to go," I reply, my voice shaking.

"Macy," he says, reaching for my hand again. I pull back so he can't reach it, even though all I want to do is stay here, in his presence. I want him to hold my hand and kiss me. I don't want to leave him, but I have to.

"Whatever it is, I can help," he adds.

"No, you can't," I refute. He stands, staring at me. I can feel my face starting to grow warm. I don't know what to say. "I'll be back," I finally reply, but even I'm not sure of that statement. Although Chastrin and his Uniforms hadn't found me yet, Malina had, and by going back to Dunchoria, I was asking to be discovered. Plus, my sister is there, in the castle. It's been years since I have seen her. My stomach turns at the possibility of not coming back. Tears begin forming in my eyes. Quickly, I whip around so I'm no longer facing him. So he can't see the tear sliding down my cheek.

My heart stops and begins pounding in my chest as I feel Colt's hand touch my shoulder. I spin around, press my lips to his and kiss him for what may or may not be the last time. I don't want to regret leaving him without a proper goodbye.

Chapter 21

IRETURN TO THE PORTAL THAT MALINA HAD used. Taking a breath, I step into the tree. My vision quickly changes from the wide trunked hemlock to the ramshackle outskirts of the kingdom.

I walk through the abandoned streets, knowing that no one else will be here. I head in the direction of the castle. The further I go, the more populated the streets become.

Being here reminds me of last time I was here and what happened to Keson. My eyes begin watering, but I blink away the tears. I can't think about him right now. It's been over a week since his death.

Finally, the castle comes into sight. As I grow closer, I can see the two Uniforms guarding the front gates. I walk straight toward them. They don't try and stop me, so I make my way inside, heading straight for the throne room. As much as I don't want to encounter Chastrin, he will know where Evlyn is, and that's my focus right now.

Chastrin's black pupils stare at me as I enter the room. "I'm here to see Evlynell," I announce, coming to a halt in front of him.

Without saying a word, Chastrin turns his gaze to two of the Uniforms standing along the wall and gives them a deliberate nod. I follow his gaze and watch as they both return his nod and walk out of the room.

A cluster of footsteps approaching causes my attention to remain on the door. Two new Uniforms enter the room with something—someone—wedged between them. As they grow closer to me, the face of the person between them becomes unmistakable.

His head is down, but bobs in consciousness. His hair hangs limply, covering those eyes I know so well. I can faintly see his lips, the same lips I kissed only a half hour ago. The sight of him causes my heart to flutter in my chest. But the feeling quickly vanishes and my heart begins to violently beat in my chest.

Colton.

I stare at him in disbelief. Colt's here, in my realm, sandwiched between two Uniforms.

I quickly turn around to face Chastrin, who is also staring at the newcomer. As Colt is dragged and dropped a few feet away from me, I try my best not to look at him.

Three long minutes later, the two other Uniforms reenter the room, a young girl walking between them. My sister. She's wearing a uniform, just like them… she's one of them. This is my fault. I left her here years ago, and just like my mother had said, Chastrin wouldn't kill her. Where else did I expect her to go?

A sweet smile plays on her lips as her light green eyes meet mine. "Hi," she says in a gentle voice, looking up at me through dark eyelashes. Blonde hair traces her soft features and falls over her shoulders. She looks so much like my dad. *Our* dad.

"Hi," I breathe, barely able to speak.

"My name's Evlynell." She extends her hand, the smile remaining on her face.

My heart leaps in my chest, colliding with its constricting walls. My pulse quickens as my thoughts race. A grin slowly slips across my lips as I survey her. She is my sister.

"My sister," I finally say. The words taste strange in my mouth. I like it. I want to hug her, embrace her and make up for the years of distance.

She nods, giggling. "Hi Rose." She steps forward and does the one thing I can't. Her arms wrap around me, the warmth of our bodies merging. I feel uncomfortable in the embrace, being watched by all of the Uniforms. It just feels wrong. They don't deserve to see the interaction between us. They took her from me. They are the ones that caused two sisters to be separated. This is their fault.

One of the older Uniforms places a hand on her shoulder, causing her to pull away from me.

Evlynell glances up at him before turning to me to say, "Bye Rose." She turns and leaves the room. I want to follow her. There's so much I want to say. But I let her walk out of view, knowing that none of those answers I can receive while standing in front of Chastrin.

"Oh," Chastrin says, his eyes focused on something at the entrance of the room. "And here comes one more surprise."

I turn to the door. This time a tall man with dark, nearly black hair and brown eyes stands uncomfortably in the entrance. His hands are clasped behind his back. As he takes an awkward step forward, my eyes trail his outfit—a nicely fitted navy blue and white uniform, covering nearly every inch of his body.

I gasp in shock. "Keson?" I whisper.

He doesn't respond, and in the otherwise silent room, the only noise is the numerous thoughts pounding in my brain as it rattles off questions that I don't know how to put into words.

After a moment, I add, "This isn't real. It can't be. You *can't* be working for them." His eyes spark with recognition before fading into pain and regret, but he quickly collects himself and his eyes darken again. "You died. You're dead."

He shakes his head in disagreement, taking a quick glance down at his feet.

He's not dead. He's standing right here, in front of me, breathing and alive. But how...?

"I watched you die." I can't grasp this. It doesn't make any sense.

Everyone remains silent, but I can feel the tension in the room thicken, becoming nearly suffocating.

"But he didn't die," Chastrin pipes in.

I spin to Chastrin. "I can see that. I just don't understand how. He had no pulse." My eyes settle back on Keson. "I felt you die. You weren't breathing. Your pulse stopped."

Keson nods. "I did die, but then somehow I started breathing again. Malina was hovering over top of me when I woke up."

Malina? I remember that I followed her into Dunchoria after I saw her in the halls of my school. But I lost her when I heard a scream coming from the woods—Keson's scream.

"Wha-How?" It doesn't make sense.

"You did that Rose," Chastrin replies, a sly smile on his lips.

"Did what?"

Keson, who has been hovering in the room, makes his way to the side of Chastrin's throne, taking his position beside him.

Chastrin doesn't answer my previous question, but instead leaves me to wonder about the answer to it. "Which is why I brought you here. Now let's deal with the boy," Chastrin interjects, switching the subject. His eyes are dark and menacing as he speaks. "What's your name and why are you here?"

Colt, who seems to have been intensely listening to our conversation, quickly snaps to attention. "Colton," he answers honestly, but glances at me, hesitating to answer the second part.

"Why are you here?" Chastrin repeats, more harshly this time.

Attempting to help Colt, I speak up. "He's a boy from my school," I admit. My heart speeds in my chest.

"Continue," Chastrin instructs.

I don't know what to say. "He must have seen me leave school when I came here. He was probably just curious and followed me, not knowing what he was getting himself into," I try to explain casually.

Chastrin nods comprehensively. "Is he human?" he asks.

"Yes," I answer, hoping that will help get him out of this world.

Chastrin nods, his gaze switching back to Colt and his eyes narrowing as they examine him. Colt stands still and stares back.

"He has no idea about this world," I continue, trying to convince him. "He's got nothing to do with Dunchoria—or me, for that matter. He's just a classmate at school." My heart sinks to my stomach at the mention of him having such little connection to me. It's a lie, but I know I have to say it. I can't let Chastrin use Colt as leverage against me.

"So he means nothing to you?" Chastrin asks, watching and trying to gauge my reaction.

"That's right," I reply, knowing it's a test. I can feel my heart squeezing painfully as I force the words out of my mouth.

Chastrin's eyes switch to the Uniforms holding Colt, giving them a single nod. I don't glance in their direction; I need to keep up this act.

Suddenly, a thud sounds and echoes through the room. There are no other gasps of shock except for mine as I turn to look at Colt's limp, unconscious body on the floor. My heart stops. One of the Uniforms is hovering above him, the man's hand clenched in a fist.

He punched Colt!

A faint purple bruise is already beginning to form on the left side of Colton's forehead. Chances are he'll end up with a black eye in the morning.

"Was that really necessary?" I ask Chastrin pointedly. I don't even try to conceal the pain and accusation in the words.

"You said he didn't mean anything to you," he replies halfheartedly.

"That doesn't mean you can knock him out!" I exclaim, my hands forming tight fists. My heart is pounding in my ears.

I know I need to calm down, but I can't.

Chastrin doesn't ponder it for too long. "We can't have a human knowing about our world, now can we? We'll alter his memories so that he'll forget about this whole experience," Chastrin reassures, but I know it's not meant to comfort me, it's meant to discourage me. My heart slows, sinking into what feels like a depressed state.

After they change Colt's memory he won't remember coming here, he won't remember what happened, he won't remember where I went or what happened to me. I frown at the thought. *At least he'll be safe*, I tell myself. At least he'll be far away from here and the Uniforms won't bother him.

"He'll be taken back to the human world," Chastrin adds. With that, Colt is lifted by one of the Uniforms, and thrown him over his shoulder like a sack of flour. It makes me uncomfortable to see Colt handled so harshly.

"Your task will be performed later tonight."

"Wait, task?"

"You didn't think I got Evlynell to bring you here for no reason, did you?" He pauses. "Everyone is dismissed," Chastrin announces.

I swing around, walking toward the large wooden door—my exit and only escape.

Just before I enter the hall, Chastrin speaks. "And Rose," he adds. I stop, slowly turning on my heels until I'm facing him. "If you try anything, I guarantee that your classmate won't be getting home any time soon. There won't be a happy ending... for either one of you."

I scowl at him, but Chastrin doesn't seem to notice. A Uniform steps between the two of us, his massive body towering over me.

"I'll take you to your room," he conveys.

My focus shifts to him. I shake my head, spinning around and walking into the hallway. I'm not in the mood for him to lay his hands on me. I'm led down the castle's maze-like hallways and shoved into a room. The door is pulled shut with a thump before I can turn back around. There's a clicking sound. I walk to the door and twist the knob. Locked. I examine my new room. I look up at the ceiling, viewing the bright blue sky above the clear glass. The ten-foot walls give me no chance of reaching the window, but I am able to stand in its sunlight and take in the heat. I walk to the bathroom and take out my colored contacts; there's no reason for me to wear them anymore and they're making my eyes itchy and dry.

For the first time in what seems like forever, I look a little like myself. This time *my* eyes are the ones that stare back at me, not the unfamiliar brown ones I've been peering into every time I see my reflection. I like the feeling of being able to recognize myself.

Not an hour later, I hear the doorknob turn and door's hinges squeak. My gaze darts to the door, where dark eyes settle on me. Familiarity fills my nerves, casting a feeling of relief, and then anger, throughout my body.

"Keson," I snarl.

Chapter 22

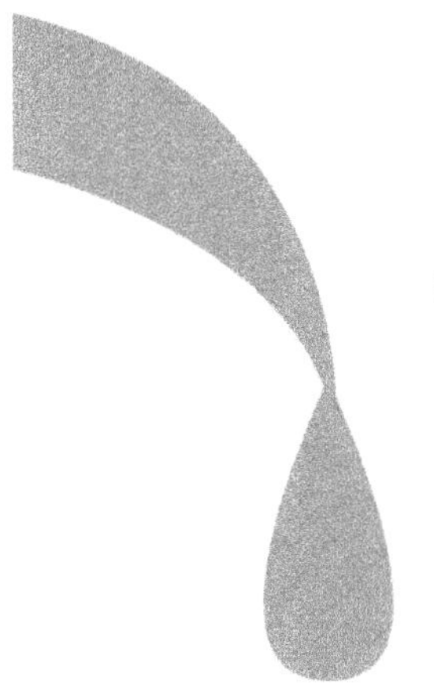

KESON TAKES A STEP TOWARD ME.

"Chastrin wants you," he acknowledges as he walks to my backside and reaches for my hands.

"What the *hell* are you doing?" I ask, whipping around to face him.

"My job." He reaches to seize my hand. I pull it away from him.

The scene from when I found him in the woods in Dunchoria last week replays in my head.

"Wait a second," I say, realizing something. "Back in the woods, before you *supposedly* died," I emphasize the word. "When I first saw you, right after you woke up, you knew right away it was me." I pause to let it sink in. "But I had a different identity. Brown hair, brown eyes—there's no way you could have recognized me that quickly. Unless—you were expecting me." I pause again, trying to understand all the implications of this.

"You were working for them then! Weren't you?!" I can feel myself getting worked up. I take a deep breath, trying to calm myself, even though I know it's not going to help much. "How long have you been one of them?" I ask, my voice steady.

"Rose," he sighs.

"Keson, don't!" I hiss. "Were you lying to me?"

He doesn't respond. All he does is stares back at me with a confused expression.

"Back in New York," I clarify. "Were you lying to me?"

His expression turns hurt, but he remains silent.

"That's what I thought," I reply. Everything begins to connect. "You knew I was headed to North Carolina because you helped me decipher the letter. And you came back to Dunchoria and told Chastrin everything. It was only a matter of time until you found out where the second safe house was. You were their spy. I trusted you."

He hesitates. "I did what I had to." With one swift movement both of my hands are locked together behind my back by large, strong hands.

"And in New York... how did you know where I was?" I ask, remembering my frantic escape from the suspected Uniform through the crowded New York streets.

I already know the answer.

He lets out a sigh. "Rose, Chastrin has had eyes on you for a while now. He knew you got that letter about the safe house. He knew you were leaving to find it. We've been watching you. Even when you think you're alone, you're not. There's always someone keeping tabs on you. You can't hide forever, especially not when you have something Chastrin wants."

"What does he want?" I ask, not sure I'm prepared to receive the answer.

"Oh, you'll find out soon enough, trust me."

I snort at the remark. *Trust* Keson... I thought I could, but I was wrong.

Keson pushes me toward the door. The hallway is empty as we exit the room. "You know I could get away from you right now if I wanted," I say.

"No, you couldn't."

"What's that supposed to mean? I could make you crumble to the ground right now." I brag about my power, even though I'm not proud of it.

"Rose, I've known you for a long time, and I know that you have too much of a heart to do that to anyone, especially if it's someone you know and care about."

"I've thought you were dead for this long. I could make it actually happen."

"But you could never bring yourself to actually do it. Not to me. Because, admit it, even though you hate me right now, you don't really want me to be dead."

I don't say anything. He's right.

We get to the throne room. The doors are propped open, framed by stoic guards on either side. Keson escorts me up to the throne, where Chastrin is sitting.

Keson releases my hands, but another big body takes his place behind me almost immediately. I don't even bother to look back at the new Uniform.

"You have a task for me?" I prompt Chastrin.

"Yes—" He continues staring at me, as if expecting something to happen.

My eyebrows lift questioningly. "The task?" I push, beginning to get annoyed.

"It's not so much a task as it is a favor." He pauses, thinking.

I don't want to do him any favors. I don't want to stay here. But Colt is here. And he shouldn't be. The only way to get him home, is to do what Chastrin wants.

I roll my eyes. "What do I have to do?"

"You'll be escorted to the hospital. Once there, your responsibility is to supervise the patients." He pauses.

"Supervise?" It seems like a strange word to use for a mandatory task.

He nods. "Yes, supervise. You have to watch them, care for them, comfort them and do whatever it is you do, or can do."

I stare at him, not completely sure why this is something I have to do. It just seems too easy.

"Um, okay."

Three Uniforms instantly surround me. They lead me out of the castle and down the gravel road to the hospital. It only takes a few minutes. Inside, there are rows of cots filling the huge room. I stop, taking a look around the room. Nearly every cot has a patient in it. I walk up to a young girl that lies still. She looks to be about eight years old. Her black hair is sprawled on the pillow beneath her head. Her skin appears pale and shiny.

I turn to the Uniforms, who are hovering close to the door. "What's wrong with her?" I ask.

They shrug.

A stark voice next to me replies. "She has an infection in her leg and a collapsed lung."

The boy who spoke appears to be a couple years older than the girl in front of me. His dark brown hair lies flat on his head, slicked back with natural oils from not showering. His green eyes stay focused on me as he repositions his body into a sitting position on the cot.

"Faisil," he introduces, shaking my hand.

"Roslanie," I respond. I watch as the girl's chest rises and falls in uneven breathes, her face contorting with every movement. "When did she get hurt?" I ask, looking back at Faisil.

"Uh—" Faisil hesitates. "I'm not sure. I can't tell days from nights here, or months from years." There's silence. "She's my sister," he adds.

"Where are your parents?"

"I don't know." He thinks for a moment. "We came here with our mom. There was an attack near our house, that's how Adelia got hurt. Mom said this was a safe place; somewhere we could heal and get better. She said that she had to leave, but she'd be back." Faisil goes silent and by the expression on his face I can tell she hasn't come back.

"How old are you? Twelve?" I ask, trying to change the subject.

He nods.

"That means you have a power, right?"

He shakes his head.

"You don't know?"

He shrugs again. "Is it possible to not have one?"

"Yes," I reply slowly. "I was a late bloomer in getting my power too. But you want to know something an old friend told me once?" I wince at calling Keson an 'old friend.'

He nods as I recite what Keson once said. "Just because you don't have a power doesn't mean you won't get one. And maybe, your power will be even better than you or anyone else expects."

He's silent for a second. "What's your power?"

I hesitate. "I can manipulate people's emotions and feelings."

"Can you make her feel better?" he asks, jerking his head toward his sister laying on the cot in front of us. "Please."

I give her a gentle shake, trying to wake her up.

Her eyes drift open tiredly. "Mommy?" she asks, her tiny hands rubbing her eyes. Her precious light brown eyes peer up at me. They're sweet and innocent at first, but I watch as they fill with fear and worry. "Faisil!" she yells, her voice shaking.

Faisil runs to my side. "Shh, Adelia. It's okay."

Adelia tries to push herself up, but ends up falling back to the cot. A moan escapes her lips and her breathing grows heavy.

"Calm down." Faisil reaches over and rubs his sister's shoulder. "This is Rose, she can help you feel better."

"Do you want me to?" I ask.

She nods and smiles at me. I focus on being happy and peaceful. Then, slowly, I ease that feeling onto her. It's unnoticeable at first, but then her smile grows and her body relaxes. I slowly cut off the feeling.

"How do you feel?" I ask her.

Smiling she says, "Good!" She looks over at Faisil, whose eyes flit between his sister and me, amazed.

"She hasn't smiled like this in a long time," he mumbles.

"Well, I'm glad… You said she had an infection in her leg?" I ask.

"Yeah. It's a deep cut that got infected."

I walk to the bottom of her cot, near her feet. I carefully roll up the fabric of her pants. There's a huge cut on the outside of her right calf. The skin around is swollen and pink, covered in dry blood and oozing puss. Her bone is visible deep in the gash. I can feel my stomach beginning to turn as I think about how a girl this age could get an injury like this.

I begin wrapping it in a piece of cloth, not sure if it'll help, but figuring it's better than nothing.

Chapter 23

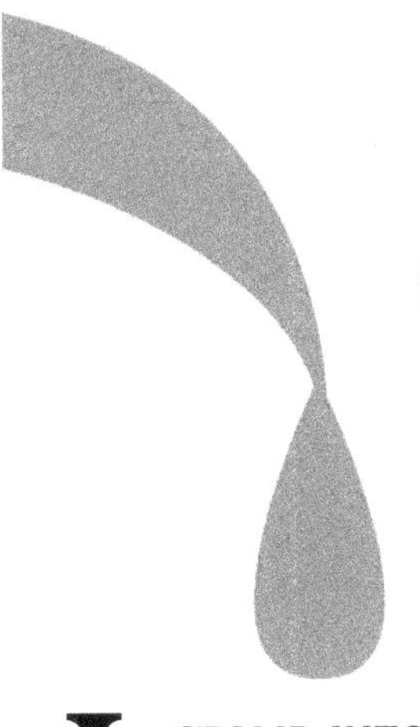

I STOMP INTO THE THRONE ROOM, WITH THE three Uniforms who had accompanied me on the walk to the hospital trailing a couple feet behind, unable to keep up with me.

"Chastrin!" I say, making every head in the room turn toward me as I make my way to his throne.

"Oh! You're back," he exclaims.

"What was that for? Why'd you send me there?"

"What do you mean?"

"You sent me there to 'supervise them, care for them, and comfort them.' And you know what I did instead?" My tone is harsh and aggressive, but I don't bother trying to cover it. I need to say this and he needs to hear it.

"What?"

"I found out that you don't do anything to help those injured people. I saw infected wounds, broken bones, organ failures, and a whole lot more. Things that could have easily been fixed if you had tried."

Chastrin doesn't reply.

"Well?" I ask. "Do you not care?"

"Of course I care."

"Then why aren't you doing anything?"

"There's nothing I can do."

"What are you talking about? You can train doctors, find cures or take them to the human world to be cured. Anything! These are your people, you're supposed to be leading them, pulling them out of hard times, and all you do is sit on your throne and let them die!" I know I shouldn't be talking to him like this. He is the king, after all, but he doesn't seem bothered by my tone or my words.

"Well," Chastrin responds. "If you think it would be so easy to take care of them, you can manage the hospital. Go right ahead."

"I shouldn't have to," I reply. "That's not my job."

"It is now."

Everything clicks. He needs me. He's tolerating my tone, words, and behavior because he needs me for this. But why?

"These," Chastrin says, lifting a stack of navy blue and white clothes from his lap. "Are yours. You can wear them while you work at the hospital."

"I'll wear my own clothes, thanks." It's quiet for a moment. "I can't heal everyone, not when we don't have any medicine or antibiotics."

A smile slips across his face. "I'm not sure about that."

"What does that mean?"

"You might be surprised how much of an effect you have on the people in that hospital."

I shake my head, not comprehending. "Did you take Colt back yet?"

"Not yet, but we will soon."

I nod as a Uniform leads me out of the throne room and back to the same bedroom I was in earlier today.

The next morning, I am led to the throne room by two Uniforms.

"Did you take Colt back yet?" I ask.

"Yes, earlier this morning."

I nod and, without saying anything, walk out of the room. A Uniform escorts me back to the hospital an hour later. When I arrive, I walk straight toward Adelia and Faisil.

"Rose!" Faisil exclaims, jumping up from his cot and running toward me.

"Hey!" I say as he comes closer.

"Check Adelia's leg."

I laugh. "Okay, okay. Let me look."

"Hi Adelia," I say when I reach her cot.

"Hi," she greets, pushing herself into a sitting position.

"Lie back down, okay?" I ask.

"Why? It doesn't hurt right now. Nothing does."

"Okay," I pause. "Well, can you still lay down?"

After some resistance, she lies back down on the cot. I push her pant leg up to her knee, unwrap the cloth, and observe the gash. The puss from yesterday has diminished, leaving only dried blood, which has since scabbed over.

I pause. "It looks better."

"Really?" Faisil asks, a grin spreading across his face.

"Yeah," I reply with a smile. "But don't get your hopes up too much; it still has a long way to go until its back to normal."

I glance around the room. "I have to go help other people now. Will you two be okay here?"

They nod in unison.

I walk around the hospital, observing the other injured people. There are dozens. I don't know what to do to help some of them. Their injuries seem too advanced for me to fix, but I sit down and talk to them, trying to distract them from the pain that engulfs their daily lives.

Walking up to a cot with a middle-aged man on it, I introduce myself. "Hello Sir, I'm Roslanie. I'm here to help you."

His gaze drifts to me and his throat emits a small chuckle. "That's a new one."

"What hurts?"

"Something on my left side and this burn on my arm." He lifts his arm to show the boiled, red-black charred skin.

"What does it feel like?"

"Cramping, aching, you know," he finishes.

I nod. "How did you end up here?"

He pauses, shaking his head.

I can feel my eyebrows pull together as I stare at him, confused. "You can tell me," I finally add after a couple seconds of silence have passed.

He snickers, a pained smile crossing his face. "I was in the military, working under Chastrin's command. He thought of us as bodies and weapons, but not people."

"Is that why most of these people are here?" I ask.

The man nods. "Chastrin sent us to our deaths by involving us in that war with the griffins a couple years back. My team and I went on a mission and got cornered inside a building, and that's when the griffins found us. I ruptured something trying to escape and got burned when a bomb went off, setting the place on fire."

I gasp, horrified. "Griffins?" *They're real?*

The man nods as he watches me. Then, he releases a laugh, but quickly cuts himself off and wraps his arms around his abdomen, his face contorting in pain. After a moment, he says, "You didn't know about them, did you?"

I shake my head. "I always thought they were just a myth." *And a horrible reoccurring nightmare.*

"Oh no, they're real all right. But they're evil monsters, massive and dangerous... Dunchoria tries to keep the citizens oblivious to the other realms because the king doesn't want people to fear them."

"There are other realms?" I question.

He nods, a smile slinking onto his face. "You wouldn't believe the realms that exist—that are hidden right in front of our eyes. It's astonishing."

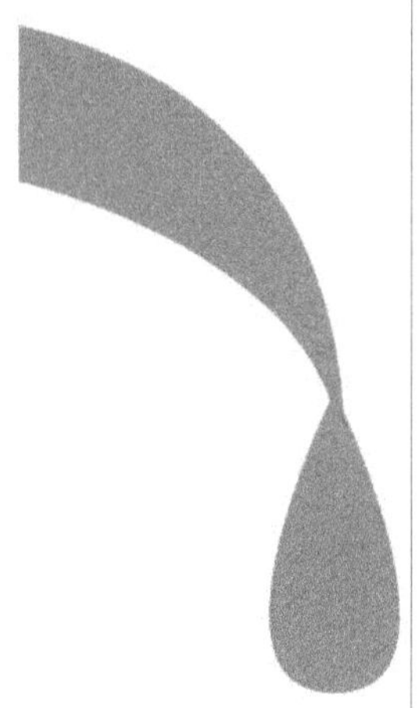

Chapter 24

THE NEXT MORNING KESON COMES TO GET me. He tells me that everyone has been ordered to report to the throne room. He escorts me there, both of us silent.

The commotion in the room, which is packed with Uniforms, diminishes as Chastrin enters the room and sits on his throne. He begins talking, but I drown out what he says, my eyes fixated across the room on where Keson now stands.

Suddenly, a thud echoes through the room, snapping my attention back to reality as the wooden doors of the throne room open. I'm pushed to the back of the crowd as a path is cleared between the doors and Chastrin's throne.

I hear mumbles come from some of the Uniforms around me. I push my way to the front of the group, curious to know what is happening. As I surface at the front, my heart lurches to a halt. Instinctively, my chest squeezes closed. My breath catches and I can't help but gasp for air. My heart pounds fast, drumming against my ribcage.

Two Uniforms hold Colt, their expression angry. Chastrin eyes Colt skeptically. His light gray eyes search the crowd and settle on me. "I thought you said he was human."

My gaze flits to Colt, confused to see him back here. "He is," I reply.

"Then why is he back here, where he doesn't belong?"

"Maybe *someone*..." I direct my words at Chastrin. "Didn't keep his promise on returning him to the human world." I know talking to Chastrin like this shouldn't be accepted, but he doesn't reprimand me or even flinch. I walk toward the Uniforms who are holding Colt. "Can you please release him?" I ask.

They both look to Chastrin for instructions. With a single nod of Chastrin's head, Colt is released.

I turn to Colt once the Uniforms have distanced themselves from us. I talk to him in a hushed voice, insuring that no one else will be able to hear me. "Colt?" I ask, knowing that depending on how much memory he lost he might not even know who I am or what this place is. "What are you doing here? Do you realize how much trouble you've just walked into?"

"I couldn't just leave you here," he whispers back. My heart leaps in my chest as I realize that he didn't forget about me or the fact that I was still here.

My eyes lift to gaze around the throne room. Dozens of eyes are watching Colt and me intently. They're observing us, deciding what to do about this human that shouldn't be able to remember this place. Thinking fast I say, "He's still a bit confused. He can't quite get his surroundings straight."

He shakes his head. "Actually, I'm fine, but thanks for trying to help." He takes a couple steps closer to Chastrin. I stare at him with wild eyes. *What does he think he's doing?*

"Well in that case, we only have one option," the king says. "This might hurt a little more than it did last time—"

"No!" I scream. A Uniform pulls me back into the crowd of bystanders.

The Uniforms grow closer to Colt. Instinctively, I rip my arm from the Uniform and sprint toward Colt. But I freeze mid-stride as Colt's eyes settle on me, flickering from brown to blue just before his body folds and drops to the ground. Clothes fly through the air.

Every person in the room stops, expressions displaying utter shock. I stumble backwards in surprise as my body goes numb. Fear engulfs every inch of me. There's dead silence.

The only sound is the breathing that emits from the massive animal standing in the same place Colt had been. The creature is almost my height. A sharp beak protrudes out of its face. *His face.* Pointed ears perch on top of its skull. Feathers cover its face, chest, and forearms. The torso and hind legs of the creature resemble that of a lion, covered in soft, thick fur. Majestic wings grow from its—*his*—shoulder blades. Animal paws support its front arms; bird talons extend from the tips of each finger. Its back legs ripple as the muscles tense. His tail swishes from side to side.

A griffin.

I thought they were only a myth. I thought my *deepest fear—my nightmares*—were only a myth. The man in the hospital had told me otherwise, but even then, I had been doubtful. Now, looking at the massive creature towering in the center of the room, I believe him.

I shiver uncontrollably, releasing shaky breaths. I can't help but feel queasy, scared, and helpless in its presence. I just watched Colt turn into a griffin? My head can't wrap around it. He's not a griffin... he can't be. I would have known. Right? Then again, I never told him about me being a Cylilian, and I didn't know griffins existed, so how would I have ever known?

The animal swings its head in my direction. Its blue eyes lock with mine. And even though they don't look like Colt's, I still feel like he's in there. It's comforting. Something in the way they stare at me. The expression appears sorry, as if he's trying to apologize for not telling me. After a long second of examination, I know that the creature, no matter how massive and how dangerous it looks, is perfectly harmless. Colt has complete control and he knows exactly what he's doing.

Flashbacks run through my head. I see Colt sitting on the couch, the music blaring in the background. I feel his lips on mine and his hands on my skin.

I remember my hand resting on his underneath the desk in class as I give it a little squeeze. Drake's menacing form hovering over top of us.

I smell him as my face is buried in his chest. We stand in the stairwell. His arms feel warm and secure as they wrap around me, holding me tight and safe.

My senses kick in. No matter how scared I am of the griffin, this is still Colt. And I need to get him out of here. He's always been there for me, now it's my turn.

Obviously, talking this out with Chastrin isn't going to work, leaving me with only one other option; make a run for it. With everyone else frozen in shock, I might have just enough time to make an escape.

I dart toward Colt in a mad rush.

The noise comes in one big wave. The Uniforms start screaming; attempting to distract the griffin and somehow gain control of it.

As I grow closer to Colt, he kneels down and tucks his wings against the sides of his body. I jump onto his back, throwing one of my legs to the other side. I grip the light brown feathers on the back of his neck.

"Go!" I scream as Uniforms charge toward us. Some of their faces grow hard, their eyes focusing on Colt. I watch as they try to force their powers onto him. He doesn't even flinch at their efforts. They don't seem to have any effect on him, which would explain why he didn't forget about me being trapped in this realm.

Colt lifts himself from the ground, races through the open wooden doors, and barrels through the hallways of the castle and to the front entrance. We make it past the castle wall and into the forest. He runs until we are in the outskirts of town. By now, we've lost the Uniforms. I'm sure they're still chasing us, but we have some breathing room.

Colt's blue griffin eyes look at me, then glance at the road behind us, then back to me. He slows his pace to a walk before I slide off his back. He trots over the side of one of the buildings.

He begins to demanifest, his griffin features glimmering in the air as they start to dissolve. As his wings disappear, Colt dives behind the crumbling house, out of sight. The sound of clothes ruffling fills the empty air. It's the only noise I can hear; everything else is silent; still.

Colt emerges from the side of the house in human form, wearing only a pair of shorts. My eyes travel down to his bare chest and well-defined six-pack. I watch as his muscles flex and shift as he walks toward me. "Always have a backup pair," he says, gesturing at the shorts and grinning. I jump at the suddenness of his voice, my eyes skipping up to his face. I can feel my cheeks beginning to burn.

I smile at him, embarrassed.

"We've got to move," he says. He grabs my hand, his fingers intertwining with mine. A tingle runs through my body. He pulls me toward an abandoned house that seems like it could cave in at any minute. Pushing open the door, it squeals in protest. As we enter, Colt heads straight for the back room. I follow without protest, my thoughts still swarming with the fact that Colt is a griffin. My attention is on his toned, bare back only inches in front of me.

There's a dark mark on his shoulder. Getting a closer look, I realize that it's different than it was at the party a few weeks ago. Now, the shape appears to be a maple leaf. *Do they all have these birthmarks? And do they all change?*

He stops near a wall, tearing me out of my trance. "What are we doing here?" I ask.

"You'll see." He begins moving the pieces of lumber resting against the wall and stacking them in the opposite corner of the room, slowly revealing a door.

Swinging open the door, Colt leads me through it. He's careful to close it behind us just before he guides me down the narrow, stone hallway. The stones grow bigger and the ground switches from wooden planks to dirt as we walk.

Up ahead, a light shimmers. It grows brighter as we get closer, illuminating an exit to the long passage. I'm temporarily blinded as we emerge from it. My eyes readjust and I can see that it looks nothing like Dunchoria. But I've never seen anything like this in the human world either. *Where are we?*

This place is filled with rubble. Houses have crumbled to the ground, leaving only the foundations of buildings. Trees are sparsely scattered around the landscape, but they offer little respite from the beating of the hot sun. The place appears both destroyed and deserted. Not one soul is anywhere in sight.

"What happened here?" I breathe.

Colt peeks at me out of the corner of his eye. "War," he answers, turning his focus back to the road in front of us.

I'm not able to say anything else as we walk down the street. All I can do is observe the neighborhoods that have long since collapsed in exhaustion.

One building is still standing. As we grow closer to it, I notice its white stone exterior. The roof is caved in and some of its walls look dented, but overall, it's in better condition than the rest of the houses in this area. Behind the building, a forest of trees rests. They look untouched, as if whatever affected this area hadn't reached them.

Colt leads me to the stone building. He takes a quick glance toward the trees before opening the doors to the building. We enter and the doors fall shut behind us. Colt, his fingers still intertwined with mine, leads me into a hallway and down a set of stairs. As we walk, I hear the sound of footsteps, ones that don't belong to us. A young man turns a corner and approaches us.

"Hey Colt," he says. Colt returns a nod before the man shifts his gaze to me. A friendly smile forms on his lips and something in his expression tells me that there's some other meaning behind his smile. "Hi Rose," he greets me. I nod, but stop short. *He knew my name. How'd he know my name? I've never seen him before.*

Colt takes me down another hallway and down another set of stairs. Everything's so unusual and different here. I look around at the peeling walls and small pebbles on the ground.

My attention is yanked back to the hallway at the sound of voices. Two men stand in front of us, talking with ease. As we grow closer, they turn their attention to us.

"Hi Rose," one greets with a smile.

"Nice to finally meet our guest of honor," the other adds in a friendly tone.

In a moment of quick, blurred movements, I'm thrust through a door and into a dark room. A deadbolt latches behind me. I'm alone.

Chapter 25

I JUMP OFF THE BED AS THE DOOR CREAKS open. I've been sitting here for hours, just waiting for someone to open the door. I'd tried everything possible to open it on my own, with no luck.

I lunge toward it, eager to get out and find Colt. I have no idea what happened to him, but I need to find out. As I reach the doorframe, a force knocks into my chest, catching me off-guard and sending me stumbling backwards. When I regain my balance, I survey the person in front of me. It's a woman with vibrant red hair. She blocks the doorway with her solid body. Her sapphire blue eyes stare at me from under thin, expressive eyebrows.

"Hi honey," she says sweetly. "Where are you headed?"

I stare at her curiously. "Where's Colt?" I ask.

She cocks her head to the side and watches me for a minute. "He's here," she finally replies.

"Where?" I ask, irritated.

"Do you want to get out of here?" she asks, avoiding my question.

"Yes."

"Well," she says, gesturing toward the door. "Come on." She moves out of the doorway, leaving it wide open. I look between the open doorway and her, trying to decide if it's a trick. Taking a step toward it, I keep an eye on her. She nods reassuringly, but it doesn't make me feel any more comfortable.

She reaches a hand out to me. I glance at it and walk by her, pushing her hand to the side. As nice as she may seem, she belongs to the same group of people who locked me in that room for hours.

"This way honey," she says.

I trail behind her silently, wondering whether this lady, and everyone else in this realm are griffins.

"I'm Kyra," she tells me as we walk.

I nod, but don't say anything.

"And you're Rose," she says.

That catches me off-guard. "How do all of you know my name?" I ask.

She throws me a glance over her shoulder. "You're very well known around here."

I pause. "What does that mean?" I ask, surprised.

"That means, don't be surprised by the number of people that know your name," she replies.

At that moment, we pass under an archway and enter a massive room.

"This," Kyra says, gesturing around the room. "Is our meeting hall."

I nod. *What is this place, really?*

Kyra walks to the far wall, slapping her hand on it. "See this?" she asks.

I turn my attention to where her hand is placed. There's a faint red color plastered into the crevices of the stone. "Yeah," I acknowledge.

"Blood," she says casually, but there a hint of anger in her voice.

I look at her confused. "How'd it get there?"

"It's a funny story actually," she starts, her facial expression rock hard. "Your people came to *our* world— Griffik— and killed *our* people. A war broke out on the streets." She points a finger to where I'm assuming is outside.

I turn to Kyra. I've waited long enough. "So, where's Colton?" I ask.

Kyra rolls her eyes. "He's around."

"Where?" I ask, irritated.

"It doesn't matter."

"What do you mean it doesn't matter?!" I nearly scream. "I need to talk to him. He's the one that brought me here. Can I at least see him?"

"Oh, you'll be seeing him in no time," she says with a smile.

I pace back and forth against the hard floor, my brain empty of thought. I've already tried getting out, yet I remain a sitting duck in yet another locked room. I'm always being locked up. And for what?

All I wanted was to see Colt, and I wasn't even granted that privilege. I'm a prisoner, not a guest. My head sinks into the plush pillow as I lay down on the bed. My eyes slide shut, exhausted by today's events.

I press my back up against the cold stone wall. A deep, familiar rumble echoes from down the hall, sending a shiver up my spine. I can't place my finger on exactly what made the sound, but I know that I have to get out of here.

Another rumble shakes the ground beneath me, obviously closer. I begin running, not sure which way will lead me outside and which will lead me to the creature I'm so afraid of encountering. My nerves tingle and, in spite of everything, I can't seem to collect myself. My mind won't focus, not enough to decide what to do next.

I come to a stop, leaning over to grasp my knees. My breathing slows slightly as I straighten, flattening my back against the wall again. Little, uneven rocks poke my skin through the fabric of my shirt. I can hear my heart drumming inside my head.

A different sound erupts from further down the hallway to my right. Its pitch is slightly deeper and smoother than the one I'd heard before.

The pace of my breathing automatically increases and I try to slow it down. I know they can hear it. They can sense it. If I can't get it under control, they'll find me, and after they do—I don't let myself consider that alternative.

I break into a sprint, darting down the hall as it curves to the left. Shooting a glance over my shoulder, I search for the creature that made the noise, not sure what I'm looking for, but knowing I'll recognize it the moment I see it.

I run into something solid. My body topples back helplessly. I manage to catch myself just before my head hits the floor, elbows slamming into the ground. It hardly hurts like I expect it to. Tracing the object in front of me, I'm finally faced with what I've been running from. The animal is tall; it would probably be my height if I were to stand up next to it. Its fur ruffles as it repositions its body. I grow numb, utterly terrified.

Blue eyes stare at me. The animal's head and neck look like that of an eagle. Light brown feathers with streaks of gold cover its head, while pointed ears protrude upwards. As my eyes follow its body downward, the feathers dissipate and are replaced by the same golden shade of fur. Its body resembles a lion's, but feathered wings fold alongside either rib cage. Eagle talons poke out of the animal's lion-like paws. Its tail looks like a lion's, the tip a mixture of feathers and fur.

My eyes falter on a white, furless patch on the animal's right shoulder, just as it releases a deep, trembling growl. I look up at it, terrified.

It lowers its head, eyes intent on me. My body stiffens, too scared to move. It sniffs me, its nose inches from my face, before raising its head again. It lets out a low noise, almost like a purr.

Then, a high-pitched, rough growl erupts from the end of the hall behind me. It's the same growl I heard earlier. The same growl I was running from. I whirl around, just as another griffin rounds the corner. Its golden fur shimmers red where the light strikes it. Its sapphire eyes stare at me. Its body lowers, ready to pounce. My body stiffens instinctively, preparing for the blow.

My eyes snap open. Panting, I throw the bed covers off of my body and jump out of the bed. My legs give out and my body slumps to the ground. My vision goes black, slowly returning to normal as my body adjusts. I sit on the floor, feeling the cold sweat running down my spine and my fingernails digging into my palms. My body gradually relaxes as the minutes go by. My fists unclench and the sweat stops dripping.

"Bad dream?" a male's voice questions from across the room. Jumping to my feet, I stare into the darkness. A figure sits against the wall, arms crossed against his chest, legs outstretched. He raises from the ground and walks toward me. In the dim light I can see his dark eyes and tall frame.

"Drake?" I ask, a mixture of anger and confusion mixing inside of me.

"Hey Princess," he greets.

"What are *you* doing here?" I nearly yell.

His body lunges toward me, hand quickly covering my mouth. "Shh!" he hushes.

I claw at his hand, attempting to get him off of me.

"Keep it down," he says before removing his hand. "I don't want everyone to know I'm here."

I pause. "Why are you here?"

He shrugs. "I guess I'm just attracted to damsels in distress."

"I am *not* a damsel in distress."

His eyes slowly trace my body, examining me. I can feel butterflies growing in my stomach. "You sure look like one to me."

I scoff. "Why are you here? You're human."

"You sure about that?"

I eyeball him, suddenly uncertain. "What are you?"

He laughs. "The same as you," he adds with a smirk.

"You're a—"

A hand falls over my mouth again as Drake's pulls me closer to him. My cheeks grow hot.

"You can thank me later, but we have to leave. Now." His eyes are alert as they bore into the door, as if someone might bolt through it.

I push his hand from my mouth. "Enough of that! I'm not going anywhere with you," I reply, planting my feet on the ground.

"Would you rather stay here?" he retorts.

"Drake. Between the bowling alley, the incident in the stairwell, and all the constant attempts to get on my nerves, I have no reason to trust you. Why on earth would I go anywhere with you?"

He's silent. "Look, I know you have no reason to believe or trust me," he starts. "But I don't want you to hate me. And I know that it probably means nothing to you right now, but you being here—it's dangerous. This isn't where you belong. You don't know what they want. Just please, come with me. I'll get you out of here. Get you to safety."

I don't reply. I can see in his eyes that he means what he's saying, but it's hard to give in. Finally, I nod.

He walks to the door, slowly cracking it open and peering into the hallway. He opens it the rest of the way. "Damsels first," he conveys, waving a hand at the door. Drake lingers behind me.

I roll my eyes as we walk into the hall. We walk through the halls in silence. I turn the corner before Drake, and a figure catches my attention. My body freezes in place.

"Colt?" I stutter.

His caramel eyes meet mine, but I can't read his expression. A blond-haired boy with striking blue eyes walks next to him.

"Where is your escort?" the blond voices starkly, his eyes scanning the hall as he aggressively approaches me.

The moment his hand lands on my shoulder, it is ripped off, causing the boy to stumble backwards in shock. "Get off of her Calum," Colt's voice emits in a deep, almost animal like, snarl as he stands in front of me, shielding Calum from my sight.

The hallway is nearly silent as the boys stare at each other. Colt's hands are clenched in tight fists at his sides. I want to reach out and grab them in mine, to ease the tension he's bottling inside, but I'm not sure if I should.

"You're weak Colt, Kyra will be interested to hear about this." I hear Calum say just before his footsteps begin echoing down the hall as he retreats.

Colt's demeanor doesn't shift, it only remains stiff and tense. He takes a step away from me, beginning to follow Calum. I reach for his arm, my fingers wrapping around his wrist. "Colt, please."

"Not now Roslanie," he says, but remains with his back to me. The way he says my real name sounds strange and unfamiliar.

"Not now?" I repeat, questioningly. "Colt, I've wanted to see you ever since I got pushed into that room. I was worried something happened to you. Are you okay?"

"I'm fine," he says, releasing a sigh before spinning to face me. "It's you that needs to be worried." His eyes switch back and forth between mine, searching for something, but I don't know what. "You need to leave. Now."

"But you're the one that brought me here."

"Rose, I didn't bring you here. I would never bring you to my world."

"Then who did? Your twin? Because he sure looked like you."

Colt draws his hands up to his face, grabbing the sides of his head as he thinks. "Look, there are things you don't know about griffins... dangerous things. I didn't bring you here, it may have looked like me, but I would *never* do that." His expression displays a mixture of worry, regret, and vengeance. It almost scares me to see him this way, but he is one of them. And it was him who brought me here.

An alarm screeches through the air, causing his head to lift to the ceiling, listening. Two deafening beats protrude.

"Intruder," Colton breathes. "You need to leave. They know." In seconds, he's running down the hall, leaving me to stand alone, staring after him. Moments later, Drake emerges from a nearby passageway, sprinting toward me.

"Time to go, Princess. Party's over." His hand finds my wrist and pulls me down the hall.

We keep running until we're outside. Drake's momentum slows, but mine doesn't. "Rose, you can stop now, we're out," he says. My feet stop, standing shakily on the dirt covered ground. I want to keep running, but I know I can't. I know he won't let me. "Rose," he whispers, approaching me cautiously, as if I'm some injured animal he might spook. I guess, in a way, I am.

Shaking my head, I try my best to keep the tears from rushing down my face.

"Rose," Drake repeats, peering into my eyes. "What happened? Are you okay?"

I laugh at the irony. "You weren't even there. You didn't even stay to help me. You *hid* and let me face him alone."

Drake's eyebrows pull together. "Rose." He lets out a laugh. "I'm the one that set off the alarm." There's a pause. "You're welcome, by the way. For saving you… again."

"Why? Why'd you do that?"

"We needed a distraction. I needed to draw them away from you. I couldn't have them catch you or me before we got out."

I nearly choke on the words. "Really? Why's that? A little throw down doesn't suit your fancy right now?

Drake versus Colton. Wonder who would win..." I begin walking, not giving him time to reply.

"If they know I'm here, they'll kill me." He pauses. "Then, the war begins."

I stop midstride, turning to look at him. "What did you just say?"

He shakes his head, his fingers wrapping around my forearm. "Just—Let's go."

Before I know it, we're in the trees, hidden underneath their dense canopies. "Where are you going?" I finally ask. "The portal's that way." I point in the opposite direction, toward the building that we just escaped from.

Drake turns to me, releasing my arm, but leaving a distinct warmth in the place his skin had touched mine. "Do you want them to catch us?"

"No—"

He smirks, his eyes narrowing as they watch at me. "Then follow me," he says. "Here's the thing Princess," he explains as we swerve through the tree trunks. "That building, that's your dungeon. And those griffins... they're your dragons—your captors and guard dogs. They're ready to throw flames and bash you with their tails the second you step out of line. Does that make sense?"

I nod. "Yes," I breathe, trying to understand what he's getting at.

His eyes survey me momentarily before continuing. "And me? I'm the handsome knight that comes to rescue the princess." He puffs his chest into the air triumphantly.

I narrow my eyes, challengingly. "Isn't there always a prize?" I want him to admit his motive behind all of this, only, he doesn't.

"Well, usually yes. But I'm a good person, so naturally, I'm just doing this out of the kindness of my heart."

I choke on a laugh. He smiles as well. "Yeah, okay," I reply as we come to a stop. "Is this the portal?" I ask.

"No. You seem to be bottling in a lot of anger, so I thought we would stop here and fight it out. That way we can have a clean slate. And so I can win." He shrugs. "Go ahead," he says, pointing to the side of his face. "You get first swing, my Lady."

I shoot him a look. "Seriously?"

He laughs. "I mean, if you want."

"Yeah, well I don't. Where are we?"

"That's fine. Forfeiting means I automatically win." There's a moment of silence before he continues.

"Anyways, this is the portal back to the human world." He gestures to a tree in front of us.

"The human world? Weren't you going to take me back to Dunchoria?" I ask, confused.

"I thought you could use some time to just figure things out. But hey! If you'd rather go back to Dunchoria, I'd be more than glad to take you there." He begins walking in the direction we came from, as if he would actually lead me to another portal if I said that was what I wanted.

"No! No. Stop. The human world is perfect."

"That's what I thought you would say." He smiles.

He grabs a hold of my hand, leading me toward the pine tree. He lifts up one of the branches and walks through, holding it until I pass under. We walk to the trunk of the tree. He takes a deep breath and begins stepping toward the tree. He stops midstride.

Looking back at me he says, "You might want to take a breath before going through."

"Take a breath? Why would I need to take—" Drake steps into the tree, dragging me with him. I suck in a breath.

Chapter 26

I FEEL MYSELF FALLING. MY TOES HIT THE freezing water first, and seconds later my whole body is submerged. Arms wrap around my waist, pulling me up to air. I gasp, shocked and cold. As Drake drags me out of the water, my arms instinctively fold across my chest, trying my best to keep the heat preserved for as long as possible.

After a moment of silence, Drake—whose clothes are also soaked—looks at me and says, "Hmm, I guess what they say about girls and wet shirts is true."

"Wh-What?" I stutter, watching his eyes gently glide over my body, lingering on the soaked shirt clinging to my skin. I feel my face growing warm, despite the freezing sensation running through the rest of my body.

His eyes return to mine. "You should wear your shirts like that more often."

I glance down at my drenched clothes. "What? Wet and uncomfortable?"

He doesn't respond, just takes one more quick look before turning so that his back is towards me.

"You know, a little warning would have been nice," I remark, teeth chattering.

"I did w-warn you."

"Psh! N-Not much of one," I reply.

"So, a b-better warning next time. Got it!"

"T-This isn't a game, Drake! Not everything's a g-game! I'm f-freezing and wet and confused and m-my life is being turned upside down."

He doesn't say anything for a while. "Okay," he finally mutters, defeated. "The c-cottage is around the corner. We'll get you dry clothes and there's a fireplace to warm up at."

He begins walking away. I look back at the water. The frigid temperatures make it hard to feel the heat radiating from the sun, which is shining brightly down, illuminating the shoreline.

"Rose?" I hear Drake's voice asking from behind me. I turn to face him. He's standing right beside me; I didn't even hear him come up. "Are you c-coming?"

"Y-Yeah." My lips can hardly move. I don't know how he's able to talk. "W-Where are we?" I ask.

"In Ohio," he responds.

"So t-that's one of the G-Great L-Lakes?"

"Yep! L-Lake Erie."

"S-Seriously?"

"No—" He cuts himself off before he can make another sarcastic remark. "Yeah, seriously."

"C-Can we g-go?" I ask, wanting to get someplace warm.

"Yeah, c-come on my little damsel," he says, wrapping an arm around my shoulder. The warmth emanating from his skin is prominent next to mine.

I ignore his belittling comment. "O-Oh my g-gosh! You're h-hot!" I exclaim, pulling myself closer to him.

"Why thank you Princess, I d-didn't realize you thought about me like that," he adds with a smirk. His shirt is still soaked, but he's warmer than I am and I'm too cold to salvage whatever remaining pride I have.

I toss him a threatening look, which only causes him to laugh. He leads me to a little log cottage just along the shore. The smell of burning wood greets me as we enter the doorway. I look over at the fireplace that's centered on one wall. The flames blaze, creating an orange and yellow shimmer that's tossed across the room.

A creaking comes from around the corner as a teenage boy appears. He looks familiar. He has brown hair and a tall, muscular build and from what I can see, his eyes are the same shade as Drake's.

"Who's this Drake?" the guy asks in a deep voice as we enter.

Drake turns to him just as another boy enters the room. He's shorter than the first, but just as muscular. Light brown hair covers his forehead. His brown eyes meet mine curiously.

A third guy with brown hair and pure hazel eyes stands at the top of the balcony and pauses. "Drake brought a girl home?" he asks in mock shock.

Drake looks at him, rolling his eyes. "Guys," he says. "This is Rose, formerly known as Macy."

"Macy?" the one with the hazel eyes asks.

"She went to Oak Landing for a little. You remember," Drake replies. He turns to me. "Rose," he says. "This is Zander." He points to the first guy who rounded the corner. The boy's dark eyes look at me. He gives me a sharp nod. "Quinn." The second boy who entered with light brown hair covering his forehead gives me a wave. "And Tanner." The boy with hazel eyes smiles.

Drake takes a breath. "They're my cousins."

It clicks. They were with him when I confronted him after the stairwell incident and I know I've seen them around school a few times.

I nod, shivering.

"Oh! You wanted some dry clothes!" he exclaims.

I look down at my still drenched body. "Yeah, that'd be nice."

"Follow me," he says, jogging up the stairs. I follow him into a bedroom. He pulls out a t-shirt and a pair of grey sweatpants from a large dresser.

"Here," he says, handing me the clothes. Simultaneously, his hand reaches for the bottom of his shirt. In a single, fluid motion, his shirt is off his body and in his hand, leaving his hair ruffled. My breath catches as my gaze traces his bare chest, which is still wet from our fall in the lake.

Drake makes a sound, as if clearing his throat. I tear my gaze from his stomach and meet his eyes. His eyebrows are raised in question, but the curve of his lips tells me he already knows what I was doing. Embarrassment swells inside of me. His dark eyes watch me, but they aren't as menacing as I remember them being back in school.

"What are you doing?" A high-pitched voice comes from behind me, breaking the silence.

I spin around. A short girl with similar features to Drake and his cousins stands in the doorway looking at us. She appears slightly younger than me.

"Rose, this is Maeve, my other cousin," Drake introduces.

"Hey," I say.

She gives a small smile and glances back at Drake straight-faced. "Why are you in my room?"

"I brought Rose through the portal and we, uh, kinda fell into the lake. She needs dry clothes."

Maeve rolls her eyes. "Okay. Just hurry."

"We're done," Drake announces, pushing me toward the door.

I look at Maeve as I pass her. "Thanks," I say.

"Hmm," she replies, shutting the door behind us.

"Sorry about that," Drake apologizes, rubbing the back of his neck. "She can get… moody sometimes."

I nod.

"Okay," he responds, stopping at one of the doors and turning to face me. His skin seems to be shining in the dim lighting. "This is my room. There's a bathroom attached to it. You're welcome to change in here and take a shower if you want. Just come downstairs when you're done."

I walk into the bedroom and close the door behind me. I take a deep breath, finally able to feel my lungs expanding. My thoughts return to normal. I flip on the light, illuminating the room. It's a cozy room with darkly stained furniture. I walk over to the bathroom and quickly shed my wet clothes.

Stepping into the shower, I start the water, adjusting the temperature. I stand, letting the bitter winter chill vanish from my body as the steam rises. I wash my hair, trying to get the lake smell off me.

Turning off the water, I pick up a towel and quickly change into the clothes Drake gave me. Drake is sitting on the couch in the living room—wearing a shirt—when I come down the stairs. His hair is wet, but he's in dry clothes. He looks up at me as I come to the bottom of the stairs.

I sit down on the couch, not saying anything.

"What?" he finally asks.

"Back in Griffik, you said something."

His dark eyes narrow, trying to think back.

"You said that it was dangerous and I didn't know what they wanted." I pause, letting the memory come back to him.

"Yeah," he says slowly.

I hesitate. "They never tried to hurt me. They didn't even show any signs of wanting to harm me. Do *you* know something I don't?" I ask.

He hesitates. "I-I don't know."

"What does that mean?"

"There's so much happening right now, Rose. I don't know what to think or who to believe."

"You mean like that jerk I decided to trust and follow?" I give him a pointed look.

"Who are you—oh... you mean me?" He pauses. "I'm glad you came with me."

I nod, continuing, "What is going on?" I ask, trying to get him to talk.

He hesitates, looking down at his hands.

"Drake?" I push.

"I can't tell you."

"But it's about me, right?" I ask.

He nods.

"Then why can't you tell me?"

"Rose." His eyes lift to meet mine. "Why would you believe me? Even *if* I told you? You don't like or trust me. You said it yourself. Why would you ever believe anything I say?"

I pause, thinking. "I don't know, honestly," I admit. "But you did just help me get out of Griffik." I take a breath. "Not everyone is who you think they are," I mutter, thinking back to Keson and Colt. Neither of them were the people I thought they were. Maybe Drake isn't either.

"So you're saying that I'm not really Drake?" he asks with a sly smile.

"I mean… I'm not Macy," I say, playing along, trying to lighten the mood.

"True. I mean you said it yourself that I'm your hot rescuer. That part is most definitely not a lie." He flashes a smile. I can't help but laugh at him. His ego is *huge*. After another moment, he starts to talk again. "There are a bunch of stories right now, about who wants you and why." He pauses. "All I know is from what my uncle has told us, or from what I've overheard."

"Your uncle?" I ask, confused.

"Yeah, he's one of Chastrin's advisors."

My eyebrows lift onto my forehead. "Seriously?"

Drake nods.

"Is that why you brought me here?" My voice begins rising, growing angry.

"What do you mean?" he asks, confused.

"Is that why you brought me here?" I stand up from the couch. "So I can sit around and wait for the Uniforms to come strolling through that door to collect me?" I point a finger toward the door.

Drake's dark eyebrows pull together. "Rose, what are you talking about? You know why I brought you here. To get away from them. They're your slippery dragons and I'm your—"

"Hot damsel in distress rescuer. Yeah, you've mentioned that," I say, suddenly very aggitated. I stay standing, hands on my hips, as he peers up at me from the couch.

"Can you please sit back down and let me explain?" he pleads, ignoring my clear attempt to attack his 'rescuer' story.

It's silent for a couple minutes while I contemplate. Finally, I sit.

"Look," he continues. "You're safe here, okay? You don't have to worry. They won't find you."

"What if they do?"

"They won't."

I stare at him. How could he possibly know that?

"Rose?" he questions quietly.

My eyebrows rise in question.

"Can you just trust me on this one?"

I search for any signs or reasons to doubt what he's saying. His irises look lighter in the flickering light of the fireplace flames. There are no signs of deceitfulness or lying in his tranquil eyes as they search mine.

I sink back down, to the couch, taking a seat on the couch. "I don't know," I reply.

He stands up from the couch. "I'll give you time to think on it," he says. He begins walking away when the door creaks open.

I watch as Drake's eyes skip to the door, then to the clock on the wall. "No!" he hisses.

Chapter 27

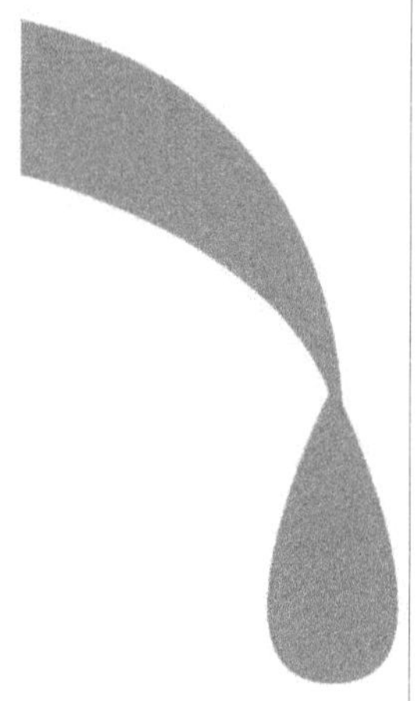

I TURN TO THE DOOR, WHICH OPENS THE REST of the way, letting the bitter air burst into the room. A middle-aged woman enters, followed by two men. She looks up for a split second, catching Drake's gaze. A small smile slips onto her lips.

"Hi Drake, we're back from—" She stops short when she notices me sitting on the couch. Placing her bags down, she says, "Oh hello. I wasn't expecting any guests." She casts Drake a curious glance, then looks back at me. "Who are you?"

I open my mouth, ready to answer, but stop short, not being able to find my voice.

"Mom," Drake begins. "This is—"

"Roslanie Callerie," a hoarse voice finishes.

I look at the person who said it. The man stands in front of the closed door, staring at me. He's older, with greying hair and plain hazel eyes.

Drake looks hesitantly between me and the man. Drake and I make eye contact, and I can tell there's something about the way he looks at me that isn't right. He takes a hesitant step toward the man.

"How long has she been here, Drake?" the man asks.

Drake hesitates, taking another step to the side, blocking my view of the door. I peer out around him, so that I'm able to see. "Uncle Mehxn—" Drake trails off.

"How long?" Mehxn asks Drake again, more demanding this time.

"Dad?" I hear a voice say from the stairs behind me. I turn to Tanner, standing wide eyed at the bottom of the stairs.

"Hi Tanner," Mehxn says with a sweet smile.

I watch as Tanner's expression grows confused, his hazel eyes narrowing as thoughts pass through his head. "Why are you here?" he asks, looking at Mehxn with a puzzled expression.

"I thought I'd come for a visit."

"But here? How'd you even know where we were?" Tanner asks.

"Well," Mehxn starts. "It is winter break, and I know you guys have been coming up here every year since Lyndell and Nox bought the place."

It's winter break already?

Quinn comes into the room then. He stops and glares at Mehxn, who remains by the door. "Quinn!" Mehxn exclaims, as if he doesn't notice the glare. "My boy! How are you?"

"Don't dad," Quinn replies, turning away and trotting up the stairs.

Mehxn, unfazed by the interaction with his son, turns back to Drake. "Drake? An answer."

"She hasn't been here long," Drake replies simply. His face is solemn, and his eyes hold the faintest sign of retaliation.

"And what exactly does that mean?" Mehxn asks, trying to get a clearer answer.

Drake stands silently in front of me.

Mehxn turns to Tanner. "Tanner? Would you like to answer what Drake obviously can't?"

"A couple hours," Tanner answers slowly, his eyes flickering to Drake cautiously. Drake doesn't glance at Tanner; he simply keeps his eyes focused on Mehxn.

"Hmm," Mehxn nods, looking at Drake. "And how long were you going to wait until you told us she was here?" he asks accusingly.

Until Drake told *them*? Them who? His parents? The Uniforms? Would he really turn around and tell the Uniforms that I was here after he promised it was safe?

That no one would know? I wouldn't be surprised. But for a split second I actually believed him when he said that. I believed every word that came out of his mouth. I should have known better.

I was blinded by the promise of safety.

"Uncle," Drake says. "I didn't bring her here so that you could come get her and take her back to Dunchoria."

At the mention of Dunchoria, my body goes cold. The last time I was there, I left with a griffin. What would Chastrin do to me if I came back? After I helped someone they were trying to eliminate?

"Now Drake," his mother pipes in, warningly.

"No mom," Drake responds. "It's true."

"Oh?" Mehxn asks, shocked. "Then why did you bring her here?"

Drake hesitates, not sure how to answer the question. "She needed somewhere safe."

His parents' expressions shift, confused. Mehxn, on the other hand, looks stoic and straight-faced.

"And why would she need somewhere safe?" Mehxn questions.

"You more than anyone should know the answer to that," Drake retorts.

Mehxn's eyebrows lift questioningly.

"The griffins?" Drake hints.

"Right!" Mehxn exclaims. "But wait—" He pauses, his eyes shifting to me. "If I'm not mistaken—wasn't that boy who came to Dunchoria a griffin?"

I nod, unable to find my voice.

"And, correct me if I'm wrong, dear—" I flinch at the sound of him calling me that. "—But wasn't that boy also your boyfriend?"

Eyes locked on him, I stare, bewildered. How could he know that? I never told them that. "Not quite... but kind of," I reply, my voice weak. I flinch at the memory of the last time I saw Colt in Griffik. The way he tore Calum's hand off me, his denial in taking me there and his insistence on me leaving. I take a deep breath, trying to calm myself. "How did you know that?"

"Know what, dear?" I flinch at the word again.

"How did you know he was more than just a boy at my school?"

Mehxn grins. "We have our sources," he replies, his gaze flashing to Drake, who stands rigid.

I look at Drake. "You? You told them?" I ask, my heart sinking.

Drake's body tenses. He turns slowly to me. "I—Rose—They—You have to understand..." he stumbles over his words. He can't seem to look into my eyes for more than a couple seconds.

"Drake. You. Told. Them." I pause between each word, letting them sink in. "How am I supposed to understand that?"

"I didn't tell them you were here, though. I didn't tell them that," he replies.

"And that's supposed to make it better?" I ask, my anger slowly intensifying. "How much longer?"

His eyebrows pull together. "How much longer until what?" he asks.

"Until you would have told them I was here," I clarify.

"I-I wasn't going to tell them you were here. I told you that," he responds.

I shake my head.

Mehxn interjects, "Oh, so you *weren't* going to tell us."

Drake glares at his uncle. "This has nothing to do with you," he says through his teeth.

"Drake!" His mom glares at him, but Drake doesn't even turn his head.

"Oh, but Drake," Mehxn counters. "It has everything to do with me. The Uniforms have been looking for her ever since she disappeared with that griffin."

My body goes numb. I knew it.

"You knew where she went, though, did you not?" Drake asks angrily.

"We did."

"And yet you didn't go to get her. You *know* what could have happened."

"It's not like we can just barge onto their land and take her back," Mehxn explains.

Drake's eyes narrow. "That's what I did."

"And you're lucky they didn't catch you." There's a pause. "We just finished one war with them. We don't need to get into another one," Mehxn states.

It clicks. Kyra's story about the war between the griffins and our people wasn't a lie. It had really happened. That explained the ruins of Griffik and Dunchoria and all the people in our hospital. *We'd been at war.*

Mehxn continues. "For getting her back, Drake, you'll be rewarded. I'll make sure of it. Now, if she just comes with me," Mehxn says, taking a step closer to us.

Drake stands up so stiff and straight, it looks painful. "She's not going, uncle."

"Oh? And why not?" Mehxn asks. "Because you have some kind of say in this?" He pauses. A smile slips over his lips. "You didn't have a problem with it before. When we asked you to help us find her."

"What?" I ask.

Drake turns to me, his expression unreadable. He doesn't say anything. When Mehxn begins speaking, Drake's eyes stay molded on me.

"He helped us all right," Mehxn confirms. "We needed to find you back in New York, and he helped us track you down. Keson and him." And just like that, my suspicions are all confirmed. Keson was playing me back in New York, and Drake is completely untrustworthy as well. "Drake actually almost caught you in New York City," Mehxn adds.

"What?" I ask, my mind going in a thousand directions at once.

"He chased you down the city streets."

The memory floats back to me. It's hard to remember every detail; it's blurry. But, as I think about it, the memory becomes clearer. I was standing in the doorway of a store when I got an odd suspicion of the boy wearing a grey hoodie and looking in the window nearby. It was too dark to see much, but I do remember him being young, about my age, his features similar to Drake's.

My eyes skip to Drake, who is still staring at me. I can see in his eyes that it's true, but I need to ask anyways. "Is it true? Was that you? Were you one of them?" I ask, my eyes pleading him to tell me no, to say that it's all just one big lie, even when I know it's not.

He nods.

My chest squeezes, tightening, suffocating me. Air whizzes through my teeth. "And all this time," I say, shaking my head. "I should have known it was just a game. Everything's always just a game to you. From the first time I met you in school. People don't change. And you're no exception."

"No. Rose. Can you just let me—"

"Explain yourself?" I interject.

He nods.

I stand up from the couch, making sure not to get close to him. "Just so that you can trick me again? Make me doubt myself?" I pause for a split second. I glare at him, eyes narrowing. "I won't let you fool me anymore. I know who you are and you will *never* change. You've made that pretty clear. I won't be a part of your little game."

"Rose—" Drake pleads.

"No. Don't even try Drake."

Everyone is silent as I rush toward the door. Mehxn shifts, stepping in front of me and blocking my exit.

"I would not do that," I growl, cocking my head at him. I'm not sure what his power is, but I highly doubt that he's a Force Field or Mind Inflictor; the only abilities that wouldn't be affected by my powers.

Drake's mother reaches for Mehxn's arm, pulling him out of the way. "Let her go, brother."

I move past them, not bothering to say anything else as I storm out of the house and into the winter air.

Chapter 28

THE BITTER WIND CASCADES AGAINST MY skin as I walk through the frigid Ohio winter. I don't look back at the little cabin sitting alone in the desolate landscape. I walk. It feels like I walk for hours. My feet are the first to go numb, then my nose and ears, fingers, and eventually my entire body. It feels as if I can't move, like I'm stiff as a rock. But somehow, I manage to go on. I consider turning around and going back to the cabin, but immediately decide against it. That's not an option.

My legs give way and I feel my body falling toward the snow-covered ground. I land on all fours, but no matter how many times I try to stand back up, I can't gather enough strength. My body is frozen; I can't feel anything. My vision grows blurry and I black out, falling the rest of the way into the powdery snow.

When I wake up, I'm lying on a bed. Looking around, I see an overall bland room, occupied by only a single couch and a door along the far wall. At first, I think I'm back at the cabin, but realize this looks nothing like the cabin. Sitting up, I feel a strain in my neck, as if I've been asleep in an odd position for hours. I observe the room, recognizing nothing. *Where am I?* I stand up and walk in circles around the room. My limbs still feel weird, as if they're still numb. My head is whirling, and even though I'm not dizzy, I feel really out of it. Looking out the window, I notice that there is no snow on the ground, meaning that I'm not anywhere near the cabin, which makes me feel relieved and worried at the same time.

The door opens as Drake enters the room. I release an annoyed sigh. "I was hoping I left you in Ohio."

"No Princess, you can't get rid of me that easily." A smile forms on his mouth.

I nearly gag at the obvious comfort he feels. "I'm assuming I'm in Dunchoria?"

He freezes, the comfort slowly morphing into unease.

"I'll take that as a yes." I stare at him momentarily, but he doesn't react. His egotistical demeanor has long since faded.

"Rose, I'm sorry. I didn't mean to—" Drake starts.

"Drake I really don't have time for your insincere apologies right now. Just please leave." I turn my back on him, walking back to the bed to sit down.

"Fine," he finally agrees. "But I brought you some water." There's the sound of glass clinking against wood just before the door closes.

I stop midstride and turn to look at the glass. I pick it up and drink it, hoping to clear my head enough to be able to get my thoughts straight. I walk back to the bed and lie down, my eyes sliding shut.

I wake to the sound of a door creaking. I sit up and focus my attention on the noise. A figure steps through the opening, her facial features so familiar that I'd know them anywhere. After all, they are my own.

The girl hovers in the doorway for a second before entering and closing the door behind her. My heart squeezes in my chest, anxious and confused about what is happening.

"Hello," the girl greets in a voice that I recognize as my own.

I must be dreaming. This can't be real. "Who are you?" I pause. "Why do you look like me?" I ramble.

A smirk crosses her face—my face. "Would you like to see?"

I nod hesitantly, positive that it's a bad idea, but fully aware that I have to know why she looks like me. Turning on her heels, the girl saunters out of the room and into the hallway. I follow, surveying my surroundings. The walls are all stone covered and lit with fire torches.

We're in Dunchoria. In the castle.

A Uniform rounds the corner, making his surveillance rounds. The girl presses her back against the wall, squeezing into the shadows of a doorway. I hide behind a nearby pole, hoping that he doesn't spot me. If I'm in the castle, it's because I'm meant to be, but I can guarantee they don't want me outside of my room, roaming the halls.

Once outside of the castle, I turn to the girl. "Why do you look like me?" I repeat.

She smiles. "Do I?" In seconds, her body is shifting, her facial features writher from mine to someone else's.

I blink, trying to understand what just happened. "Well, now you don't." I pause. "How did you do that?"

Her smile grows. "That's only the beginning." Her long legs carry her further down the cobblestone street.

"Wait, where are you going?"

She peeks over her shoulder, but doesn't reply. My feet move quickly as I catch up with her. We walk in silence for what seems like a while. The town slowly fades, morphing into deserted streets that contain an occasional house. This is the lumber and farm land. I don't come out here much, there's never any reason to.

The further we walk, the more anxious I grow. *Why is she bringing me the whole way out here?* Glancing back at me, the girl ducks under a warped tree and vanishes. I stumble, startled. She was there a second ago, but after she went under the tree she disappeared. That can only mean one thing. *It's a portal.*

I pass under the curved trunk, knowing that I have to keep following this girl. I have to know who she is... *what* she is.

The scene transforms into something alien. I see the girl a couple feet away, staring at me. "What took so long?" she asks, but before I can answer, she spins and weaves through the trees.

I copy her movements, but my eyes are on everything except her as I survey my surroundings. It looks like any other forest; trees and foliage. Except, there's a lone house resting to my right. It appears to be lived in with good upkeep. I've never seen it before, I know that. *Where am I?*

I remember the man at the hospital talking about all the realms that Dunchoria keeps secret. The thought worries me. I shouldn't have followed this girl… but I need to know why she can shift her appearance.

A break in the trees reveals a vast plain splayed against the pale blue sky ahead of us. A crumbling stone building sits in the center of the emptiness. At that moment, a creature appears from behind the building, slinking across the deserted soil. I freeze, my heart stopping.

Its black fur ruffles as it breaks into a trot. A lion-like tail trails behind its strong frame. Wings unravel from its sides just as it sails into the sky, flapping momentarily to gain altitude.

A griffin.

Griffik.

My eyes settle on the girl trekking toward the building. I jog until I am beside her. "We're in Griffik," I breathe. Her eyes flit in my direction, but she doesn't respond. "I'm assuming that means you're a griffin."

A small smile forms on her lips in response.

I gulp, knowing I'm in trouble. No one knows I'm here. I shouldn't be here. Colton's words form in my mind. He didn't want me in his world. He was scared for me. But why?

As much as I know I should turn and run away from this place, I'm curious. I need answers. For starters, why do the griffins want me?

We enter the building. A chill runs down my spine. Something is different. After rounding a couple corners, the sound of voices become prevalent. The girl leads me through a doorway and into a room where nearly a dozen people stand.

Kyra speaks before I get the opportunity to say anything. "Oh good! Roslanie, how wonderful it is to see you again. I'm glad you decided to come back." The corners of her lips lift upwards as she attempts to hide a smirk. "Where have you been?"

I know that it is not meant to be an actual question, but I can't help to choke a laugh. "Wouldn't you like to know?"

"Clearly, we managed to find you. It didn't take too long to figure it out," she adds.

I shrug. "Why did you bother looking for me after I left?"

"First off, you weren't meant to leave." There's a hint of spite in her tone. "And secondly, we never got to hold our welcome ceremony."

I stop short. "Welcome ceremony?"

"Yes, we were going to hold one to welcome you to Griffik," Kyra asserts.

"How hospitable of you," I spit.

"We will be holding it tonight, so don't worry, you won't miss out on it. It will be centered around our esteemed guest of honor. You." Something in the way she says it sounds deceiving. There's more context to the sentence than the words imply. "Calum will take you to your room."

My eyes scan the room until they settle on Calum, who is taking long, determined strides toward me. My stomach turns uncomfortably as I remember his aggressive nature toward me last time I was here. The way Colt had to step between us.

Colton. Where is he? Shouldn't he be here?

"Let's go. This way," Calum's hoarse voice commands, placing a hand on my shoulder. Instead of the painful clench I was expecting, I am greeted by his gentle touch on my skin as he gingerly pushes me toward the exit.

In the hall, his hand drops from me. We walk in silence for a couple minutes. "Are you okay?" Calum's words fill the empty hall.

"Why do you care?" I hiss.

He laughs. "Rose, calm down. It's me."

I look at him, watching as Calum's exterior melts into a more familiar one. The blue eyes darken into a caramel brown. The pigment of his hair shifts into a deep brown as his body stretches, growing taller.

I gasp. "Colton?"

He smiles and I feel every nerve in my body relax. "Hey Rose."

"What the—how did you just do that?"

His eyebrows furrow. "What? The shifting?"

I nod, both amazed and horrified.

"I told you there were things about griffins that you didn't know."

What he said last time I was in Griffik drifts back into my mind. The girl that brought me here looked like me before she shifted into her normal form. "Everyone here can shapeshift," I connect. "The person that brought me here a couple days ago…"

"Wasn't me." Colt acknowledges, watching me carefully as he speaks. "It was someone who shifted to look like me. But it wasn't me, I swear to you."

I nod, trying to let the concept sink in. I've seen it happen twice now, but it still doesn't feel real. How could it be? It's not humanly possible. Then again… these aren't humans, or Cylilians. They're griffins.

We push through the doors and into the hot bare earth. As we near the forest, a stark voice comes from behind us. "Colton!"

My stomach flips and a chill runs through my body.

"What do you think you're doing?" Calum growls.

I can see Colt's body stiffen beside me. "Rose, I need you to do something for me."

"What?" I ask, concerned by the request.

"No matter what, keep walking. You know where the portal is, right?"

"Yes. A couple."

"Okay good. Find one and leave, okay?"

"Okay," I agree. "But you're going with me."

Our eyes meet. "Not if Calum gets his way." He pauses. "I will keep you safe." His hand reaches for mine and I can feel the warmth being shared between us.

Colt's body whips around as a force yanks him backwards. I stop, turning to face Colt and now Calum, who has caught up to us.

"She is not supposed to leave the facility." Calum points at me. "You know that."

"I do," Colt confirms, his chest broadening as he straightens into a confident stance, a clear demonstration of power. Calum matches Colt's position.

"If you know, why did you let her out?"

"She doesn't belong there."

"And clearly, neither do you," Calum snickers. "Give her back to me." He extends a hand toward me, causing me to take a step backwards, avoiding his touch.

Colt seizes his wrist, then tosses it to the side. "Don't touch her." A growl emits from deep in Colt's throat, sounding very much like an animal. Like a griffin.

Colt's head turns in my direction, but his eyes remain on Calum. "Walk." I don't move at the command. "Now!" he screams, the ending of the word sounding as if it has protruded directly from a griffin's sharp killer beak, rather than a human mouth.

My feet carry me in the opposite direction of the boys and toward the trees. At the tree line, though, I stop to watch the face-off. I'm not leaving Colton that easily.

They circle each other, mouths moving as if they're speaking to each other, but I can't hear the words being said. Calum lowers to the ground and in a split second his body has transformed from a modest human to a menacing griffin. He leaps at Colt, who remains in human form, knocking him to the ground. Calum's golden griffin pins Colt to the ground with a single claw and as much as Colt tries, he can't seem to push Calum away from him.

I emerge from the trees and, as bad of an idea as I know it is, I run straight for Calum's griffin.

"Hey!" I holler, gaining speed.

The griffin's light blue eyes focus on me, narrowing and emanating a noise similar to a laugh. In one fluid motion, it lifts into the air, releasing Colt, but soaring toward me.

"Shoot!" I mumble, spinning on my heels and retreating as fast as I can toward the trees. I'm almost there. Almost under the cover of the trees. The sensation of air beneath my feet instead of solid ground and the slowly shrinking height of the trees causes my heart to stall in my chest.

I glance down, seeing the ground as it grows further away. Pressure forms against my chest. The fabric of my shirts tightens around my neck. I pull at it, trying to keep it from choking me.

Hot air glides down my back and I hear what sounds like a grunt come from above me. I'm too scared to look up. I already know what's above me. What's pulling at my shirt. What's holding me in its mouth; in its beak.

I can't escape. I can't get free. I can't fight it off.

The griffin—Calum—flies above the trees, high enough that if it were to drop, I would die. I would die. What if—

No.

I'm not dying.

Not today.

And not like this.

I begin struggling, kicking my legs and reaching up to where the animal's beak is, pushing firmly against it. I hear it snarl, but I don't stop. It begins lowering, getting closer to the ground. My hands fumble with its beak, my fingers feeling the fabric of my shirt clamped inside. Gripping the fabric in my hand, I yank.

Calum growls, clearly upset; making me even more determined to get free. He begins lowering himself above a large, open clearing in the middle of the woods. I pull on my shirt one more time. It rips loose. Air rushes around me as I fall to the ground.

My feet feel the impact first, then my ankles, knees, and arms. My head collides with the ground. My vision goes black momentarily, my world going dark. It comes back, slow and fuzzy. Before it has completely recovered, I'm back on my hands and knees. I push off the ground, standing upright for a fraction of a second before crashing back down to the earth beneath me.

My legs scream in protest and my head begins to throb. I shake my head, attempting to clear it. Taking a panicked breath, I try to push myself back off the ground, but I can't.

A snarl comes from behind me. I twist around to glance at the animal. His body is in a crouch, standing low to the ground. His golden fur is standing straight up on his back. The dark beak opening and shutting as he approaches, creating clicking noises. His eyes stare at me, narrow and focused—as if the griffin is stalking its prey.

My heart stops. And it doesn't restart. It just stalls. My chest tightens. My throat closes. I can't breathe. My legs grow numb. A chill runs through my entire body. The hairs on my back stand upright. I can't move. I can't function. My body has frozen, but my mind hasn't.

A story my mom used to tell me as a kid replays in my head.

Once upon a time, a young boy named Caius lived in Cylilia. He didn't have a power, but he was very curious. For years, people had told stories of a world where griffins lived—animals that looked like a mix of a lion and eagle. Huge, strong, and dangerous. Their feet had sharp talons that could tear through anything in a matter of seconds. Their faces had pointed beaks that could puncture any object with the slightest touch. Their ears let them hear even the lightest of footsteps; their wings could lift them into the skies; and their legs could push their body to incredible speeds.

For years, people avoided these animals. Until one day...

Caius was a quiet, shy, modest boy, but he loved to explore. And that instinct to wander made him walk right through a portal—one leading to an unknown and unfamiliar world.

Caius walked this world as if it were his own, not knowing any better, he began exploring. As he roamed the woods, he heard a sound. He looked around, but saw nothing. Just as he was about to begin walking again, he caught sight of something moving in front of him. He stalked towards it, careful not to spook it. As he grew closer, he began to notice some of its features: a large, fur-covered body; strong legs, a flicking tail.

Curious and entranced, Caius reached out to touch the mysterious animal. His hand lay on its side for a split moment, and in that moment, Caius felt the beauty and warmth of the living creature.

But just then, the animal sensed him, and swung around, releasing a startled grunt. Caius froze as the animal made eyes contact with him. Its eyes were large; shocked by the interaction. The animal's body lowered to *the ground aggressively. Its nostrils flared, angrily puffing out air. The animal's big eyes narrowed, its pupils growing small as it sunk into predator mode. Opening its pointed beak, it released a loud snarl.*

Caius stood, frozen, in front of the animal.

The story always ended abruptly, and when I asked my mom, she said that was all there was to it. There was no more to be said. That world had been a myth to me. I had always believed it to just be a bedtime story, one meant to scare kids into not wandering through realms. To teach us as children that even the seemingly most innocent of things can snap in a split second, transforming into something you would have never expected. You never know what is hiding underneath a façade.

It always stuck with me though, the terror of Caius facing the animal. It resulted in my caution when exploring, but also my fear of griffins. They are beautiful, and strong, and magnificent, but they are also ill-tempered, and aggressive, and in some cases—or most cases—deadly. They can cause so much damage with such little effort.

I stare up at the griffin now standing above me. Its eyes watch me. Its ears flat against its skull, making them parallel to the ground, creating a menacing look. A deep growl rumbles in its throat. Its talons dig into the ground at my sides, clawing up the loose soil.

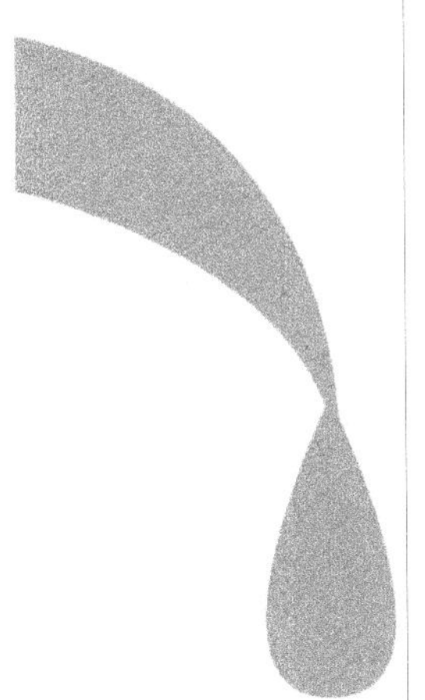

Chapter 29

MY HEAD STILL FEELS WOOZY, AND EVEN if I had the physical strength to sit up, I don't think I could bring myself to move. Every inch of my body has frozen.

I hear a thud. The griffin that was hovering over me is no longer there. It takes me a moment to realize what happened. Propping myself up on my elbows, I see a blur of brown and gold movements coming from the other side of the grassy field.

My head whirls as I try to distinguish the shapes. My eyes slowly focus, settling on the two animals. I watch as they tumble in the grass, wings flapping, beaks pecking and talons ripping. From what I can see, it looks as though the golden one is winning. Calum is winning. I watch as his talons tear a gash in the brown griffin's back leg. A shrill scream escapes the brown griffin's beak. I wince, but can't manage to close my eyes, too terrified to intentionally blind myself from what's going on, even for just a second.

A short growl leaves the golden griffin's mouth just before it lifts into the sky and disappears. The brown griffin stands motionless, except for its panting. The sun shimmers against its fur, making it appear as though it is shining. Its head swings toward me, staring at me for a moment. It begins walking toward me, crouching low to the ground, passively. Its brown eyes watch me. I look it over as it gets closer to me. It is not menacing or aggressive in its approach, and its eyes are so familiar that I'd know them anywhere. Colton.

The numbness in my legs begins to dull. The pounding of my heart slowly subsides. There's a vague limp in the way he walks. His ears are drooped, and his sides expand and contract as he pants. When he's a couple feet away, he stops, his head rising, his ears perking up. He looks toward the sky. I listen, but don't hear anything abnormal.

I try to predict what he is thinking. My eyes linger on a furless patch on the animal's shoulder. The more I stare at it, the more I can distinguish a shape. A talon with a drop of liquid clinging to the tip, ready to fall.

The griffin glances at me once more, then quickly turns and starts running in the opposite direction. My heart speeds in my chest. *Why is he running? Is he running from me? Or something else?*

Just as he disappears into the trees, my legs start moving. I twist my body, pushing off the ground. I sway for a moment, my legs still sore and wobbly.

I start rushing—as fast as I can manage—in the direction he disappeared. Halfway there, a figure emerges from the trees. *Colton.* My heart skips hopefully. The only article of clothing he wears is a pair of shorts. The bare skin on his chest and arms shows toned muscles and tanned skin. His eyes are focused on the ground as he walks. His brown hair lays ruffled on the top of his head. He runs a hand through it as he walks. His eyes lift, meeting mine.

"Colt, are you okay?" I ask.

A small, uncomfortable smile forms on his lips. "It could be worse." He continues walking toward me slowly and with a limp. A trail of red runs down his leg, starting at his thigh and flowing down his calf.

"Oh my gosh!" I exclaim. "You're bleeding!" I gesture to his leg.

He glances down at it, then looks back up at me. "Sure looks that way," he replies, his voice tired. "We need to get you out of here." Colt grabs my hand, dragging me behind him and into the trees. I stare at his back mindlessly, eyeing the dark shape on his shoulder. A claw with a drop dangling off it. It's the same one I noticed at the party weeks ago.

"Do all griffins have a mark on the back of their shoulder?" I suddenly ask.

"What?"

"Do all griffins have these marks on their shoulders?" I ask, pointing to the one on his shoulder.

He nods.

"Are they all the same?" I ask.

"No." There's a moment of silence. "We all have different ones."

The multiple marks I've seen on Colt's shoulder reform in my mind.

"Do they ever change shapes?" I ask.

He stares at me curiously. "Nope, never."

"Then why..." My voice trails off as my mind goes crazy trying to connect the dots.

Everything clicks.

If a griffin's marks are always the same that means that is their identifying factor. That is the hole in their camouflage. I remember the mark on Colt's shoulder at the party. It was a claw. The same claw that rests on his shoulder in this moment. He is the same Colt I first met in school.

This Colt transformed into a griffin with brown fur and brown eyes, looking very similar to his human appearance. Implicitly, griffins take on the same basic physical appearance as their human forms.

The Colt that came to Dunchoria and first brought me to Griffik had a maple leaf birth mark and shifted into a griffin with golden fur and blue eyes. Although he looked like Colton in human form, his griffin characteristics and birthmark are nothing like Colt.

The griffin in the field moments ago—Calum's griffin—looked the exact same as the one from Dunchoria. Golden. Light blue eyes.

"It was Calum," I whisper, more to myself than to Colt.

He looks down at me and although he doesn't say anything, his eyes tell me I'm right.

"Now you know why I need to get you out of here, Rose."

"Why *we* need to get out of here," I correct.

He shakes his head in disagreement. "Rose, I have to keep you safe. Me coming with you will not do that."

"But Colt, if you stay here, what are they going to do to you?" I pause. "You helped me get away... twice."

He smiles. "And I would do it a thousand times over in a heartbeat. Don't worry," he says. "I'll catch whatever they throw my way. As long as I know that you're safe, I will be fine." He reaches down, grabbing my hand in his. His thumb rubs circles gingerly on mine.

We come to a stop in front of a tree with a large trunk. My attention shifts from our hands to the tree. "Is this the portal?" I ask.

"Yes, it'll take you back to Dunchoria." He pauses. "You can't go back to Coos Bay."

"Why not?"

"You can't be alone in the human world. The Griffins will know you're there, they'll be on high alert for you. If you go back, don't go by yourself. Stay with your own people for now. That's your safest bet."

I scoff. "That's not who I would have—" The look in his eyes makes me stop short, I don't move. I don't want to leave him. "Please come with me."

"Rose," he sighs. I can tell by the way he says my name he wants to. He's so close to breaking. He just needs a little push.

"Colt I can't just leave you." I pause. "This entire situation has been so confusing. I didn't know what was going on. I didn't understand why you were avoiding me, or why you treated me like you didn't want me—"

"I do want you Rose," he interjects. "I avoided you to keep you safe."

"Then come. Please. It's my turn to keep you safe."

His beautiful brown eyes skip between mine. Slowly, he lifts a hand to my face and brushes a stray hair off my cheek and behind my ear. His fingers trace my jaw until they come to a stop at the bottom of my chin.

I know what comes next, and I have never wanted it more than I do in this moment. Lifting my body onto my tip toes, I lean into him. I let his presence fill me with the sense of relief and security. A soft pull on my chin brings my lips only centimeters from his. For a second, we stand, staring into each other's eyes. Then, we're connected, hopelessly tangled together as our lips silently speak the words that we want to say. His hands find my shoulders first, progressively lowering until they are wrapped around my waist, tugging me even closer to him.

I focus only on him. On this feeling. On the butterflies tapping gently in my stomach. On my heartbeat fluttering and leaping in my chest. On the sensation of his lips against mine.

The sound of someone clearing their throat interrupts us and we pull away from each other.

"Well, would you look at that, Beauty and the Beast... literally," the familiar voice says.

My eyes skip around us until I locate Drake, who is leaning against a nearby tree. Blood trails from the corner of his forehead to the edge of his jaw before dripping onto the collar of his shirt. There's a large, animal-like tear in the sleeve of his shirt, as if... a griffin had done it.

"I hate to interrupt but—"

A deep growl cuts him off. The ground shakes at the nearness of the noise. Colt straightens, growing tense at the sound.

"Drake what in the—" I start.

"You guys need to leave. Now. They're here," Colt interrupts before I can finish. His eyes wildly search the forest.

"What about you?" I ask, horrified. If they attacked Drake, what are they going to do to Colton?

For a moment, Colt's eyes freeze on me. "I promised to keep you safe." He looks to Drake. "Take her. That's the portal. I'll handle it from this side."

I can hear Drake moving through the trees toward me, but I don't take my eyes off Colt. I can't.

"Rose," Drake's voice comes from behind me. "Let's go."

His hand touches my arm, attempting to get my attention, but instead it just infuriates me. Of course he wants me to leave with him. He hates Colt and doesn't care what happens to him. But I do. "Drake! Leave me alone." I rip my arm away from him.

Colt turns to me at the sound of my outburst. "Rose," he says, taking a step closer. "I need you to go with him, okay? I'll be fine. I'll see you soon."

I stand, unmoving, but after a couple seconds I nod and turn to Drake. Passing him, I walk toward the portal.

A snarl erupts, breaking the previous silence. Turning, I watch as three griffins emerge from the brush. Only one is familiar—Calum. Colt manifests, just as Calum and one of the other griffins leap onto him, knocking Colt's large griffin frame to the ground.

Drake's hands are on my shoulders within a second, pushing me through the portal. The setting changes, shifting from Griffik to Dunchoria, but the image of Colt being attacked by the three other griffins remains in my mind. A nauseous feeling bubbles in my stomach, slowly growing until the feeling of helplessness and weakness consumes me.

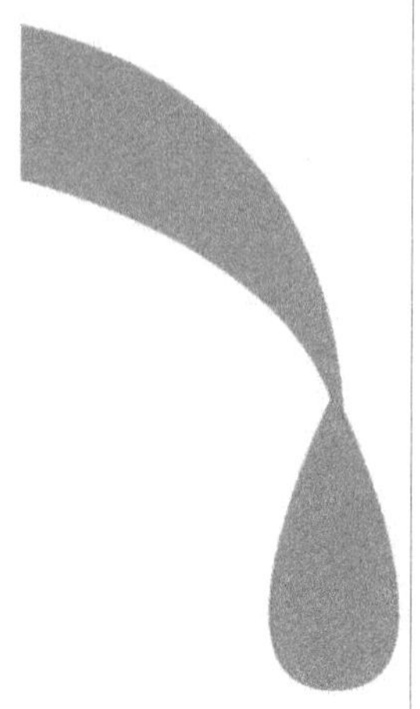

Chapter 30

T HE STREETS ARE EMPTY AS WE WALK, OR more accurately, as Drake forces me to walk. My mind is foggy, but physically I am okay, unlike Drake who is heavily bleeding.

Rounding the corner of a nearby building, we are encountered by a large group of people blocking the road.

"Oh my!" one of the ladies exclaims, her dark blue eyes on Drake. "Oh dear, what happened?" she asks, taking a step forward.

I scowl at her, unwilling to answer. Drake remains silent, but not because he doesn't want to answer, more because he doesn't know how.

"Why are you letting him bleed?" the woman questions me, her expression judgmental.

I stare at her, uncertain what she means.

"Heal him." She tilts her head slightly, causing her mid-length brown hair to fall over her shoulder.

"Excuse me?" I ask, suddenly confused.

"You're letting him bleed out."

"'*Letting* him' is an interesting way of putting it," I mumble, peering over at Drake, who is also intensely listening.

"Well, you can heal him, can't you?" The woman watches me, waiting for me to reply, as if she already knows what I'm going to say.

"I don't know what you're talking about." I pause, looking her over. "Um, who are you?"

"Oh! I am so sorry. My name is Reign."

"Do I know you Reign?" My eyebrows furrow together as I run through faces in my mind, seeing if any match hers.

She laughs. "No dear, I guess you don't know me. But I know you."

"How?" Now I'm curious.

"Have you ever heard of Celestia?"

I hesitate. "No... should I have?"

She laughs again. "No, I guess not." Turning to her associates, she adds, "This realm seems to be oblivious to almost everything."

I don't like the comfort she feels in being here. Her relaxed nature makes me anxious.

Reign shifts her focus back to me. "So... you can't heal him?"

I tilt my head, not at all understanding what she's trying to get at. "Maybe with some bandages..."

"Oh honey! You don't need bandages." She stops speaking, but stands at attention, as if she wants to say something, but doesn't.

"I'm sorry, but what are you—"

"You don't know, do you?"

"Know what?" I string out the words as if the answer may come to me as I'm talking.

"About the prophecy."

"Excuse me?" I'm seriously lost.

"It has to be true," she murmurs, her posture beginning to dwindle in uncertainty. "I saw the people in the hospital."

My attention sparks. "The hospital?" I pause. "What about it?"

Reign's body straightens, confident once again for knowing something that I don't. "We just visited the hospital. I've been coming for years to try to help those people."

I stare at her. "What do you mean you've been coming here for years? You're not from here."

"Oh my dear! You're right, I'm not. But your King Chastrin asked me to be the head doctor. It's my natural talent in Celestia and so Chastrin and I made an agreement."

My eyebrows lift, questioning her.

"If I healed his wounded soldiers, Chastrin would ally with my realm."

I have to hold back a laugh. "Chastrin's not one to keep promises."

She nods slowly, her eyes narrowing as she looks at me. "I heard of this prophecy that exists here. Recently, I've been hearing rumors of a special Dunchorian girl. The one that fits into this prophecy. I wanted to see it for myself. I went to the hospital and, unsurprisingly, found that many of them were healed. Miraculously, even. With the injuries they had, there was no way they could have healed properly... not without supernatural help."

"How does this involve me?"

She smirks. "Well, I'm assuming you're the one that did that."

"That healed them?" I question. "Are you insane? That's impossible! That's not my power."

"I'm not so sure." She spins and ushers her associates back through the streets and out of sight.

I don't know what else to do or what to say. It doesn't make sense, and yet she believes I can somehow heal.

I turn to Drake, who stands watching me, swaying as he attempts to keep his balance. "We need to get to the hospital."

"The two kids?" Drake asks.

I stop. "Yeah," I reply. "How did you know that?"

He looks down, then back up at me. "Mehxn is my uncle... it's not hard to get information."

Drake follows me, a couple steps behind as I trek through the streets in the direction of the hospital.

When I get to the hospital, it looks exactly the same as it did the last time I was here. Beds clutter the room. Now that I know about the war with the griffins, I understand why this space exists. It was meant for casualties of the war.

Griffik. Colt's realm. *Colton.* Where is he now? Did he get away? Is he safe? My mind races with questions, exploring all the possibilities, hoping that he is okay. My stomach twists at the alternative, making me want to throw up.

I shake my head, attempting to clear it—focus for a moment on the task at hand—as I scan the empty beds. Where did everyone go? Are they really healed? Faint talking travels from somewhere nearby and I search for the source. My eyes settle on a cot a couple yards away. A young girl, about my age, sits on the edge, looking at the arm of an elderly patient. The girl's orange hair is pulled back into a tight braid that trails down her back. I stop dead in my tracks.

Malina.

I haven't seen her since I followed her through the portal to Dunchoria.

I turn to Drake, who stands beside me. "Sit down. I'll go get the supplies."

He nods and sinks to the cot. I walk to the edge of the room and rummage through the cabinets for the cleaning supplies and bandages. I kneel next to Drake's cot, my hands working quickly as I pour alcohol over his wounds, wiping away the thick dark red blood and wrapping the opened wounds. The gash on his forehead is too deep for a simple cover, so I begin threading a needle and stitching. Although I numbed the skin prior, I can feel him wincing underneath my touch. I finish relatively quickly, but leave Drake to rest while I take a lap around the hospital, checking in on a couple patients.

The sound of my name being hollered from across the room stops me. A boy with oily dark hair runs towards me. His green eyes are lit with excitement. Behind him runs a small, petite girl. A smile stretches across her lips and her precious brown eyes are locked on me.

"Rose!" Adelia exclaims joyfully as she comes to a stop in front of me.

"Hey," I reply, smiling. I crouch down so that I am her height. "You shouldn't be out of bed. Or running."

"Why not?" she asks with a pout.

"Because you aren't feeling good."

"Yes I am! Look!" She pulls up her pant leg. The gash that had been on the outside of her right calf is completely healed, only a scar remains as evidence that it had ever happened.

It looks amazing! "Oh my gosh," I say under my breath. "What about your lungs?"

"They're fixed too."

"That's amazing," I breathe, unable to believe it.

Faisil smiles next to us. "You helped heal her."

"Me?" I look at him. "All I did was put a cloth over the cut and helped distract her. I didn't heal her," I say, thinking back to what Reign said only minutes ago in the street.

He shrugs. "You did something. And it worked."

I force a smile, conflicted. "I'm glad."

"Rose?" a familiar voice says from behind me.

I twist to see Malina. I look back at Adelia and Faisil. "Hey guys, can I talk to Malina for a minute?"

They nod in unison and walk back in the direction they came from. I stand up, facing Malina.

"Hey," she says, her voice small.

"Hey," I reply, my thoughts distant. "Was there a woman with brown hair and blue eyes in here a little while ago?"

Malina stares at me, not answering. "Yes," she finally responds.

"What was she doing?"

"Just walking around, looking at the patients. Nothing out of the ordinary." She pauses. "Why? What's wrong?"

"Nothing."

"Rose." She smiles, shaking her head. "I know you. I can tell by that look on your face that something is wrong."

I sigh. "There's just a lot on my mind right now. Sorry." I think for a moment. "What are you doing here?" I ask.

"I'm tending to the patients."

"Why?"

She hesitates. "Because this is what you did."

Not expecting that answer, I stutter, "Wait… what?"

"I heard what you said to Chastrin and I know that you were big on trying to make the hospital better and help the patients. I wanted to help too, so I volunteered."

"You did?" I gawk at her, shocked.

"Yeah." Her face grows red, embarrassed. "I know I won't be as good as you, but I figure I'll try."

My arms fly around her. I can't help it. The fact that she wanted to help—wanted to follow the footprints I had already formed—is just one more indication that I have not lost her, that she is still my friend, and that she still wants to help.

My arms wrap around her as I hug my childhood best friend.

"Why are you hugging me?" she asks through giggles.

"Because you went through the effort of finishing something that I couldn't." I hesitate. "I do have a question, though."

"Yeah?" She pulls away to look at me.

"How did you find me in the human world?"

She smirks, nearly laughing. "Rose, you act as if you don't know me."

"Your tracker abilities," I confirm, remembering the way that she would always win when we used to play hide and go seek. She always knew where I was because she could track me. And because she is my best friend, she can sense and find me much quicker than any other tracker would be able to.

She nods, solidifying my assumption.

"But why?"

She shrugs her shoulders. "I hadn't seen you in a while. I meant to talk to you, but the humans were overwhelming. When we got back to Dunchoria, the whole thing with Keson happened and you then disappeared."

"Keson said you were standing above him when he woke up."

"Yeah, I was." She pauses. "I came when I heard you scream. I realized you weren't following me and I was really worried. I watched everything."

I gawk at her, not believing what she's saying.

"I watched you wake up and try to help Keson. I watched him die in your arms."

"Only," I continue. "He didn't die."

"I know." Malina averts her eyes as if she's suddenly uncomfortable.

"I don't understand," I mutter. "How is that possible? I felt his heart stop. I watched his lungs stop breathing."

Malina shakes her head. "I don't know. After you left I went to go check on him myself. I was there for maybe ten minutes and suddenly he started coughing and breathing. It was the strangest thing I've ever seen."

I shake my head. "Odd." Reign's words slide into my head, replaying. Maybe I can... No! That's insane. I can't do that. "I have to go."

"Okay. Well, hey, stop by and visit me sometime. We have a few years of catching up to do!" She offers a smile before spinning and walking away to tend to more patients.

I return to Drake's cot, helping him up, and leading him back to the castle.

Chapter 31

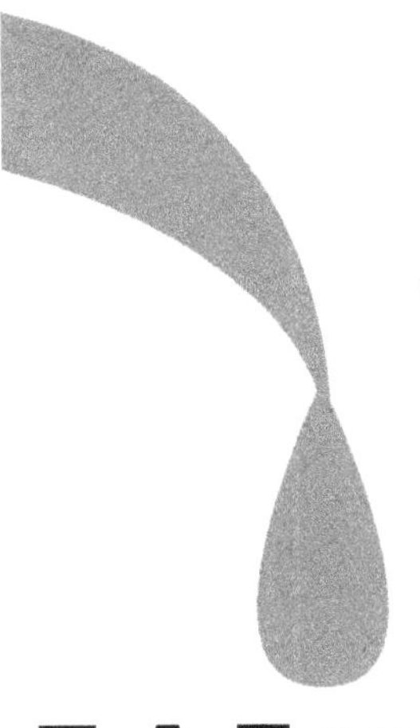

WE ARE A COUPLE BLOCKS AWAY FROM the castle when Drake finally breaks the silence. "About what Reign said…"

"What about it?" My heart skips, anticipating what he's going to say next.

"Did you understand what she was getting at?"

"No, did you?"

He shrugs. "You're a freaking miracle worker, duh."

"Drake," I nearly hiss in frustration.

He chuckles. "Rose, loosen up."

"Why? Because I have that luxury? I don't even know what is going on. Colt is out there somewhere probably fighting for his life, while I'm just here doing nothing. Meanwhile, everyone else seems to think I really am this miracle and I don't understand why. I'm no different than any other Dunchorian."

"No?" Drake's eyebrows raise onto his newly stitched forehead.

"Do you know something that I don't?"

"Maybe, maybe not."

"Drake! Seriously. If you know something, you have to tell me."

"Oh Princess, it doesn't work that way. How about this? I'll tell you, but you're going to have to give me something in return." A smirk crosses his face.

I glare at him. "What do you want?"

"Not sure yet, but when I figure it out, I'll let you know."

"You think everything's a game, don't you?"

"If life weren't a game, everyone would be winners and that's just not reality Princess."

"So, Reign," I state, attempting to get him back on track.

"I don't know a whole lot, just the things I've overheard my uncle and the Uniforms talking about." He pauses. "There's a prophecy in Dunchoria. Supposedly every century or so there is one person born with two powers that complement each other."

"What does that even mean? Cylilians only get one power."

"*Most* Cylilians," Drake corrects.

"Except this one every hundred years?" I question, not understanding how that's possible.

He takes a breath. "Okay, remember how in the human History class we learned about the Curse of Tippecanoe? It's the theory that every 20 years, the President of the United States dies in office. It's a reoccurring event. An odd, but undeniable occurrence since it began in 1840."

I nod. "Yeah, I think I remember learning about that."

"Well, it's the same idea." He pauses. "This prophecy occurs every hundred years. It's strange, but not unheard of. A reoccurring tradition here in Dunchoria."

We pass through the front doors of the castle, our conversation quickly dying.

The day passes and as much as I want to go back to Griffik and make sure that Colt is okay, Drake won't let me. He's always with me, never letting me out of his sight. As much of a nuisance as he is, he's kind of funny and I don't mind his presence. He's a good distraction in an otherwise anxious and stressful situation. When Drake isn't exceptionally entertaining, I do my best to stay distracted, knowing that if I'm not, I'll start thinking and I don't want that.

Drake offers to go on a walk with me, which I quickly accept, not wanting to sit in the castle any longer.

We're a block from the castle, which explains the large number of people walking along the streets. My eyes dart around the street aimlessly, not knowing what I'm searching for, but knowing that when I see it, I'll know.

My thoughts wander back Colton, and I once again feel sick. I shouldn't have left him. I could have helped him.

Dark, almost black eyes meet mine. I flit past them, only to cast my gaze on them once again for a second glance.

Keson.

My heart sinks as he walks toward me, all thoughts of Colton vanish. Keson is not what I was looking for, I know that. I try to swerve around him, hoping to get past him. He shifts his direction as well, intersecting his path with mine.

"Rose." His voice is gentle and soft, but still audible over the noise around us. "I'm sorry about what happened. I wanted to tell you that I was one of them but—"

"Keson!" I interrupt him. "Stop! Okay? I don't want to hear it!" *Especially not now.*

His eyes widen slightly, surprised. It's quiet between us. The only noise comes from the people bustling around us.

"Can we talk?" he suddenly asks, breaking the silence. He stares down at me with pleading eyes.

I tilt my head at him questioningly, but don't answer.

"It'll be quick," he adds, his eyebrows lifting slightly.

"Fine," I reply, even though I don't want to. In this moment, all I really want to do is get out of here, away from him, away from all of it, and retreat to my solitude.

He looks around. His eyes finally settle on me. "Not here."

My eyebrows pull together.

Without saying anything, Keson grabs my wrist and begins pulling me down the street, leaving Drake to stare after us. I want to push away from Keson, to break free, but I don't.

We turn a couple corners before we stop. There's the distant sound of voices and noises, but not a soul roams the street we are on. We are alone.

"What?" I ask, annoyed.

He begins talking, "Do you remember that night—in the woods—and the man with the knife?" He pauses, watching me.

I nod, still confused. I can feel my heartbeat beginning to grow faster. An uncomfortable feeling settles in the pit of my stomach.

"That guy—Tizek. We used to be friends. He was a classmate of mine, a few years back." He pauses, hesitating slightly. "And that's why I got so worked up when I found out that he had stabbed you," he admits.

"But he stabbed you too," I point out.

He hesitates. "We, um, weren't on such great terms. We used to fight a lot in school, and then he disappeared to the human world for a little while after Chastrin took over, just like a lot of other Cylilians did. We hadn't seen each other for a while. We ran into each other that night and went to have a talk. I thought it was because he wanted to try to resolve things. Turns out... he wanted a fight." Keson pauses, his eyes staring at something somewhere in the distance as he retells the story. "We began fighting. It started off as a fist fight—until he pulled out a knife."

The feeling in my stomach intensifies. I know what comes next.

Keson's eyes come back into focus. They slide down to gaze at me. "Just so happened that you were nearby and you heard me scream when he stabbed me. And you came running."

"Then he stabbed me," I say, the memory sliding back into my thoughts.

I can vaguely see a chill run through Keson's body as I say the words. I ignore it. There's a moment of silence, then something clicks. "Wait! The guy in the woods, the one that stabbed you and me, he was a Cylilian?"

Keson nods his head. "Yeah."

"Are you sure?" I ask, not understanding.

"One hundred percent sure," he responds.

It doesn't make sense. It was a Cylilian that stabbed Keson? That stabbed me? Keson knew him? I thought it had been either a Celestian or Griffin, not a Cylilian.

"I have to go," I say, swiftly spinning around and hurrying off in the direction Keson dragged me from. Thankfully, he doesn't try to chase after me. I need some time to think.

Emerging onto the crowded street, I spot Drake and Malina talking. Growing closer, they both stop to look at me. "Hey Malina," I greet, coming to a stop.

"Hey Rose! I was just asking Drake where you were." She nearly jumps into the air in excitement. "I'm having a party at my house tonight if you want to come." Her eyes shift to Drake. Her face shifts into a scowl. "You can come too, I guess." Despite her unpleasant expression, she releases a small playful laugh.

"I may," I reply.

"You better! You owe it to me."

I laugh. "Do not!"

She smirks. "Okay, maybe not, but you still better come." Turning to Drake she says, "And you? I could take it or leave it."

"Malina! I'm the life of the party, come on now," he exclaims.

She giggles, shaking her head before walking away, leaving Drake and me in the street.

Chapter 32

THE SUN HAS LONG SINCE SET BY THE TIME Drake and I leave the castle, walking in the direction of Malina's house. Music shakes the otherwise still air as we approach the house. Seeing her house brings back memories of when Malina and I were young and had play dates and sleepovers. Those days are long gone, it's time to make a new memory.

Through the windows I can see the dim lighting and the bodies moving back and forth throughout the interior. I can feel my stomach cramping, the uncomfortable sensation spreading throughout my body. A name nags in the back of my head. I know whose name it is. I know what it's trying to tell me. I shouldn't be here. I shouldn't be attempting to have fun with everything else that's going on right now. Not without him.

But I need a break. I need a breather.

Drake clasps his hands, rubbing them together. A smirk crosses his lips. "Time to get this party hoppin'." He glances down at me. "You're with me tonight, Damsel. If anything goes wrong, you find me."

The door swings open as we enter. My eyes scan the room, searching for familiar faces. People clutter the rooms, their bodies swaying slowly with cups in their hands. Drake walks to the guy standing behind an assortment of keyboards and equipment. I'm assuming the guy is a Vocal—typically known for their amazing singing voices and ability to manipulate music into beautiful pieces.

The two talk for a moment before the guy smiles and Drake gives a single nod. In an instant, the music comes to a screeching halt and suddenly becomes electric. The high-pitched noises come in short, exciting bursts, gradually manifesting into deeper, longer segments. The music is unpredictable and thrilling. I can feel my body begin to sway to the sounds, matching the movements of the other Cylilians in the room.

Suddenly, the lights flicker so quickly that my vision looks as if I am taking single pictures every second. People appear to be moving in robotic-like motions throughout the room. I look around, searching for Drake. Finally, I spot him, leaning against the doorway leading to the kitchen. He watches as the Cylilians dance.

The music slows and with a single swipe of Drake's hand, so do the lights. They drift into an array of colors, slowly changing from one to the next as the seconds tick by. Only a Bender could do this. They have the ability to bend light, creating whatever setting they want. And that is exactly what Drake is doing right now.

When the bass drops, so do the lights. The room goes black, but only for a moment. The lights come back blazing white, illuminating the entire house, as the music reclaims the silence.

I reach Drake's side, just as Malina rounds the corner. "Hey Drake," she hollers over the music. "Let's not blow out all of my lights, okay?"

He smirks. "Do you want a party or not?"

Rolling her eyes, she turns to me. "I'm so glad you came!"

I laugh. "Did I really have a choice?"

Her arm wraps around mine. "No, not really. Now, let's get you something to drink."

"I would like that," I reply, thinking that a drink may help to distract my thoughts from the single subject I'm intent on staying away from.

As she yanks me toward the kitchen, I watch as a Passive walks through the wall, appearing moments later in the living room. Arriving in the kitchen, Malina looks at the girl behind the very amateurly built bar. "One classic Cyli," Malina says.

The girl nods. Grabbing a clear cup, she pours four different liquids into it. Keeping her attention on the cup, she raises a single finger and twirls it midair. The liquid matches her motion. Her finger slowly comes to a stop. She lifts the glass and places the same finger on the base of the cup. Bubbles instantly rise. She's a Lique—liquid manipulator, essentially—which makes her the perfect bartender. "Here you go," she acknowledges, passing me the cup.

"Thank you!" Malina responds before we walk back onto the dance floor.

Sipping the drink, I can taste the perfect blend of native fruit juices from Cylilia and Canreli—our version of alcohol. The drink fizzes in my mouth as the carbonation slowly subsides.

I finish the drink and begin dancing with Malina. After the song she looks at me, holding up a single finger. "I need to go check on something," she says loud enough for me to hear. "I'll be right back."

I nod, but remain on the dance floor, awaiting her return. Although there are dozens of people surrounding me, I can't help but think about one. The one I left behind, back in Griffik. The one I abandoned as he was being attacked by other griffins. What if that was the last time I see him? What if they killed him? My eyes begin to water at the thought. I command myself to stop, to hold it in, and to not show the tears—they are a sign of weakness. But inside, I feel alone.

A body presses against mine, causing my attention to snap back to reality. Spinning around, I see Drake hovering above me.

"Hey Princess, need a dance partner?"

"Aren't you supposed to be handling the lights?" I ask, trying to avoid the question.

"I can multitask." The corners of his lips curl up in a smile and as much as I hate myself for it, butterflies flap in my stomach and my heart flutters. Without any further questions, one of his hands wraps around my wrist, pulling me closer to him. A nauseous feeling fills me as I struggle with what to do next. I know that Drake acts as if he's interested in me, but is any of it real? Is it worth falling for his tricks to figure it out?

My free hand collides with his chest, attempting to stop the ever-growing nearness of his body. But instead of resisting and pushing away, I find myself thinking back to when he first saved me in Griffik. His muscular stomach against my chest as he held a hand over my mouth, listening. The toned muscles beneath his wet shirt after he pulled me out of the lake in Ohio. Seeing him in the cabin, with his bare chest and ruffled hair, standing in front of the fireplace. I can feel my face growing warm at the thought. "What are you thinking about?" His voice breaks my train of thought.

My eyes shift slowly up to his. I don't respond, I just stare into his chestnut irises and feel his chest expand as he breathes beneath the palm of my hand. His head dips, all the while his eyes remaining on me. I can feel his breath skimming the skin on my cheeks as he grows closer. His lips are only centimeters from mine.

An abrupt memory of Colt and I sitting on the couch at the party in the human world flashes through my mind. His hands on my back, the look in his eyes, the sensation of his lips on mine all overwhelm my senses. Then, every memory I have of him seems to flood my head, making me feel as though I might explode. The day I ran into him with the door downtown... Our first conversation in the halls of the school... English and Math class... Yanking me away from Drake in the stairwell after school... Large, protective hands holding mine… His fatigued body sleeping on the couch in my hospital room… Shapeshifting into Calum to help me escape from Griffik… The griffins attacking him for saving me… Maybe killing him for it…

It's all my fault.

I snap out of it, finding myself staring up at Drake, his lips so close to mine I can nearly feel them.

"Stop!" I exclaim, pushing away and stumbling backwards.

The lights flicker momentarily, losing rhythm as Drake straightens, startled.

"I-I can't."

"That's okay." Drake steps toward me, but I counter it with another step backwards. I need to keep my distance. I almost kissed him. I wanted to kiss him. Despite everything with Colt. I forgot about all of it for a moment. I was ready to let Drake in and replace Colton. I shake my head, attempting to push the thought of his nearness and touch out of my head, but it doesn't leave easily. I turn, slinking into the crowd, needing to get away from him and clear my head.

A hand lands on my shoulder, catching me off guard. Jumping around, I am surprised to find myself staring at Keson, and not Drake.

"Hey Rose, I didn't expect to see you here."

"This is my best friend's party."

"Fair, I didn't think about that." He pauses. "How long have you been here?"

"About an hour or two," I answer, my eyes studying the room. Drake is no longer lingering nearby.

"Hey, I just wanted to thank you for your help in the woods. I realized that I never thanked you."

I stare up at him in shock. *Why is he thanking me?*

"If you hadn't been there, I don't know—"

He's cut off by the sound of glass breaking and screams. I rush toward the noise, intent on seeing what is happening. Two boys wrestle each other on the ground, rolling over shards of glass. The one with a bigger, bulkier build gains the advantage, pinning the smaller one to the ground. He throws a punch at the smaller kid. Then another. Blood trails almost instantly from the pinned boy's nose.

"Hey!" I exclaim, stepping forward. I place my hand on the big male's shoulder. He shrugs me off almost immediately, but I touch him once again. The sensation of being calm and peaceful fill my body and slowly flood into the boy's. His muscles relax until he finally stands up, chest heaving, and takes a step back from the boy on the ground.

Before I can react, the smaller boy is up on his feet, swinging wildly at the larger one. "No, no, no!" I reach for the boy, who turns to me, throwing a fist into my rib. The blow doesn't hurt, but I stumble backward in surprise. Trying again, I place both hands on the boy, spinning him to face me. His eyes bore into me, angry and relentless. His forearms are bleeding from the glass shards. "Sh," I hush, letting tranquility flow from me and into him. Our eyes remain locked and I watch as he grows more calm. As we stand, staring at each other, I see the blood from his nose stop dripping and the cuts on his face shift from red to pink to normal skin color. Then, the scrapes are gone, his skin nearly perfect, as if nothing had ever happened.

I pull my hands off him, taking a step backward, and drawing a deep breath.

Did I really just see that? He just... healed. Right before my eyes.

I have to leave.

Twirling on my heels, I bolt from the house, ignoring the questioning looks and surprised mutters as I push past everyone in my frenzied escape.

Chapter 33

WINTER BREAK IS OVER, MEANING IT'S time to return to the human world and "reality." Despite what Colt had previously said about not returning to the human world, I have to go. I have to see Colt… to see how he is. Drake, Quinn, Tanner, Zander, Maeve, and I walk together through the portal to school the next day. Drake and I walk awkwardly side by side, neither of us sure how to act after the incident at the party a couple nights ago. The cousins trail behind us, wrapped up in intense gossip.

A pinch of guilt forms in my stomach. I had been dating Colt before everything happened, and now there's some chemistry between Drake and me. I push down the feeling, not sure how that is going to help anything.

"Hey," Drake's voice rumbles as we grow closer to the school. "I'm sorry about the other night."

"Not now, Drake. Please."

"No, seriously. I am sorry. That was my fault. I don't know what today is going to bring, but I want you to know that I've got your back if you need it." He pauses. "After all, I'm always down for a good damsel in distress rescue." A smirk slides across his face and I can't help but laugh.

"Yeah okay, see you in fifth."

The first bell rings. I follow the crowd of teenagers as I walk to class, separating from Drake as we enter the building. Bree is already there when I arrive. She looks up, her eyes meeting mine. A smile slips onto her lips, her entire face lighting up.

"Macy!" she exclaims, excitedly.

It's been so long since someone's called me Macy. It's weird to be called that again.

"How was your break?"

My heart drops as I think about everything that happened. It wasn't much of a break. "It was okay. How was yours?" I ask, trying to push the attention back on her.

"It was okay. The usual," she replies simply.

The class starts and finishes fairly quickly. About an hour later, I walk into English, bracing myself. Colt will be here. *If* he made it. The thought makes me sick. I left him in Griffik by himself. He had to defend himself against three other griffins to save me. Suddenly, my stomach feels unstable and my head is throbbing.

I look around frantically as I enter the room. Colt isn't here yet, but I take a seat in my normal chair, waiting. Finally, he enters the room. I release a sigh of relief, my heart lifting gratefully. The sick feeling in my stomach subsides as he takes his place at the desk next to me. The weight that I didn't realize had been placed on my body lifts, making me feel light.

Mrs. Taylor begins class. Colt and I don't speak much, but I'm happy he's here.

Bree and I walk to math together and sit in our usual spot in the back. Colt walks in the door a minute after we do.

"Colt!" Bree exclaims, putting her hand in the air and waving him over.

"Hey guys," Colt greets as he pulls out the chair and takes a seat next to me.

Drake saunters through the doorway. His eyes scan the room observantly. They settle on me and we lock eyes. His gaze then skips to Colt. Drake's pace slows, his eyes examining the situation. I give a single acknowledging nod, signifying that everything is okay. The second bell rings. Drake takes a seat in his chair on the other side of the room and faces the front.

The students quiet down as the class begins. I place my hand on Colt's and lean toward him. I speak under my breath. "Hey, I'm really glad you're okay."

His eyes flit to me, but they don't hold the adoration and overall emotion that I expected. He offers a single nod before averting his attention back to the front.

I sit back in my chair. I let out a long, slow breath, but my mind is running wild as I overthink his reaction. He should have been happy. He should have smiled. But instead he shied away. He locked me out. Is it because I left him in Griffik? Should I have stayed? He told me to leave.

The bell signifying the end of the period rings, tearing me from my thoughts. The remainder of classes sail by, all the while, my mind is on Colt. Walking outside at the end of the day, I spot him strolling toward the parking lot among the large herd of other students. Jogging toward him, I holler his name, "Colton!"

I grasp his arm in my hand when I'm within reach. "Hey," I greet.

He glances at me. "Hey," he responds quietly, his tone flat as his eyes scan the area. "Where's your friend?"

"What?" I ask, suddenly confused by his tone. "What friend?"

"Drake."

"I don't know..." My gaze follows his, looking for whatever he is. He's acting weird.

"He was with you in Griffik, where is he now?"

I shake my head. My stomach drops to my feet, the sick feeling beginning to set in once again. "Can I get a ride home?"

He hesitates, but eventually nods. "Sure, get in," he says, jerking his head toward the passenger side of the vehicle.

We get into the car and he begins driving. The atmosphere feels weird. Everything feels tense and hostile and I'm not sure why. I know I left him behind, but this... this is too much.

My house is the next right, but instead of getting in the turn lane, Colt stays in the center. "My house is that way." I gesture to the street.

Colt nods. "Right, sorry." The car quickly swivels into the correct lane and turns onto the street.

He's driven me home so many times. How could he forget? That's not normal. Everything feels wrong.

I give him directions nearly the whole way back to my house.

Just before I jump out of the truck, I turn to him. "Are you okay?"

"Yeah, just fine." His eyes remain straight forward, staring at the garage door in front of the car.

I pause. "Okay." Leaning over, I peck him, but instead of reacting by kissing me back, he sits, not moving. I place my hands on his shoulders, gently moving my fingers in small circles. I kiss his neck, slowly pulling his shirt off his shoulder as I maneuver across his body. A dark patch reveals itself. Observing it, I can tell it's not a claw with a drop hanging from it. Instead, I find myself looking at a leaf... a maple leaf.

Shoot!

This is Calum.

And if this is Calum, where's Colton?

My heart stalls in my chest. I pull back from 'Colt,' dropping my hands from his body.

"I'll see you later," I comment, attempting to keep my voice as steady as possible. I hop out of the car, eager to put distance between the imposter and me.

Once inside, I press my back against the closed door. I can feel the panic rising inside of me. Why was Calum disguised as Colt? What happened to Colton?

My breaths come out in short bursts.

"Macy?" Linda's frame emerges from the kitchen doorway.

"Hey, sorry. I'm back."

"I noticed," Linda comments with a smile. "I'm glad you're safe."

I laugh at the irony. I was just in a car with a griffin. He looked like the one I like, but his birthmark says otherwise. His birthmark says he's the one that carried me over that field. The one that wants me dead. "Yeah, I'm fine," I lie. I have to tell someone about Calum, but I don't know who. Certainly not Linda. She wouldn't be able to help, she's just a human.

Drake. He'll know what to do. He always does.

I resist laughing at myself for having that thought.

"I have to go back to Dunchoria," I tell Linda. "I'll be back."

"Is everything alright?"

"Yes." I nod. "It will be." Before I finish the sentence, I'm rushing out the door and back to the portal by the school.

Chapter 34

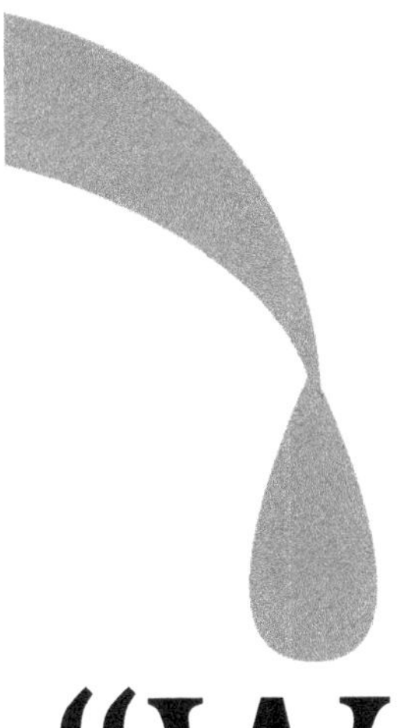

"**W**AIT, WHAT?" DRAKE'S CHESTNUT eyes bore into me as I explain the situation.

"Drake," I hiss, annoyed. "Please, just listen. Try to understand."

"It's just that I've never heard of griffins being able to do that."

"I know. That's because Chastrin doesn't want us to know."

Although Drake doesn't respond, I can tell he's considering. "Okay." He strings out the word as his thoughts slide into place. "Let's say you're right... what are you going to do?"

I shrug. I hadn't thought about it a whole lot. "Confront him? Talk to him?"

"Rose." He stares at me, making butterflies lift in my stomach. My chest tightens and I can feel a force pulling me towards him. "Are you sure that's the right thing to do?" His words snap me out of the trance.

"I have to figure it out. I have to know what happened."

He sighs. "Alright, Princess. I've got your back."

Relief fills my body at the sound of those words.

The bell rings, ending fourth period. Walking to fifth, I can feel my heart flipping as I anticipate what comes next. Entering the classroom, I find 'Colton' already sitting at his normal desk.

"Hey," I greet as I approach him. I sit next to him. My knee bounces anxiously as I wait for Drake to enter the room. Seconds turn into minutes and I begin to worry, contemplating my next move if he doesn't show up. Finally, after what feels like eternity, Drake comes into view, gliding into the classroom flawlessly.

I lean over to Colt, lowering my voice. "Can we talk?"

His expression contorts, eyes shifting to examine me. "About?"

My heart pounds in my chest. "Something happened and I don't know who else to talk to," I lie. My words quiver, but I attempt to keep my voice steady.

He nods, slowly standing. I lead him into the hallway, knowing that Drake will follow us.

When we're alone in a stairwell, we stop. I turn to him.

"What is it?" he asks, almost too interested.

I exhale, the air coming out in a single, shaky burst. "Where's Colt?"

His face scrunches in on itself. "What?" He pauses.

I force a laugh. "You and I both know you aren't him. What are you doing here Calum? And where is Colton?"

He doesn't cave, but his expression does shift to curiosity. "How would you even know that?"

I drop my head, then look back up at him. Taking a step closer, I pull at the neckline of his shirt until his shoulder is exposed. His birthmark is prevalent, even in the dim light.

"A maple leaf," I reply with a knowing smile. "Birthmarks don't change. And Calum's birthmark is a maple leaf, not Colton's."

He curses under his breath. "Did that bastard tell you that?"

"Depends… Where is he?" I barter.

"That's none of your business," Calum hisses, stepping toward me aggressively.

For a second, I'm scared, but then I remember that Drake is right around the corner. My confidence elevates. I'm not afraid to aggravate him. I need answers. "Oh? It's not? I believe Colt was with me. He was trying to protect me. So it is my business."

Colt's familiar laugh fills the air, but there's something sinister in this one. "You might as well have signed his death warrant."

I freeze. "What?"

"He lost sight of his mission. He helped the enemy. He was weak. We had to get rid of him."

I can feel my knees growing weak, about to give way. I clutch at the wall, attempting to find security in it, but instead, I feel it closing in on me and I can't breathe. The world begins spinning. My head grows light as my vision begins to go. "Y-you killed him?" I spit out the words, barely able to speak them.

He nods. "Take a good look Roslanie. This is the last time you'll be seeing Colton." After a moment, Colt's features begin to warp, pulling and pinching until they are completely different. I stand, staring at Calum. His features, while not unfamiliar, look strange to me. I'm still searching for Colt. I want to see him again. I want to see his face and his body and his smile. Only, this isn't Colt. It hasn't been since we got back from winter break.

It's been Calum the whole time. He cocks his head to the side, observing me. "Oh honey, heartbreak and despair aren't a good look on you. But the fact that I made you feel that… well, I like it."

My expression hardens at his words, as if to defy them. Every emotion seeps from my body, leaving me feeling empty.

"Well, I've gotta run. See ya around, Rose," Calum says before disappearing into the hall.

Drake comes into sight seconds later. His eyes are on me, watching me, determining how he should react. His arms are around me, holding me tightly to his chest. Instead of feeling suffocated by his touch, I feel protected. My chest heaves as dry sobs escape my lips. I don't want to cry right now. I don't want Drake to see me cry, but I can't help it. My desolate body sinks to the ground. My head swims, as if it's drowning in a deep pool of water. I assume, in a way, it is.

Drake's arms reach around my feeble body. "Let's get out of here," he says, lifting me into the air.

A familiar face hovers over top of mine, interrupting my gaze. Chestnut eyes stare down at me. They look me over before returning to my face.

"What are you doing?" he asks. I can hear the smile playing out in his words.

I stare at him, my expression blank. "Laying on the bed," I answer.

"Princess and the Pea… seems fitting," he comments with a smirk. "Mind if I join?"

My eyebrows furrow together, not in the mood for his princess jokes. "Yeah, I do actually."

His head disappears from my view. For a minute, it's silent. The mattress beneath me shifts slightly as a new weight is introduced.

"I told you no."

He lets out a breath. The mattress bounces slightly, signaling that he has moved. "What's wrong, Rose?" he asks.

I look at him from the corner of my eye. "I'm not in the mood for your games."

"Fine. Then we don't have to play games," he asserts.

"You? Not playing games? I don't even think that's possible," I reply.

"Try me." A smirk crosses his lips.

"Exactly my point."

"What is?"

"This. Even this is a game to you."

"Come on, Rose. Lighten up." His voice is soft and gentle, but it still hits a nerve.

I turn my head to look at him, propping myself up on my elbow. "Lighten up?!" My lips press into a tight line as I stare at him. His eyes grow slightly bigger, surprised. "You *know* what just happened! Aren't I allowed time to mourn him?" My chest squeezes, and my throat begins to burn. I can feel the tears beginning to surface. I can feel my body breaking down.

Drake's expression grows sympathetic. "Of course you are," he whispers. Reaching an arm out, his hand grazes the exposed skin on my arm.

I pull away from him, nearly falling off the edge of the bed. "Please don't touch me."

"Rose." His voice is low.

"Not today." Although I say the words, I can't help but want to feel his skin on mine. My mind ventures back to the cabin in Ohio and Malina's party in Dunchoria. I snap myself out of it as quickly as I can. I feel guilty thinking of Drake like that. He's a jerk, and I just lost Colt... permanently. What is wrong with me?

I grow stir crazy. My body itches to move. My mind races, wanting to think about everything and nothing at the same time. I need to get out. I need to do something. I can't just sit here and wait for something to finally happen.

I jump off the bed, my vision blurring momentarily. I walk out the door and move down the castle hallway. Drake had thought it was a clever idea to bring me to Dunchoria instead of my house in the human world so I could have a support team, but I think it was more for safeguarding and making sure I'm in the Uniform's reach, just in case I try anything. Which is exactly what I'm about to do.

As I twist and turn through the halls, making my way to the exit, I intersect paths with Drake. Keeping my head low, I attempt to evade his attention, but it's no use. "Rose! Nice to see you're finally up." He changes his direction so he can walk beside me. "Where are we headed?"

"*I* am going to Griffik," I correct.

His footsteps falter in surprise. "Wait, what? Why?" He pauses. "Can we think about this for a second?"

"There's nothing to think about."

"What are you talking about? Of course there is."

I shake my head, my pace unfazed by his words.

"Fine. But at least let Chastrin know what you're doing."

"Why?" I ask. "So he can lock me in a room and claim it's 'to keep me safe'?" I use my fingers to air quote the words.

"No, but he might be able to offer help."

"How?"

"Power in numbers," Drake replies with a shrug.

Chapter 35

THE SUN IS SETTING AS WE WALK OUT OF the castle, heading toward the portal to Griffik. Chastrin hadn't liked the idea, but after he saw that I wasn't going to give up—that I would go, whether he approved or not— he finally caved.

He selected ten Uniforms to accompany Drake and me, Keson being one of them.

The twelve of us walk through the portal and head straight for the stone building positioned on the horizon.

I walk to the large stone-walled room where I first met Kyra. Kyra stands at the far end of it, staring at the wall.

"Kyra," I announce, my words echoing in the nearly empty room.

"There you are," Kyra says, turning to look at us. "Calum told me we should be expecting you." His name makes my stomach turn. "You brought friends. How lovely."

I stop in the middle of the room, not replying.

"You're here about Colton," she concludes.

I stare at her, remaining silent. She already knows the answer.

Her lips pucker. "Yes. Well, that is a very unfortunate circumstance. I wish it didn't have to be this way."

I have to resist laughing at the irony. "It didn't," I hiss.

She shakes her head, sucking at her teeth to create a clicking noise. "But you see, it did. You're not from here, so I wouldn't expect you to understand the way things work."

"Killing? You don't expect me to understand meaningless killing," I clarify.

"It wasn't meaningless." She cocks her head. Her eyes trace my body, examining my expression and stance as she speaks. "He was beginning to have feelings for you. Why? I'm not really sure. You don't seem like anything special to me... but either way, it prevented him from doing what he was meant to do."

"He had feelings for me?"

She cackles, throwing her head back. "Such a naïve little girl."

I can feel the anger begin to bubble inside of me.

"That's really all you got out of that explanation? Of course, all you would care about is if he liked you or not." Her voice mocks that of a five-year-old, poking fun at my question. "What a typical teenage girl. His death must be heartbreaking. You guys knew each other for what? Two months? Such a long time." She purses her lips. My stomach grows hard and my chest tightens as she speaks. "You poor thing. Well, if it makes you feel any better, he did put up quite a fight. He said he wouldn't do it. I offered him an alternative. I tried to give him one more chance to kill you himself, but he denied it. What a pity. I thought he was such a good soldier until he met you. But he lost his drive." She shakes her head from side to side in fake melancholy. My hands ball into fists at my sides. "You did this to him, Rose." Her eyes sink as she accuses me. "You are the one that caused this."

My jaw clenches, teeth grinding in my mouth. My breathing vibrates in my lungs as I inhale and exhale short, uneven breaths. My stomach turns to acid. My blood begins to boil. The color on my face shifts from its normal tanned color to a deep red. Muscles tense, eyes focused, I glare at Kyra. My thoughts jumble together until there's just one single thought remaining.

I want her dead.

I want Kyra dead.

My eyes bore into her, attentive and intense. I think about all the horrid things she's done. About Calum's griffin lifting me into the sky. About the three griffins attacking Colt as he helped Drake and I escape. About his last words to me. Our last kiss. I want that back. But she has stolen that from me. From us. And I will not let it go. Ever. She'll pay for it. I will kill her.

"Oh Rose, did I upset you?" Kyra asks, her eyes surveying me.

A hand touches my shoulder lightly, but pulls back instantly. "Ouch!" I hear Drake exclaim behind me. "Rose, you need to calm down. Your emotions are *seeping* right now." He leans closer to me, but keeps a slight distance, careful not to encounter my bleeding feelings. "Deep breaths," he whispers in my ear. A chill runs through my body, cooling my blood ever so slightly.

"Why are you so bothered by the death of one griffin? Your kind came in here and murdered hundreds of our kind without so much as a blink," she notes, patting her hand on the wall. I know she's touching the blood that's permanently plastered into the cracks of the stone. "And why? Just because I said a couple 'wrong words' to

Chastrin—your leader?" she asks, her eyebrows raising on her forehead.

Keson scoffs behind me. "It was more than just a couple wrong words. You threatened our entire realm. You sent your griffins to destroy the outskirts of our town to make an example. To prove your dominance. You asked for the war. You killed our people. Innocent people just to try to prove your point." He shakes his head. "Some leader you are," he adds, laughing.

I absorb Keson's words. I hadn't known how the war started until now, but it makes me even more eager for vengeance against the griffins. I turn my attention back to Kyra and speak. "But this *is* different, now isn't it?" I pause.

Kyra doesn't say anything, she just looks at me. A man walks in just then, joining Kyra. He looks familiar, but I'm not sure where I've seen him before. I can't focus on him right now. He is the least of my concerns at the moment.

"You want revenge," I say, wanting to confirm what I'm sensing. "That's why it was a problem that Colt liked me. That's why killing him ultimately wouldn't set you back in your plan."

Once again, Kyra doesn't say anything; she just continues to stare at me.

"You want revenge on Dunchoria. Because we came and killed your people and you want to do the same to us. That's why you're doing this."

A small smile forms on her lips and her eyes darken, knowing I'm getting close.

A whisper comes from behind me. I turn to look. Keson stands, stick straight. His skin is pale. Sweat has gathered on his forehead. His expression is blank, but at the same time, every feature is filled with fear. His eyes are focused, unblinking. His blue lips move, speaking, but I don't catch what he says.

The words slowly float to me. "You stabbed me."

I can feel the blood drain from my face. I turn slowly, following Keson's gaze to the man standing by Kyra's side. He's smirking as he looks at Keson. Then, it all comes together.

"You," I say. His eyes look at me. "You're Tizek. The one from the woods. The one that got into the fight with Keson. The one that stabbed him. The one that stabbed me." His smile grows.

"Well, aren't you a clever girl? That's correct."

"But you're a Cylilian?" I question, remembering what Keson had told me about them being classmates.

"That's right," he says.

"Why are you here? Why are you doing this? Working with them?" I ask.

"I guess I wasn't fond of the new ruling in Cylilia," he says with a shrug.

The memory of what happened in the woods plays in my head.

As I looked up at him, tiredly, his pupils had seemed to grow even larger, blackness claiming his irises. "It's done," he had whispered, more for himself than for me.

"You're a Visionary. Aren't you?" I ask, looking into the eyes of the man.

He nods. "You noticed," he says, sounding satisfied.

"I've been noticing a lot of things lately," I acknowledge. "You transmitted a vision of me after you stabbed me," I recall.

"Mhmm," he confirms, his eyes sliding to Kyra.

"You transmitted it to her," I speak slowly. It makes sense. It's finally beginning to come together.

"But why? How does any of this involve me?"

"Chastrin needs you. Your ability to heal benefits him. Because you benefit him, and we want revenge, we have to kill you," Kyra explains.

Not them too. They believe the prophecy is true. Thinking back to the boy at the party, I remember his cuts disappearing before my eyes—healing in front of me. I shake the memory out of my head.

Because of this prophecy, the griffins want me dead. They want to kill me and I'm currently standing in the middle of their facility. I'm on their turf. I'm right where they want me to be.

I take a step back, but my back bumps into something solid, stopping me short. I turn to look at the person behind me. Drake's chest heaves in and out, breathing hard.

"We need to leave," he says, voicing what I am thinking.

I nod eagerly.

We turn to leave, facing the large entryway that we came in through. People block the exit, making it impossible to leave.

"You're not getting away that easily," Kyra says. Although I'm not facing her, I can hear the smile in her voice.

I focus on the people blocking our exit. My body floods with the hurt and sadness and anger that I'm feeling. Then, I release it, letting it seep through my pores.

I take a step forward, away from the other Cylilians accompanying me, and towards the griffins blocking the doorway. I turn to the other Cylilians and say, "When they go down, make a run for it. Understand?"

The Cylilians look at me, expressions confused as they attempt to predict my next move. I begin walking, one foot in front of the other, toward my worst fear. Except this time, I have the upper hand.

As I get closer, I extend my arms, reaching for the griffins that approach me. As my touch comes in contact with their bodies, they coil to the ground. Their bodies shake on the floor as they fight the pain flooding through their veins.

The pathway out of the room clears as the last of the dominoes drop to the ground. I stop, looking behind me at the faces of the other Cylilians. My gaze flits to Kyra, standing at the far end of the room. Her jaw protrudes as she clenches her teeth; her eyes are narrowed, staring at me, ready to kill.

"Run!" I exclaim.

All the Uniforms look at me, shocked.

"Run! Now!" I repeat, louder.

They all burst into a sprint, charging out of the building. Keson and Drake trail behind, waiting for me to move, but I don't. I continue staring at Kyra. She narrows her eyes further. Her body begins shaking. She drops to the ground and before I realize what's happening, she shifts into a large orange colored griffin.

"Rose!" Keson exclaims, snapping me out of the daze. The boys both dart toward me, quickly closing in. Drake's hand wraps around my wrist just as I cut off the transmission of pain. We dash out of building and run toward the portal.

A growl erupts from behind us, shaking the dry, desert ground as we run. A large, animal-like shadow covers our figures as we gradually close the space between us and the remaining group of Cylilians.

"No!" I holler. Out of the corner of my eye I can see orange fur. *Kyra.*

Her shadow covers the three of us as she suddenly nosedives toward the ground.

Her body makes impact with the dry earth, causing the otherwise solid dirt beneath our feet to jolt. I lose my footing and fall to the ground, rolling across it and quickly losing momentum.

"Callerie!" Keson screams, his body shifting direction as he backtracks. His arms wrap around my body, yanking me upwards. "Come on—" A cry erupts from his throat as his body drops.

A huge griffin hovers a couple feet behind his fallen body. Her front paw is covered in a deep red liquid. Blood. Keson's blood.

She lowers to the ground, gaining a predatory stance as she stares at me. My heart stops. The world freezes as we stare at each other. She's going to kill me.

A beam of light centers on the griffin, gradually traveling along its body until the bright light is in its eyes, blinding the monster. The griffin snarls, shutting its eyes and moving its body in a motion that is supposed to shake the light. But the light doesn't move from the creature. The griffin's annoyed grunts quickly grow into pained howls as the heat from the light begins to make its eyes smolder.

A body walks up next to Keson and me. Looking up, I see Drake standing, one hand outstretched toward the griffin, flicking his wrist ever so slightly. He's the one doing this. The animal hollers, its cry curdling my blood. Once again, I can feel my body heating in anger. Even now, in this moment, I want to kill it. I want her dead. This merciless monster that not only killed Colton and so many other Cylilians, but also injured Keson. She hurts—and kills—everyone close to me. I can feel every emotion inside of me funneling to her, everything I wish

I could make her feel bottles inside of me. The pain. The sadness. The vengeance. The helplessness.

"See?" Drake says from above us. "I told you I'm drawn to damsels in distress… and their acquaintances." His gaze shifts to Keson, who is grasping his leg with a very uncomfortable expression playing on his face. "We've got to go."

He helps me get Keson off the ground and carry him across the remainder of the desert and into the trees. When we arrive in Dunchoria, Drake and I come to a stop, Keson still between us. The rest of the Uniforms stand near the portal, waiting for us. Everyone looks stunned. No one says a word.

Chapter 36

"**A**H, GLAD TO SEE EVERYONE MADE IT back!" Chastrin exclaims.

I roll my eyes at the casual tone in his voice.

His eyes trail across the twelve of us, stopping on Keson who is being supported between Drake and me. "What happened to Keson?"

"Kyra attacked him, gashed his leg pretty badly," Drake replies shortly.

Chastrin's eyes linger, but slowly drift to me. I can feel my expression shift to curiosity. *Why is he staring at me?*

"Rose. You can heal him."

I exhale, frustrated. "Why does everyone keep saying that?" I pause.

A smile crosses Chastrin's face. "Because it's true. You're the prophecy."

"Even if that were true," I fume. "I don't know how to heal." I think back to the fight at Malina's party a couple days ago. I remember the scratches on the boy disappearing. I did that. I know that I did. I just don't know how.

"You are the prophecy," Chastrin repeats.

Keson hisses through his teeth as I examine the gash in his leg. I can see the bone a couple inches under. My stomach flips nauseously as I stare at it. I want to help him. I want to heal him. But how?

I try to remember what I did at the party.

I place my hands on Keson's shoulders, focusing on the feelings of being relaxed and calm. I sense the tension in his muscles dispersing as the moments pass. His jaw gradually unclenches as his back rests against the wall.

I peer down at his leg. Nothing has changed.

Okay, I think to myself. *Focus. Healing. Getting better. Sealing his wound.*

I close my eyes and think about the gash. I imagine the bleeding slowing. The skin going from bright pink to its normal olive shade. The bone being covered by flesh as it seals itself. The puckered skin pulling together until it is just a line on the surface of his skin.

I hear Keson sigh under my touch and feel his shoulders slump. Opening my eyes, I watch his content expression and slowly shift my attention to his leg. My eyes widen, a gasp escaping my lips as I stare at it. While it's not completely healed, it is much less severe than before. I can no longer see the bone and the skin surrounding his injury is not as swollen as before.

I did it.

I close my eyes once more. Thinking harder. Focusing more. My thoughts are centered solely on his cut. Solely on healing.

When I open my eyes once again, the gash is nearly gone, just a long, nearly unnoticeable line remains on his skin. My body feels tired, drained from the effort. It's almost as if by healing Keson, I gave him some of my own strength.

My heart skips excitedly. Satisfaction fills my entire body. A smile forms on my mouth, spreading to my entire face.

I did it!

Like on previous days, Drake, his cousins, and I walk through the portal from Dunchoria to the human world on our way to school. But unlike other days, today is quiet. My thoughts are racing about what it will be like to encounter Calum again. Will he even come to school now that I know?

I don't know which is worse, Calum pretending to be Colt, or having an empty seat where Colt should be. A fake or a reality check. My chest tightens at both alternatives. I don't want either.

During third period, I sit, waiting anxiously to see which I will be facing. The minutes tick by. The second bell rings, signaling the start of class. The teacher shuts the door and class begins without Calum.

My body fills with wave of mixed emotions. Thrill and desperation, excitement and sadness, satisfaction and disappointment. I sit, allowing the emotions to swarm my body and overwhelm my senses. I let them take over my body, not knowing what else to do. The class slugs by. Where is Calum? Why isn't he here today? Is it because I found out he wasn't Colton?

My chest is tight, lungs immobilized, and hands shaking by the time I exit the classroom. The day blurs, my thoughts on everything except school.

In fifth, I sit, slumped at my desk. My eyes stare at the blackboard, fingers fumbling with a pencil. My mind has long since gone blank. I don't want to think.

"Hey," Bree says as she plops down beside me. I offer a single nod in reply, but continue staring forward. "Where's Colt?" she asks after a moment.

I feel myself flinch at the sound of his name. My insides shrivel up. My stomach squeezes until I feel like I'm going to vomit. My head swims, attempting to come up with a response. "I-I don't know." My throat burns, as if the words were flames, slowly eating at my lie. My pathetic attempt to hide the monster eating at me from the inside out.

She nods. "Odd," is all she says.

Drake's frame enters the room. His eyes quickly scan the room, stopping on me. We make eye contact as he crosses the floor. My stomach twists and I can feel myself drawn to him. I want him to come to me. I want him to hug me and make me forget, even if just for a moment.

His eyebrows lift and he gives a slight jolt of the head in recognition. Then, he turns his attention to his desk as he lowers his body into the chair. Suddenly, I feel guilty and embarrassed. I shouldn't need his comfort. I shouldn't *want* his comfort.

The days pass and Colt's seat remains empty. He is nearly forgotten, as if he was never here. Bree chats with me, unfazed by his absence, but it never leaves me. There is a constant nagging feeling in the back of my head. It begs me to pull it forward, but I know it will break me if I do. So instead, I push it further back, never letting it surface.

The final bell rings, releasing us from the last class of the day. I walk in the direction of the portal, blocking out the noises around me until they are a distant buzz.

"Macy!" A male voice breaks through my daze. Swiveling my head, I turn to look at Drake as he jogs toward me. My heart stops. I wasn't expecting to see him. Why? I'm not sure. After all, he walks to Dunchoria after school as well. "Macy, hey," he says as he slows his pace to a walk and throws an arm over my shoulder.

My heart skips in my chest at the sensation of his touch. "Hey Drake. What's up?" I greet. I try my best to add emotion to my voice, but it still comes out monotone and apathetic.

He acts as if he doesn't hear it, although I know he does. "I've got news."

I toss him a glance. "What kind of news?"

"The kind of news you'll be interested in hearing," he replies.

After a couple seconds of silence, I peek up at him. "Are you going to tell me?"

He laughs. "Princess, we're still surrounded by…" He leans down, his mouth next to my ear. "*Humans*," he whispers, sending chills throughout my body. Straightening he continues, "I'm not sure that would be wise." He drops his arm from my shoulder.

My eyes dart to the people around us, surveying the numerous teenagers on the sidewalk. We continue walking in silence until we are nearly at the wood's edge.

Drake stops and turns to face me. "So the news," he starts. "It's not being made public because they don't want to appear weak… vulnerable."

"Who doesn't?"

Drake stares at me. "The griffins," he finally answers, watching me carefully for my reaction.

I can feel a shiver run down my spine. I haven't heard anything about them for days. I straighten, both anxious and concerned to hear the news. "What happened?" The words shake in the air as they drip from my tongue.

He pauses. The quiet lingers for what feels like forever. "Kyra is dead." A smirk slinks across his lips as he looks at me.

The sentence echoes on repeat in my head. My heart stalls.

She's dead? She's dead.

I don't know if I feel relief or anger. Why would I feel angry? I wanted her dead. I wished she were dead.

"How?" I voice.

He shakes his head, shrugging. "Random. She just dropped dead. Apparently, she wasn't showing any signs of sickness or being unhealthy. They just found her dead."

I take a deep breath, willing myself to calm. "When?"

He smiles. "That's what's so strange. It was the night we left." His lips curve even more, his smiling growing more intense.

Epilogue

I STARE AT MY REFLECTION IN THE MIRROR. I'm in a bathroom somewhere in the castle. My blue-green eyes glare back at me. There's a spark behind them, one that I've never seen before. Something sinister and hungry rests directly under the surface.

Kyra died the same day we went to Griffik. We didn't fight her. We didn't hurt her. Or did we? Did I? I think back, remembering the power I felt inside me as she talked about Colt. Her passive, casual attitude towards killing him had upset me. Thinking about it now, I can feel the angry heat rising inside of me. My blood pumps furiously, carrying with it the desire and intent to hurt, or even kill, her.

The power is overwhelming. The longing to make her feel my pain engulfs my body. Only, she's no longer alive to feel it. She will never understand what I felt.

Unless, of course, I made her feel it. Back in Griffik. It's not completely impossible. Granted, I didn't touch her, but I can manipulate emotions... *and* bodies. If I can give people life, what says I can't take it away?

I watch my arms tense as they grip the sink. My fingers brush against the cold stone, the same way they did when they touched Colton's skin as we kissed on the couch at the party. My palm flattens, as if it were once again colliding with Drake's hard chest and toned stomach underneath his shirt. My jaw locks, just as it did when I was wishing Kyra dead. My lips, the ones that constantly spew deceptive words as I pretend to be someone I'm not, press into a straight line.

Everyone claims that I'm a miracle. I'm the prophecy. Able to manipulate emotions *and* bodies. I have two powers. But everything comes with a price. Every miracle comes with its own curse.

And I'm no exception.